ARTHURIAN STUDIES XLVIII

MERLIN AND THE GRAIL

ARTHURIAN STUDIES

ISSN 0261–9814

Previously published volumes in the series
are listed at the back of this book

Merlin and the Grail

JOSEPH OF ARIMATHEA
MERLIN
PERCEVAL

The trilogy of prose romances attributed to
ROBERT DE BORON

Translated by Nigel Bryant

D. S. BREWER

First published 2001
D. S. Brewer, Cambridge
Reprinted in paperback 2003, 2005

Transferred to digital printing

ISBN 978 0 85991 616 5 hardback
ISBN 978 0 85991 779 7 paperback

D. S. Brewer is an imprint of Boydell & Brewer Ltd
PO Box 9, Woodbridge, Suffolk IP12 3DF, UK
and of Boydell & Brewer Inc.
668 Mt Hope Avenue, Rochester, NY 14620, USA
website: www.boydellandbrewer.com

A CiP catalogue record for this book is available
from the British Library

This publication is printed on acid-free paper

Contents

Three for three:

Sally, Jevan and Will

Introduction

'With the obvious exception of Chrétien de Troyes, the most influential writer within the French romance tradition may well be Robert de Boron.' So Norris J. Lacy has written;[1] and it is surely no exaggeration. Not only in the development of the Grail legend, but in the evolution of Arthurian literature as a whole, it would be hard to overstate the importance of this trilogy of prose romances. Relatively short though they may be, these works attributed to Robert de Boron not only gave a vital new impetus to the story of the Grail left unfinished by Chrétien de Troyes, but were also to prove an inspiration to later writers, showing the way forward by combining a series of narratives to create the very first *cycle* of Arthurian tales. For the redactor of the version translated here was not content merely to take the Grail as the object of a chivalric quest and go back in time to tell the story of its origins in the Biblical past; nor was he content to move on and see the Grail quest brought to a conclusion; he went further, and gave his audience a resolution to the whole Arthurian story by finishing his *Perceval* with an account of the betrayal and death of Arthur and the end of the knights of the Round Table. This trilogy is astonishingly ambitious, original and complete in its conception.

The Modena manuscript

The *Joseph of Arimathea* has survived in seventeen manuscripts, most of which also contain *Merlin*, but only two go on to contain the entire trilogy of *Joseph*, *Merlin* and *Perceval*: manuscript E.39 of the Biblioteca Estense in Modena, and nouv.acqu.no.4166 of the Bibliothèque Nationale, Paris (formerly named the 'Didot' manuscript after a past owner – hence the title *Didot-Perceval* often applied to the third part). These manuscripts have not necessarily been used as the bases for modern editions: both Richard O'Gorman in his parallel

---

1 'The Evolution and Legacy of French Prose Romance', in *The Cambridge Companion to Medieval Romance*, ed. R.L. Krueger (Cambridge, 2000), p. 169.

edition of the verse and prose versions of *Joseph* (Toronto, 1995) and Alexandre Micha in his edition of *Merlin* (Geneva, 1979) argue at length for the
superiority of other manuscripts, each editor finally opting for a different
text. But Bernard Cerquiglini, in his edition of the complete trilogy,[2] follows
the text simply of the Modena manuscript. Uncritical though some may feel
this to be, it has the great virtue of presenting a medieval reality: it gives a
single, complete text as it would have been experienced by a contemporary
audience.

Of the two manuscripts that contain the complete trilogy, the Modena text
is unquestionably the better – notably in the *Perceval* section. In his fine
edition of the *Perceval*, William Roach refers to the Modena redactor as 'a
careful and thoughtful workman . . . [whose manuscript] gives a straightfor-
ward, clear text, admirably suited to conveying the impression that the *Joseph
– Merlin – Perceval – Mort Artu* tetralogy is a unified and harmonious whole
. . . [while the Paris 'Didot' manuscript, although it tells essentially the same
story, contains] . . . hopelessly garbled passages. . . . The text of the [Didot]
manuscript is so corrupt that the reader may often wonder whether some of
its readings do not represent misprints or errors of transcription on the part of
the editor.'[3]

This, therefore, is a translation of the trilogy (or tetralogy, if you think of
the *Mort Artu* as a separate section) as compiled by the anonymous writer of
that specific manuscript, now in the library at Modena, and as it would have
been read – or, more probably, performed and heard – by a specific group of
people in the thirteenth century.

Authorship and sources

But what exactly did the redactor whose work is preserved in the Modena
manuscript do with Robert de Boron's material? What exactly did Robert
himself write?

A simple account would have it that this trilogy is a translation into prose
of a trilogy originally written by Robert in verse. However, only one manuscript of his verse version survives,[4] and it contains only *Joseph* and the first
502 lines of *Merlin*. Whilst it might be reasonable to conjecture that Robert
wrote a complete verse *Merlin* that is sadly lost, this is by no means certain;
and there is no reason at all to suppose that he ever wrote a verse *Perceval*.
Indeed, there is a very good reason to think that he did not: in the course of
this prose *Merlin* we come across a passage in which the redactor comments

---

2   Robert de Boron, *Le roman du Graal* (Paris, 1981).
3   William Roach, ed., *The Didot Perceval, According to the Manuscripts of Modena and Paris*
    (Philadelphia, 1941), pp. 37, 4, 5, 317.
4   Edited by William Nitze: Robert de Boron, *Le roman de l'Estoire dou Graal* (Paris, 1927).

that 'my lord Robert de Boron, who tells this story, says, like Merlin, that it is in two parts, for he could not know the story of the Grail' (below, p. 63). It is true that an ambiguity in the sentence structure at this point makes it just about possible that it is Merlin who 'could not know' – but it would be a strange thing to say about a being who has knowledge of all things past and future, and I have translated the sentence to make it clear that it is Robert who 'ne pot savoir le conte dou Graal'.

But what exactly did he 'not know'? Some scholars have suggested that Robert did not even know Chrétien de Troyes' unfinished *Perceval* which, in the mid-1180s, introduced the Grail to an intrigued world. However, given the degree of excitement generated by Chrétien's tantalising, unresolved theme, which prompted the composition of no fewer than four direct Continuations and other brilliant developments in, for example, *Perlesvaus* and *The Quest of the Holy Grail*, it does not seem likely that any writer interested in Arthurian matters in the 1180s and 1190s would have been unaware of *Perceval*. In any case, if Robert did not know Chrétien's work – or they were writing simultaneously – it would be difficult to explain the phrase 'and so the rich Fisher King departed – of whom many words have since been spoken' (below, p. 43, which corresponds to a similar passage in the verse *Joseph*, vv. 3456–8).

It must be said, however, that it is almost certain that neither the Fisher King nor the Grail was exactly Chrétien's invention. Robert refers to a 'high book' as his source (below, p. 22), just as Chrétien in his dedicatory prologue speaks of 'the book' given to him by his patron Count Philip of Flanders as the basis of his *Perceval*. Many motifs and narrative elements in Arthurian romances have been attributed to Celtic oral tradition, and this has long been assumed to apply also to the Grail. R.S. Loomis was notably sure that 'Chrétien did not invent his story, and later romancers, even when they knew and drew upon his poem, drew also on an amorphous mass of traditional material. . . . The legends of the Grail are a conglomerate of materials paralleled in the literature and lore of Ireland, Wales and Brittany.'[5] It is certainly possible that Robert drew on this independently of Chrétien; but I believe it most likely, amidst all the speculation, that he knew the contents of Chrétien's *Perceval* as well as something of the 'amorphous mass of traditional material', and was prompted by both to the idea for his hugely influential story of *Joseph of Arimathea*. I would suggest, therefore, that the prose redactor's reference to his 'not knowing' the story of the Grail was to Robert's being unable, perhaps because of his own death, to know the way the Grail theme had subsequently been developed in, for example, the Second Continuation, from which several episodes in the prose *Perceval* are derived.

[5] 'The Origin of the Grail Legends', in *Arthurian Literature in the Middle Ages*, ed. Loomis (Oxford, 1959), pp. 274–94.

Robert's inspirational idea was to make the Grail clearly, unambiguously Christian by giving it a Biblical early history. It is very easy, especially when coming to Arthurian literature for the first time, to forget that the so-called 'Holy Grail', connected with Christ, the Last Supper and the Crucifixion, is not explicitly Christian in the first Grail romance. It is not the famous holy chalice – in fact it is not a chalice at all, and not exactly referred to as holy.[6] In Chrétien de Troyes' *Perceval* it is even introduced on its first appearance with an indefinite article – 'un graal' – and in a most downbeat way at the start of a sentence:

> Un graal entre ses deus mains
> Une damoisele tenoit.[7]

What kind of vessel this grail is Chrétien never specifies, though he does tell us that it is made of pure gold and encrusted with surpassingly beautiful jewels, but in a later passage Perceval's hermit uncle tells him:

> Don't imagine that [the one who is served from the grail] is given pike or lamprey or salmon; he's served with a single host. . . .[8]

Chalices are not ideal for serving fish: Chrétien's grail is implicitly a dish or platter.[9]

Some might go as far as to say that nothing, in fact, in Chrétien's 'grail procession' is explicitly Christian – and certainly, nothing is in an orthodox sense: there are golden candlesticks, the grail, a silver trencher, and a lance that sheds blood from its tip.

But the 'unchristian' nature of Chrétien's grail and its accompanying procession can be – and has been – overstated. In relation to the bleeding lance, for example, although it is true that Chrétien makes no definite mention of the lance that pierced Christ's side on the cross, and although there has long been the suggestion that the bleeding lance is an echo of a pagan fertility ritual,[10] I think it inconceivable that an audience in the 1180s would have failed to think – instantly – of that relic sensationally found on the First Crusade, the Holy Lance. Moreover, Chrétien's grail contains a

---

6   In a late passage in Chrétien's *Perceval* there does appear the line 'Tant sainte chose est li graals' (Roach's edition, v.6425), but it could be argued that in context 'sainte' means 'holy' only in the sense of 'sacred', and is not specifically Christian.

7   Verses 3220–1 of Roach's edition (Geneva, 1959).

8   Chrétien de Troyes and his Continuators, *Perceval, the Story of the Grail*, translated by N. Bryant (Cambridge, 1982), p. 69, corresponding to Roach's edition, vv.6420–3.

9   If, as seems likely, the word derives from the Latin *gradalis*, it would imply a wide, fairly deep vessel. See Mario Roques, 'Le Nom du Graal', in *Colloques internationaux du Centre National de la Recherche Scientifique* (Paris, 1956).

10 See Jessie L. Weston's famous (but now the object of much scepticism) *From Ritual to Romance* (Cambridge, 1920).

host.[11] Now, Leonardo Olschki, in his forthright monograph *The Grail Castle and its Mysteries* (Manchester, 1966), declares that 'there is not the slightest reference to Christian liturgy in the whole procession' (pp. 14–15) and emphatically denies that the grail and its host are eucharistic: he is convinced that Chrétien had in mind the doctrines of the Cathars. His grail, he says, 'is a heterodox symbol, sacred, but not liturgical, and as such belongs to a ritual vaguely connected with the traditions of Christian worship, yet with a profoundly different meaning. The host contained in [Chrétien's] Grail signifies something quite different from the Eucharist of Catholic worship, which in the twelfth century was itself still an object of theological debate and widespread doubt concerning the concepts of the 'corpus verum' and 'corpus mysticum' of the 'impanatio' and 'transubstantiatio': all of which were resolved only after a great deal of controversy by the Lateran Council of 1215 . . . Chrétien's host brings to mind the consecrated bread that was broken and distributed to the faithful in the sacramental banquets that constituted the sole ceremony normally celebrated by Catharist communities. . . . This was the so-called 'supersubstantial bread', only apparently related to the historical Jesus and quite different from the 'corpus Christi' of Catholic worship . . .' (pp. 24–5).

Stimulating and intricately argued though Olschki's monograph is, it is ultimately hard to see why Chrétien, who was able to refer to 'the false Jews, who should be put down like dogs',[12] should be so mild and reasonable towards heretics, especially given that he was writing at the behest of a patron, Philip of Flanders, who, in Olschki's own words, 'after 1168, when he took over control of Flanders . . . proceeded to take more effective and more violent measures of repression against this centre of heretical expansion than the king of France had hitherto dared to employ' (pp. 60–1). Is there really anything dangerously undesirable or untoward about the Grail Castle, the contents of its procession, or the Fisher King himself? If they were intended to represent, in Olschki's words, 'the religious aberrations that menaced the

---

[11] In fact, Chrétien makes no reference to the host when Perceval first visits the Grail Castle. It is not mentioned until later, when Perceval meets his hermit uncle. This passage is thrust so briefly and abruptly into the middle of lengthy adventures centred on Sir Gawain that some scholars have suggested it is an interpolation. There is in my view nothing stylistically or thematically to substantiate this, though if it were the case, it would simply make Robert's idea of the Grail's Biblical origins even more remarkable.

R.S. Loomis ingeniously suggested that the presence of a host in Chrétien's grail was explicable in terms of a misunderstanding of the Welsh word '*corn*' (a horn – King Bran's magical horn of plenty in an old Celtic story) when translated into the French word 'cors', the equally magical, all-feeding *body* of Christ (R.S. Loomis, op.cit., p. 288). I am inclined, however, to think that Loomis's philological speculation is unnecessary, and there is certainly no need to think in terms of a misunderstanding: Chrétien merely needed to have some knowledge or memory of the Celtic tale, because to make a deliberate translation of a magic feeding vessel into a vessel containing a host is simultaneously brilliant and, in terms of symbolism, very simple.

[12] *Perceval*, tr. N. Bryant, p. 67; Roach's edition, vv.6292–3.

orthodoxy of courtly society' (p. 45), one would expect Chrétien to be rather less gentle in his correction of them. And Olschki's argument becomes much less convincing when he refers to Perceval's hermit uncle as 'the one who has found the way of salvation by remaining within the true faith, to which he causes Perceval to return, while the magic castle [of the Fisher King and the grail procession] disappears forever, as a symbol of that illusion and error which the young hero, now redeemed, definitely renounces:

> De Perceval plus longuemant
> Ne parole li contes ci.[13]

Such,' says Olschki, 'would appear to be . . . the basic allegory of Chrétien's poem' (p. 30). This is very odd. The two lines Olschki quotes do not conclude business at the Grail Castle at all; there is no reason whatever to say that it 'disappears forever': Olschki is somewhat bizarrely overlooking the two verses which immediately follow, in which Chrétien says 'You'll have heard a great deal about Sir Gawain before I tell of him [Perceval] again.'[14] There is every reason to suppose that, had Chrétien's death not prevented the poem's completion, the Fisher King would then have been revisited. Chrétien's Continuators certainly thought so: none of them saw matters finished like Olschki; they are all at pains to bring Gawain and Perceval back to the castle to do what Perceval had left undone.

And one thing is certain: when these later poets do revisit the Grail Castle, they are significantly under the Christianising influence of Robert de Boron, incorporating his idea of the Grail and its Biblical origins as described in his story of Joseph of Arimathea – without a hint of heresy. The decisive Christianisation of the Grail is Robert's vital contribution; because although I doubt that Chrétien was making deliberate and systematic heretical references and creating, in Olschki's words, 'a drama between heresy and faith' (op.cit., p. 46), Olschki may well be right to show how open Chrétien's mysterious story could have been to non-orthodox interpretation. It must be said that it is very noticeable that Robert de Boron goes out of his way in the opening paragraphs of *Joseph* (which are, significantly, uncharacteristically heavy handed) to emphasise absolutely orthodox ideas about the incarnation of Christ, the power of baptism in water and the authority of the ministers of Holy Church – all rejected by the Cathars, who were soon to be the objects of the Albigensian Crusade launched by Innocent III in 1209. Even more insistent are Robert's positive references to the Holy Trinity: as early as the 1140s Bernard of Clairvaux had found a denial of the Trinity prevalent in the Cathar heartland of Toulouse. Could it be that Robert was indeed aware of the possibility

---

[13] Corresponds to Roach's edition, vv.6514–15.
[14] *Perceval*, tr. N. Bryant, p. 70.

of non-orthodox interpretations of Chrétien's extraordinarily potent story, and saw the need to claim it absolutely for orthodoxy?

Whether or not this is the case, I believe that Chrétien's combination of the mightily suggestive lance (even though Robert does not mention it in *Joseph*) and a radiant vessel suddenly, briefly and tantalisingly revealed to be containing a host inspired Robert de Boron to his crucial idea of making the mysterious grail unequivocally Christian by giving it an origin in the Biblical past.[15] This idea makes his *Joseph of Arimathea*, in the words of William Roach, 'one of the most important documents in the history of the legend of the Holy Grail'.[16]

Robert, drawing partly on the canonical gospels and importantly on fragmentary stories of Joseph of Arimathea in the apocryphal *Gospel of Nichodemus*, created in his *Joseph* an ingenious early provenance for the grail. In writing what could almost be described as a new apocryphal gospel – carefully validated in a passage (below, p. 23) in which he explains why the other gospels do not mention certain incidents involved – Robert makes the grail the vessel used by Christ at the Last Supper, given to Pilate and passed on by him to Joseph of Arimathea, who uses it to collect the blood that flows from the crucified Christ's wounds; then, when Joseph is subsequently imprisoned, Christ brings the vessel to him and entrusts it to him and his successors. The reader will then see how Robert introduces the Fisher King (and explains the name) and carefully accounts for the vessel and its guardians finding their way to Britain.

But it is a Britain in which Arthur, let alone Perceval, is yet to be born, and the *Merlin* proceeds to bridge the gap in time by telling a rich story of the land's early history. Significant parts of this material (and the *Mort Artu* section of the *Perceval*) are derived from Geoffrey of Monmouth's Latin *History of the Kings of Britain* and/or from one of its adaptations into French

---

[15] Dating the composition and establishing the interconnection of Arthurian romances are notoriously difficult, but I believe it most likely that:

(a) Robert knew Chrétien's *Perceval*. He may also have been aware of other material relating to the Grail. (R.S. Loomis offers one small but possibly telling example when he points out how the name of Robert's Fisher King, Bron, though linked to the Biblical Hebron, is remarkably close to Bran, a corresponding infirm king with a mysterious vessel in the eleventh-century Welsh *Branwen* [Loomis, op.cit., p. 280] – if it is a coincidence, it is an extraordinary one.) Inspired to make the sacred vessel unambiguously Christian, Robert wrote his verse *Joseph of Arimathea* quite shortly after Chrétien's poem – early enough, I would suggest, to influence even the First Continuation to the extent of turning the grail in that anonymous author's mind into the 'Holy Grail' (though I am aware that the First Continuator was almost certainly influenced in his thinking by Celtic stories of magic vessels of plenty).

(b) The final composition of this prose trilogy was shortly after 1200, late enough for the *Perceval* section (which, although Robert doubtless intended to resolve what he had begun in *Joseph*, is in my view the work of a talented redactor and in no way from Robert's pen) to be influenced in turn by the Second Continuation.

[16] 'The Modena Text of the Prose *Joseph d'Arimathie*', in *Romance Philology*, Vol. IX (1955–56), pp. 313–42.

such as the *Roman de Brut* by the Jerseyman Wace. One of the central ideas in *Merlin* is the Biblical 'source' of the Round Table, as Robert states that it is a symbolic reflection of the table of the Last Supper. Interestingly, Wace was the first to mention the Round Table in vernacular literature, and although its origins probably lie in Celtic tradition – perhaps from the memory of chieftain and warriors seated in a circle around a central fire – it is intriguing that an amazing relic, a round table reputed to be that of the Last Supper, had been reportedly seen by Crusaders in the Holy Land.[17]

Sacred relics

Just as intriguing, and likewise connected with the subject of relics, is the care with which Robert traces the handing on of the Grail: at one point the bequeathing of the vessel from one guardian to another is even to have a witness arranged by God (below, p. 43). The insistence with which the Grail's provenance is marked might suggest that the authenticity of holy relics was a matter of deep concern for contemporary audiences. We should not be surprised by this. Throughout the twelfth century, ever since the First Crusade, Christians had returned with relics from the East: apostles' bones, dust and stones from holy places and above all items connected with the Passion had found their way to Northern Europe. How reliable was the provenance of thorns from the Crown of Thorns, the nails that had pierced His hands and feet, or the hairs reputedly collected by John after Mary, in grief, had torn them from her own head at the foot of the Cross? Famously questioned was the authenticity of the dramatic discovery by Peter Bartholomew, guided by his vision of the apostle Andrew, of none other than the Holy Lance with which Christ's side had been pierced. This relic is particularly interesting in relation to the story of the Grail, of course; because although, as discussed above, Chrétien does not give an overt Christian explanation for the lance with the bleeding head, the presence of this relic in the public consciousness makes it almost inevitable that his audience would have made an instant connection. It is not in the least surprising that Chrétien's first anonymous Continuator has Gawain learn that the bleeding lance is indeed the lance used at the Crucifixion – the lance of Longinus – as stated likewise here in the prose *Perceval* (below, p. 155).

But indeed, the very existence of precious relics, let alone their authenticity, was becoming a cause for concern: given the disastrous progress of the Crusades in the late twelfth century, the loss of holy places and their attendant relics to the Infidel was surely much on the minds of Robert's listeners.

---

[17] L.H. Loomis in *Modern Language Notes*, Vol. 44 (1929), pp. 511–15, quoted in *Arthurian Literature in the Middle Ages*, ed. Loomis (Oxford, 1959), p. 100.

As recently as 1187 the True Cross itself had been lost to Saladin at the catastrophic battle of Hattin. It is interesting to notice the stress placed on the rarity value of anything connected with Christ in Robert's handling of the story of Veronica: her cloth is emphatically 'the only thing they found which had touched Our Lord' (below, p. 28).

The preoccupation with holy relics in the twelfth century could well be an important element in the appeal and motivation of the Grail story. And what price a relic as wonderful as the vessel used by Him at the Last Supper – containing, moreover, the Holy Blood? The family to whom such a relic was bequeathed would be special indeed,[18] and the redactor whose work is preserved in the Modena manuscript, in adding *Perceval* to *Joseph* and *Merlin*, is extremely careful to draw the connection between Joseph of Arimathea, Bron, Alain li Gros and Alain's son: 'a line devoted to Our Lord, and He has so exalted them that He has given His flesh and His blood into their keeping' (below, p. 131).

The trilogy's construction

Careful connections, not only between characters but also between the different sections of this prose trilogy, have been underestimated by some scholars: Pierre Le Gentil, for example, has written of 'astonishing discrepancies between the two earlier romances and the *Perceval*'.[19] Admittedly, the trilogy is, in Le Gentil's words, 'loose in construction', but only two significant elements that Robert promises in *Joseph* will be resolved remain unfulfilled by the end of the trilogy – the exact fate of Moyse after plunging into the abyss (though a resolution is very satisfactorily given to the motif of the perilous empty seat), and the further exploits of Petrus. The Modena redactor is otherwise very precise in drawing his stories together. His main device is Merlin himself, who, having knowledge of all things past, present and future, knows everything about the stories of Joseph, Bron, Vortigern, Utherpendragon, Arthur and Perceval, and dictates them all to his scribe Blaise. He thus provides a link between the three parts, an explanation of how they came to be together in one book, and indeed an authority. And authority for the story was, perhaps, not unconnected to authenticity for the relic.

The 'astonishing discrepancies' are far less noticeable than the connections. In *Joseph of Arimathea*, Joseph is told to make a table 'in the name of' the

---

[18] In this connection it is worth noting Mary E. Giffin's article 'A Reading of Robert de Boron' (*Publications of the Modern Language Association of America*, Vol. 80 [1965], pp. 499–507), in which she argues that local concerns, place-names and personal names relating to Robert's patrons and his area of Burgundy correspond in a surprising way to proper names in *Joseph*.

[19] 'The Work of Robert de Boron', in *Arthurian Literature in the Middle Ages*, ed. Loomis (Oxford, 1959), pp. 251–62.

table of the Last Supper (below, p. 35), and it is part of Robert's plan that another table, with another perilous empty seat, will be made in its name (below, p. 38). Sure enough, the redactor (or Robert himself, if he did write a complete verse *Merlin*), carefully connects apocryphal Biblical matter with the mythical–historical material about early Britain by having Merlin order Utherpendragon to establish a similar table 'in the name of the Trinity, which these three tables will signify' (below, p. 92). At this point the redactor (or Robert) also plans ahead to the *Perceval* by predicting that the empty seat will be filled by the son of Alain li Gros.

And having combined Biblical matters in *Joseph* with mythical British history in *Merlin*, the connection with the world of chivalric romance in *Perceval* is fully prepared at the end of *Merlin* by the idea of knightly deeds and great feats of arms at tournaments being necessary for the successful completion of the Grail quest (below, p. 113). If there are any lingering doubts about the clarity of the trilogy's conception, it should be noted that the final pages of *Merlin* even prepare us for the *Mort Artu* section by Merlin's prediction about Arthur conquering the Romans (below, p. 112), a conquest which, he says, will be dependent in turn upon the successful outcome of the Grail quest (below, pp. 112–13).

The trilogy's construction may be 'loose', but it is an ingenious melding of disparate materials, compressing and connecting historical time in a strikingly meaningful way, and its inconsistencies, far from being astonishing, are in the circumstances remarkably minor.

Style

Robert has also been unduly criticised for his style. Fairly typical is Le Gentil's view that he was 'a poet endowed with boldness and piety but with mediocre talent' (op.cit., p. 251). No-one would argue that the octosyllabic lines of his verse *Joseph* are the most sprightly – they do not remotely compare with, for example, the verse of Chrétien de Troyes or Gerbert de Montreuil. But looking at the style of this prose redaction it is hard not to be impressed by the pace, fluency and vigour of the storytelling, and by how brilliantly it could be made to work upon the *ear*. For it must not be forgotten that what we have here is a script for performance. It cries out to be read aloud.

There are innumerable indications that this early prose literature was intended for the ear rather than the eye. Indeed in this trilogy there is not a single reference to 'reading' the story: the word used is – invariably – 'to hear'. And the writer of the manuscript refers not merely to 'all who hear this *tale*' (below, p. 65) but also, more strikingly, to 'hearing' the *book*. 'I'd like you to set it down in a book,' Merlin tells Blaise, 'for many people who hear my words will benefit from them' (below, p. 61); later he assures him that '*The Book of the Grail* will be heard most gladly' (below, p. 71); and the trilogy ends with Merlin's prayer for God's blessing upon 'all who would willingly hear his book and have it copied' (below, p. 172). That is not to underestimate the importance of writing, of the book; indeed it is very clear, as Evelyn Birge Vitz argues, that the creators of these stories valued texts 'as bearing authority. . . . They recognised the clout of the written word . . . [but] we cannot begin truly to appreciate the interpersonal and interactive, nor indeed the dramatic and musical, qualities of medieval romances unless and until we actually perform them, and hear and see them performed'.[20]

The oral nature of the writing – to coin a paradox – is crucial in appreciating the style of this prose trilogy. In the hands of a talented performer this material has tremendous potential. Time after time the reader may be inclined to think phrases – or whole passages – strangely matter-of-fact and underwritten; but it is the very spareness of the phraseology which, in performance, could be most intensely dramatic. The conception of Arthur, for example, appears on the page to be absurdly understated:

> Utherpendragon and Igerne lay together that night. And he begat an heir who was later to be called King Arthur.   (Below, p. 100)

But a good performer would understand that, coming immediately after the possibly erotic, very nearly comic 'as soon as Igerne heard that the duke had come she had taken to her bed, and when Uther saw her lying there in all her beauty, the blood stirred throughout his body. Merlin and Ulfin removed their lord's boots as fast as they could, and put him to bed,' the simplicity of the sentences quoted above is startling, potentially full of sudden gravitas, ending wonderfully with the resonant name of Arthur.

Equally underexploited at first glance is Gawain's death (below, p. 170), which could seem ineptly brief: 'ill befell Gawain: his helmet was not laced on, and a Saxon wielding an oar dealt him a blow to the head that struck him dead'; but it is totally unexpected – as is the pathetic, ignoble nature of the weapon – and timed well by a good performer this would be deeply shocking, especially because it is followed by a brilliant, abrupt change of tone as the performer is required to launch into an anguished lament.

Most extraordinarily underwritten of all, perhaps, is the exchange between Kay, Entor and Arthur about the drawing of the sword from the stone (below, p. 108). A modern novelist would almost certainly describe for the solitary reader, curled up alone in a chair, the looks on the characters' faces, exactly what went through their minds and how they felt. The medieval writer had no need to do this, because he knew that a skilled performer would reveal the subtextual emotions and reactions in his delivery to the gathered, communal

---

[20] Evelyn Birge Vitz, *Orality and Performance in Early French Romance* (Cambridge, 1999), pp. 33, 282.

listeners.[21] Once again the spareness with which it is written, apparently simplistic, is due not to artistic naivety[22] but to an experienced, highly developed sense of what would work startlingly and movingly when performed. Kay's initial impulse to be deceitful, then his inability to lie to his father, then Entor's instant realisation of the truth of the situation, cannot be quoted because they are not on the page; they are between the lines, waiting to be revealed by the performer. And for any sensitive performer, when Entor tells Arthur that he is only his foster-father, the stunningly simple sentence

> When Arthur heard this, he wept

is perfectly judged. The pacing of this passage, from a performance perspective, is masterly.

In terms both of structure and of style this trilogy has been judged far too much in terms of modern expectations. Its diverse contents make it a remarkable piece of work, combining a new apocryphal gospel (*Joseph of Arimathea*) with a retelling of mythical British history (*Merlin*) and with chivalric romance (in *Perceval*) to create the earliest complete 'Arthurian cycle'. Stylistically, it is a finely paced, vigorous piece of storytelling which, for a talented performer, would provide a highly accomplished and potent script.

Nigel Bryant

Further reading

BAUMGARTNER, Emmanuele. 'Robert de Boron et l'imaginaire du livre du Graal', in *Arturus Rex, Acta Conventus Lovaniensis, 1987*, Vol. 2, ed. W. Van Hoecke, G. Tournoy and W. Verbeke, pp. 259–68, Louvain, 1991.
CERQUIGLINI, Bernard. *La parole medievale*, Paris, 1981.
————. 'Sur la prose du *Joseph d'Arimathie*: Forme et statut de la parole', in *Perspectives Medievales* 3 (1977), pp. 43–8.

---

[21] In her excellent *Orality and Performance in Early French Romance*, Evelyn Birge Vitz emphatically states that 'for the late twelfth and early thirteenth centuries [there is] no evidence at all of private or silent reading of romance. . . . As Joyce Coleman has shown in *Public Reading and the Reading Public in Late Medieval England and France* [Cambridge University Press, 1996], people who read privately were long viewed with disapproval, as being anti-social' (pp. 220, 210). And Sandra Hindman, in an interesting study of manuscripts and their illuminations, writes that 'written texts continued to be used in performance, creating "hearing" as a middle ground in the axis between oral "seeing" and literate "reading". . . . The manuscripts of Chrétien's romances occupy this middle ground, used in a culture unlike our own that was not yet accustomed to individual or silent reading of vernacular texts' (Sandra Hindman, *Sealed in Parchment*, Chicago, 1994, p. 8).

[22] He can write intricately enough if he needs to: in describing combat, for example – which, of course, is significantly not performable.

DUGGAN, Joseph J. 'Oral Performance of Romance in Medieval France', in *Continuations: Essays in Medieval French Literature and Language in Honor of John L. Grigsby*, ed. Norris J. Lacy and Gloria Torrini-Roblin, Birmingham, Alabama, 1989, pp. 51–61.

———. 'Performance and Transmission: Aural and Ocular Reception in the Twelfth and Thirteenth Century Vernacular Literature of France', in *Romance Philology* 42 (1989), pp. 49–58.

GOODRICH, Norma Lorre. *Merlin*, New York, 1987.

GOODRICH, Peter, ed. *The Romance of Merlin, an Anthology*, New York, 1990.

GOWANS, Linda M. 'New Perspectives on the *Didot-Perceval*', in *Arthurian Literature VII*, D.S. Brewer, Cambridge, 1987, pp. 1–22.

HARDING, Carol Elaine. *Merlin and Legendary Romance*, New York, 1988.

LACY, Norris J., ed. *Medieval Arthurian Literature: A Guide to Recent Research*, New York and London, 1996.

LACY, N.J., KELLY, D., and BUSBY, K., eds. *The Legacy of Chrétien de Troyes*, 2 vols, Amsterdam, 1987–88.

MACDONALD, A.A. *The Figure of Merlin in Thirteenth Century French Romance*, Lewiston, Queenston and Lampeter, 1990.

MEISTER, P., ed. *Arthurian Literature and Christianity*, New York and London, 1999.

MICHA, Alexandre. *Etude sur le 'Merlin' de Robert de Boron*, Geneva, 1980.

PICKENS, Rupert T. ' "Mais de çou ne parole pas Crestiens de Troies" – a re-examination of the *Didot-Perceval*', in *Romania* 105 (1984), pp. 492–510.

SCHMOLKE-HASSELMANN, Beate. *The Evolution of Arthurian Romance*, Cambridge, 1998.

ZUMTHOR, Paul. *Merlin le Prophete. Un theme de la litterature polemique, de l'historiographie et des romans*, Lausanne, 1943, reprinted Slatkine, 1973.

Joseph of Arimathea

ALL SINFUL PEOPLE should know this: that before Our Lord came to Earth, He made the prophets speak in His name and announce His coming to this world. At the time of which I speak all people went to Hell – even the prophets. And when the demons had led them there they thought they had scored a great victory; but they were woefully mistaken, for the people took comfort in the coming of Christ. And Our Lord came, choosing to come to Earth incarnate of the Virgin Mary.

Our Lord was gentle and kind indeed, that to redeem His sinners from Hell He made His daughter His mother; but it had to be so if He was to redeem the descendants of Adam and Eve. Hear now how He did so: He redeemed them by the Father and by the Son and by the Holy Spirit, and these three beings are one. It pleased God the Father that the Son should be born of the Virgin Mary without sin or foulness, and should take human, earthly flesh. This Lord was full of humility, willing as He was to come down to Earth and die to save the work of His Father – for the Father made Adam and Eve. But Eve had sinned through the cunning of the Enemy, and in sinning had caused Adam to do likewise. And when Adam had sinned he felt naked and ashamed, and conscious of lust; he was instantly cast out of paradise, and fell into a state of torment and wretchedness. In this state they conceived; and all their children, and the children of their children, the Enemy was determined to have; and so he did, until the Son of God came to save His Father's work on Earth. This was Christ's purpose in coming to this world, being born of the Virgin Mary at Bethlehem. Much could be said of this, for the fountain of His goodness is inexhaustible. So I must digress now, and turn to this work of mine, in which I pray He may by His grace direct my thought and understanding.

It is certain truth that Our Lord travelled through the land and was baptised in the River Jordan. And he decreed that all who were baptised in water in the name of the Father, Son and Holy Spirit would be free from the powers of the Enemy until they laid themselves open again by their own sinful deeds. Our Lord conferred this power upon Holy Church, and gave His commandments to my lord Saint Peter. And so Our Lord cleansed man and woman, father and mother, of their sinful ways, and the Devil lost his power over men – until they chose to sin again. And Our Lord, knowing that the fragility of man was such that he was sure to die [in sin], bestowed upon Saint Peter another form of baptism: confession. He ordained that if they were willing to repent and abandon their sin and keep the commandments of Holy Church, they might come to be granted grace[1] by their Father.

At the time when Our Lord was upon the Earth, most of the land of Judaea was answerable to Rome. The Romans held sway over the region where Our Lord dwelt, and the governor's name was Pilate. This Pilate had in his service a soldier named Joseph [of Arimathea], who followed Jesus Christ to many places and loved him deeply in his heart, but dared not show it for fear of the other Jews, for Our Lord had many enemies and adversaries set against him – and also one disciple who was not as a follower should be. And because this man was not as gracious towards his fellow disciples as they were towards each other, he began to distance himself from them in his actions, misbehaving and being more cruel towards them than he had been before; they were very wary of him. But Our Lord, being God, knew all. This disciple's name was Judas, and his hatred towards Our Lord was conceived on account of an ointment; I shall tell you now of his treachery.

At this time it was the custom that a chamberlain received a tenth of all moneys that came into his lord's purse, and when my lady Saint Mary Magdalene poured an ointment upon Our Lord's feet Judas was enraged, counting in his heart that the ointment was worth three hundred pence. He did not want to lose his due; he reckoned his tenth was worth thirty pence, and was determined to recover that amount. At the earliest opportunity he sought to recover those thirty pence from God's enemies.

Three nights before the Passover, Christ's enemies were at the house of a man named Caiaphas, discussing how they could capture Him. Joseph of Arimathea was present as they talked, and to him their words were sinful: they grieved him terribly. In the middle of their discussion Judas appeared, and when they saw him they fell silent, for they distrusted him, believing him to be a good disciple of Jesus. Judas, seeing them fall silent, spoke out and asked them: 'Why are you assembled here?'

And they replied: 'Where is Jesus?'

And he told them where He was and why he had come to them. And when the Jews heard Judas's disloyalty they were overjoyed and said: 'Tell us how we can take him prisoner!'

And Judas replied: 'I'll sell him to you if you wish.'

'Yes indeed,' they said, 'most gladly!'

And he said he would give them Jesus for thirty pence. One of them had

---

1 The Modena manuscript reads 'belief'. This seems to be a scribal misreading of *creance* for *grace* (as suggested by the verse *Joseph* v.192).

the money to hand, and paid it. And so Judas recovered a tenth of the three hundred pennies' worth of ointment.

Then they discussed how they would capture Jesus: they fixed the day and an early hour; Judas would inform them where Jesus would be, and they would be armed and ready to seize Him. And Judas warned them to be sure they did not seize James, for he looked very much like Jesus – understandably, for James was His cousin. And they asked him: 'How then will we recognise Jesus?'

And he replied: 'Take the man that I shall kiss.'

And so it was resolved.

Joseph of Arimathea was present throughout all this, and it weighed heavily upon his heart, but he dared do nothing. They went their several ways and waited till the Thursday.

On the Thursday evening Our Lord was at the house of Simon the Leper. I cannot and should not tell you everything He said to His disciples, but this much I can say for sure: He told them that eating and drinking with Him was one who would betray Him. Hearing Our Lord's words, some of the disciples were afraid and swore they were not guilty. But Christ assured them it was true, and Judas asked Him: 'Am I the one you mean?'

And Jesus answered: 'You say so.'

Then Jesus told them other parables; and He washed all the disciples' feet in the same water. My lord Saint John privately asked Jesus: 'Lord, would you please tell me one thing? Dare I ask you?' Our Lord gave him leave to ask, and he said: 'Lord, tell me why you've washed all our feet in the same water.'

And Jesus replied: 'This is a parable for Peter. Just as the water was soiled by the first feet I washed, so no-one is clean of sin, and for as long as they are sinners they shall be unclean. But sinners can always cleanse away sin, just as I washed your feet in the dirty water. The first feet to be washed and the last look as clean as each other. This parable is for Peter and other ministers of Holy Church: unclean though they may be, through their uncleanness they will cleanse sinners of their sin. So long as they are willing to obey the Father, Son, Holy Spirit and Holy Church, their uncleanness can do them no harm. And no-one could know which of you I had washed, unless they had been told.'

Thus Our Lord Jesus Christ explained this parable to Saint John the Evangelist.

Then all those whom Judas had informed gathered at the house of Simon the Leper, and when the disciples realised this they were filled with fear. And once the house was full, and Judas was sure they had the upper hand, he stepped forward and kissed Jesus. Seeing this the Jews seized Him from all sides, and Judas cried to them: 'Hold him fast!', for he knew how great was Christ's strength. And they led Jesus away, leaving the disciples filled with grief.

So the Jews had accomplished part of their purpose in their capture of

Christ. And the vessel in which He had made the sacrament was at Simon's house, and one of the Jews took it and kept it until the next day.

Jesus was taken before Pilate, and many words were spoken there, the Jews charging Him with everything they could. But their power was not great: they could find no justification for putting Him to death. But the weakness of the law was such, and Pilate felt so powerless before all the Jews, that he had to accept it. Then he spoke as governor, saying: 'To which of you shall I refer if my lord [the emperor] asks me about this matter? For I can see no reason for this man to suffer death.'

And they all cried out together: 'May his blood be scattered upon us and all our children!'

Then the Jews seized Him and led Him away. Pilate stayed, and called for water and washed his hands, and said that, just as his hands were clean, so was he clean of responsibility for that man's death. Thereupon the Jew who had taken the vessel from Simon's house came to Pilate and gave it to him. Pilate took it and kept it safe.

When the news came that they had put Jesus to death, Joseph was filled with grief and anguish, and he came to Pilate and said: 'Sir, my knights and I have served you for a long while, and you've given me nothing for my service.'

'Ask,' said Pilate, 'and I'll give you whatever you wish in payment.'

And Joseph replied: 'Many thanks, sir. I ask for the body of the prophet whom the Jews have wrongfully put to death.'

Pilate was astonished that he should ask for such a poor reward, and said: 'I thought you'd ask for a greater gift. If that's the payment you desire, you shall have it.'

And Joseph answered: 'Many thanks, sir. Give orders that it should be mine.'

'Go and take it,' said Pilate; but Joseph replied: 'Sir, the Jews are strong in numbers, and will not want to give it to me.'

'Yes, they will,' said Pilate; so Joseph made his way to the cross. When he saw Jesus Christ he was filled with pity and wept most tenderly, for he loved Him deeply. He came to the Jews who were guarding Him and said: 'Pilate has given me permission to remove the prophet's body from this shameful place.'

But all the Jews together said: 'You're not having it, for his disciples say he's going to revive. But however often he comes back to life, we'll kill him!'

'Let me take him, sirs,' said Joseph, 'for Pilate has granted him to me.'

But the Jews said: 'We'd sooner kill you!'

Joseph left them and returned to Pilate and told him of the Jews' response. Pilate was amazed; but he saw before him a man named Nichodemus, and he commanded him to go with Joseph and take Christ's body from the cross himself. And then he remembered the vessel that the Jew had given him, and he called Joseph and said: 'Joseph, you love that prophet dearly.'

'Yes indeed, sir,' Joseph answered, and Pilate said: 'I have a vessel of his, given to me by one of the Jews who were present at his capture, and I've no wish to keep anything that belonged to him.'

And he gave the vessel to Joseph, who received it with great joy. Joseph and Nichodemus departed together, and Nichodemus went to a smith to get pincers and a hammer; then they came to the place where Christ was on the cross, and Nichodemus said to the people there: 'You've done wrong in dealing with this man as you demanded of Pilate. But now he's clearly dead, and Pilate has granted the body to Joseph and has commanded me to give it to him.'

They all replied that he was sure to come back to life, and refused to let the body go; but Nichodemus said that nothing they could do would stop him taking it. So they all marched off to Pilate, while Joseph and Nichodemus climbed up and took Jesus Christ from the cross.

Joseph held Him in his arms and laid Him on the ground, cradling Him tenderly and washing Him most gently. And when he had washed Him, he saw His wounds still bleeding and was dismayed, remembering the stone that had split at the foot of the cross when the drop of blood fell.

And then he remembered his vessel, and thought the drops of blood that were falling would be better in the vessel than elsewhere. So he placed it beneath Christ's wounds; and blood from the wounds in His hands and His feet dripped into the vessel. After gathering the blood in the vessel Joseph set it to one side, and took the body of Jesus Christ and wrapped it in a sheet that he had bought for his own use, and covered it.

Meanwhile the crowd who had gone to Pilate gained his agreement that, wherever Joseph might put the body, it should be closely watched in case it came back to life, and they arranged for a large armed guard. When Joseph departed, they remained.

While all this was happening, Our Lord descended into Hell, broke in and set free Adam and Eve and as many others as He pleased. And He returned to life, unknown and unseen by those who were standing guard, and He went forth and appeared to Saint Mary Magdalene and to other disciples where He chose.

When the Jews heard He had come back to life they all assembled to hold council, and said to each other: 'This man will do us great harm if he's truly alive again!'

And those who had been guarding the body declared that they knew for sure it was not where Joseph had put it. 'It's his fault we've lost him!' they said. 'And if harm befalls us it'll be because of him and Nichodemus!'

And they discussed how they could reply if they were asked for the body, or if it was requested by the master [the emperor] to whom they were subjects; and they agreed to say they had handed it over on the orders of Nichodemus.

'But if anyone says "You had the body guarded where it was laid to rest – ask your guards what happened," what answer could we give?'

And one replied: 'There's a way around that. Let's seize Joseph and Nichodemus tonight in secret, and put them to a grim death. Then after, if anyone asks us for Jesus's body, we'll say we gave it to them!'

They all agreed to this, and praised the man for his cleverness. So it was agreed they would seize them by night.

But friends of Nichodemus were present, and they informed him of the plan and he fled; and when the Jews arrived at his house they found no sign of him. So they moved on to the house of Joseph, and seized him naked in his bed; they made him dress and then led him to the house of one of the richest men in the land, where there was a tower with a dismal dungeon. Having Joseph there on his own, they beat him and asked him what he had done with Jesus.

'Those who were guarding him will know,' he replied, 'for I did nothing secret or underhand.'

'You've stolen him from us!' they replied, 'for he's certainly not where we saw you put him. We know you've taken him. We're going to throw you in this dungeon, and you'll surely die there unless you tell us where the body of Jesus is.'

And Joseph, knowing nothing of its whereabouts, said: 'I'm willing to die, if that is the will of the Lord on whose account I'm your captive.'

Then the Jews seized him and beat him dreadfully, and cast him down into the dungeon. They sealed it with a stone, so that if anyone came in search of him, they would never find him.

And so it was that Joseph was abducted and imprisoned. When Pilate knew that Joseph was missing, he was most distressed and heavy-hearted, for he was the best of friends to him. Joseph was missing for a long time.

But the one in whose cause he had suffered did not forget him. Being Lord and God He watched over him, and came to the dungeon where he lay, and brought him his vessel. Joseph saw a great light, and was filled with joy and with the grace of the Holy Spirit, and he marvelled and said: 'Almighty God, where can such a brilliant light come from unless from You?'

And Jesus answered: 'Joseph, Joseph, do not be afraid, for my Father's power will guard you.'

'Who are you?' Joseph asked Him. 'You're so fair – I don't know you – I cannot look upon you.'

And Jesus said: 'Joseph, listen to me. I am Jesus Christ, the Son of God, who has sent me into this world to save sinners. I came to Earth to suffer death at the command of my Father, who made Adam and from Adam made Eve, but the Enemy deceived Eve and made her sin, and she caused Adam to do likewise. They were cast into misery; and they conceived and had children and descendants, and when they died the Devil was determined they should all be his, until it pleased my Father that I should come to Earth and be born of woman. It was through a woman that the Enemy took possession of men; and as a woman had caused man's soul to be imprisoned, it was right and necessary that it should be recovered and redeemed through a woman.

'Now you have heard how the Son of God came to Earth, and why He was born of the Virgin Mary; and you have seen the torment I suffered and the great pain the Son bore in obeying the Father. Just as the tree[2] bore the apple, so the Son of God died on a tree[3] to save His Father's creation. I came on Earth to work this salvation, and was born of the Virgin Mary and suffered worldly pain. Blood flowed from my body in five places.'

'What, sir?' said Joseph. 'Are you then Jesus of Nazareth, son of the Virgin Mary the wife of Joseph? The one Judas sold for thirty pence, who was seized by the Jews and led before Pilate and crucified? The one I took from the cross and laid in a stone tomb, and who the Jews say I've stolen?'

'Joseph, I am the very same,' said Jesus. 'Believe what you have said and seen, and you will be saved and have lasting joy.'

'Oh Lord,' said Joseph, 'have pity and mercy on me: it's for your sake I'm imprisoned here. I've always loved you dearly, but never dared to speak to you, for I feared, Lord, that you wouldn't trust me because of the people I conversed with, keeping company as I did with the ones who meant you harm.'

'Joseph,' Our Lord replied, 'it's good to have a friend amongst enemies: you can see that for yourself – when a thing is obvious there's no need for explanation. I knew you were a good friend to me; that's why I left you with them because of the love you felt for me, knowing that you would feel dismay and grief at my torment and would come to my aid when none of my disciples could. I knew you would help me out of love for my Father, who had given you the heart and will to do the service for which I was given to you.'

'Oh, dear Lord,' said Joseph, 'don't say that you're mine!'

'But I am,' Our Lord replied. 'I belong to all the good, and all the good are mine. And do you know what reward you'll have because I was given to you? Lasting joy will be yours at the end of this mortal life. I have brought none of my disciples here because none of them knows of the love between us. You have loved me in secret as I have loved you. But know this: our love will be revealed to all – and will be a curse to the wicked – for you shall have the sign of my death in your keeping: see, it is here.'

And Our Lord took hold of the precious vessel with the most holy blood that Joseph had gathered from His precious body when he washed Him. When Joseph saw the vessel and knew it as the one he had hidden in his house, unknown by any man on Earth but he, he was filled with the love of

---

2 i.e. in the Garden of Eden.
3 i.e. the cross.

Christ and certain faith, and he went down on his knees and cried for mercy, saying: 'Lord, am I worthy to keep such a holy thing as this vessel?'

And Our Lord replied: 'Joseph, you must be its keeper, you and whoever else you may command. But there must be no more than three keepers, and those three shall guard it in the name of the Father, Son and Holy Spirit – and you and all who guard it must believe and know that these three powers are one and the same being in God.'

Joseph was on his knees, and Our Lord handed him the vessel and he took it, and Our Lord said: 'Joseph, you are holding the blood which contains these three powers, which are one and the same being in God. Do you understand your reward? Your reward is that the sacrament shall never be made without remembrance of your good work by those who recognise it.'

'Lord,' replied Joseph, 'please tell me what I did, for I don't know.'

And Jesus said: 'Joseph, you took me from the cross. And you know well that I took the Last Supper at the house of Simon the Leper, where I said that I was to be betrayed. As I said at that table, several tables will be established in my service, to make the sacrament in my name, which will be a reminder of the cross; and the vessel of the sacrament will be a reminder of the stone tomb in which you laid me, and the paten which will be placed on top will be a reminder of the lid with which you covered me, and the cloth called the corporal will be a reminder of the winding-sheet in which you wrapped me. And so your work will be remembered until the world's end. And all who see the vessel and remain in its presence will have lasting joy and fulfilment for their souls. And all who take these words to heart will be more gracious and admired both in this world and in the eyes of Our Lord, and will never be victims of injustice or deprived of their rights.'

Then Jesus spoke other words to Joseph which I dare not tell you – nor could I, even if I wanted to, if I did not have the high book in which they are written: and that is the creed of the great mystery of the Grail. And I beg all those who hear this tale to ask me no more about it at this point, in God's name, for I should have to lie. And from lies, you may be sure, they would gain nothing.

And so Christ gave the vessel to Joseph. And when he had taken it, Our Lord spoke sacred words that He had prepared for him, and said: 'Whenever you wish or have need, seek the help of the three powers that are one being, and of that blessed lady Holy Mary who gave birth to God the Son, and ask for whatever counsel your heart desires, and you will hear the voice of the Holy Spirit. I shall never lie to you about this: it would not be right. And you will not remain imprisoned in this dungeon, in the darkness you have suffered since they put you here; do not be dismayed – your deliverance will astound your wicked captors. Show love for the one who will come to free you, and tell him of the three powers just as the words come to you, for the Holy Spirit will be with you and will teach you things of which you know nothing.'

And so Joseph remained in prison. Of his imprisonment nothing is said by the apostles or those who established the scriptures, for they knew nothing about Joseph except that, because of his affection for Christ, he had asked to be granted His body.[4] Some of the apostles did hear of Joseph's disappearance, but they did not speak of it, since they committed nothing to the scriptures except what they had seen or heard themselves; and having seen and heard nothing of Joseph they had no wish to write about him – and they did not want his disappearance to make people uneasy about the faith, but such fear is wrong, and Our Lord says why when he speaks of the false glory of the world.

Joseph stayed imprisoned for a long time.

*

Meanwhile there was a pilgrim who had been in Judaea at the time when Our Lord was going through the land performing miracles and other works of marvellous power upon the blind and the lame. The pilgrim saw these miracles, and stayed in the land long enough to witness Jesus being charged and taken and crucified under the government of Pilate. This worthy man journeyed through many lands until at last he came to Rome, at the time when Vespasian, the son of the emperor, was sick with leprosy; and his stench was so great that no-one, however much they loved him, could bear it. It deeply grieved both the emperor and all those who loved him, but it was impossible to tolerate his presence. He was shut away in a stone chamber with only a tiny window through which they passed his food. The worthy pilgrim came to Rome and took lodging with a rich man in the city. In conversation that evening, the rich man told his guest how pitiful it was that the emperor's son was sick and shut away, and said that if he knew of any possible remedy, he should say so. And the pilgrim replied:

'No, I don't; but I can tell you that in the land of Judaea there was a prophet through whom great God worked many miracles. I saw lame who couldn't walk and blind who could see nothing whom he healed and restored to sight. I can't tell you of all the miracles he worked. But I can assure you that he healed anyone he wished to heal, so that the rich and powerful of Judaea came to hate him because they could do nothing to match his words and deeds.'

And his worthy host asked him: 'What became of this good man, and what was his name?'

'I'll tell you,' the pilgrim replied. 'His name was Jesus of Nazareth, the son of Mary. And those who hated him offered such a great reward that he was seized and abused and beaten and mistreated in all possible ways. Then they

---

[4] Curious syntax in the Modena manuscript could suggest that Christ wanted Joseph to be given His body because of His affection for him. I've opted for the more likely reading.

put him to death by crucifying him. And I swear to you,' said the pilgrim, 'by my body and soul, that if he were still alive and were brought before the emperor's son, if he wished to cure him he would certainly do so.'

And his host said: 'Did you ever hear why he was crucified?'

'No,' said the pilgrim, 'except that they hated him.'

'Where did this happen, under whose jurisdiction?'

'Pilate's,' said the pilgrim, 'the emperor's governor in that city.'

'Truly now, would you come with me and tell this to the emperor?'

'I'd tell it to anyone,' he replied.

When his worthy host had heard the pilgrim's tale, he went to the emperor and took him to one side and told him word for word what the pilgrim had said. The emperor was astounded, and said: 'Could this be true?'

'I don't know,' he replied, 'but that's what my guest told me. I'll bring him here to speak to you himself if you wish.'

'Fetch him immediately,' said the emperor; and he went to his guest at once and said: 'Good sir, come with me to the emperor and tell him what you told me.'

'Gladly, sir,' said the pilgrim, and when they came before the emperor the pilgrim said: 'My lord, you sent for me.'

'Indeed I did,' the emperor replied, 'to tell me what you told your host.'

'Willingly,' he said, and told him exactly as he had told it before; and when the emperor had heard it he assembled all his counsellors and told them the pilgrim's story. They were utterly amazed, for they had always thought Pilate a good and wise man who would never have permitted such an outrage.

'Well, he did so, most certainly,' said the emperor, 'and it was very wrong of him, allowing the prophet to be unjustly put to death in the land where he was governor.'

And one of them said: 'I love Pilate dearly, and I can't accept that he would have permitted the killing of such a good and wise man, and such a great healer, if he could have prevented it.'

So the pilgrim was summoned and ordered to repeat his tale, and he told them of the miracles and the great wonders that Jesus Christ had worked while on Earth, and he assured them that the Jews had put him to death in the land governed by Pilate; and had he been alive he would have healed the emperor's son if he had wished.

'And I say this, too: if anyone were to say this isn't true, I'd wager my head and my body that Pilate would not deny it. I also believe that if anyone found anything that had belonged to the prophet, and brought it to the emperor's son, if he had faith and touched it, he would be healed.'

They were all astounded at his words, and no-one dared speak in support of Pilate; but one of them said: 'If my lord sends me to learn the truth, what would you have us do with you?'

'Keep me fed until your return, and if you say my story isn't true, I shall accept death by beheading.'

They all agreed he had said enough, and they had him taken and placed in a chamber under guard. Then the emperor said he would send people to verify the pilgrim's words, and to see if they could find anything that had been touched by the prophet, for if his son could have it and touch it, it might heal him, and nothing would give him greater joy than his son's cure. Then one of Pilate's friends said: 'Send me, my lord, for I'll be a better judge than anyone.'

'I'll send you and others,' the emperor replied.

Then the emperor spoke to his son Vespasian, and told him everything the pilgrim had said, and how he had imprisoned him until such time as his messengers returned with word of whether his story was true or false. Vespasian was overjoyed at the news and his sorrow was greatly lightened, and he begged his father to send the messengers as soon as he could. The emperor did so, and gave them letters to lend credence to what they would say of the prophet's death. He sent the wisest men of his court to confirm the pilgrim's story and, if the prophet was dead, to bring back something he had touched to heal his son.

The emperor's messengers set out over the sea to the land of Judaea. And once across, Pilate's friends sent him a letter saying that they were amazed by his foolish, wrongful act in allowing the unjust death of the prophet in his land. The emperor's messengers had arrived, they said, and he should come to meet them, for he could not flee. When Pilate heard his friends' message he was astonished and alarmed, and ordered his men to mount, for he would go and meet the emperor's messengers. Meanwhile the messengers were riding to where they expected to find him, and Pilate was riding to meet them, and so it was that the two parties met at Arimathea.

When the messengers saw Pilate there was no rejoicing, for they did not know whether or not they would be taking him back to Rome to execute him. They gave him the emperor's letters, which told him everything the pilgrim had said. Pilate knew it was all true: the emperor had received good information. He turned back to the messengers, looked kindly upon them, and said:

'Sirs, everything these letters state is true: it was exactly as they say.'

The messengers were amazed that he should admit to the story, and they all said: 'You're acknowledging great folly. If you can't excuse yourself, you'll surely die.'

Pilate called the messengers into a chamber, and made sure the doors were firmly shut so that they could not be overheard by the Jews. Then he began to tell them everything he knew or had heard about Christ's life: how the rich had come to hate Him; how He had healed whoever He wished; how the Jews had accused Him and bought His betrayal by a disciple who did not love Him. And he told them of the foul treatment they had dealt Him, and how they had brought Christ before him and demanded that he condemn Him to death.

'I saw no reason to sentence him, but they were so many, and so wicked and aggressive and rich and powerful; and they vowed they'd kill him, and it grieved me. I told them that if the emperor asked me about it, it would be on their heads, and they replied that they wished Christ's blood might be scattered on them and their children! Then the Jews seized him and led him away and did with him as you've heard. I couldn't save him, and because I wanted it known that I was blameless, and that it grieved me more than it pleased me, and because I wanted to be clean of the sinful deed, I fetched water and washed my hands and said: 'May I be as clean of this man's death as my hands are clean in this water.' When he was dead, one of my soldiers in the city, who had served me with five other knights ever since I came to this land, wished for no other payment than the prophet's body, and I gave it to him, though I'd thought to give him a greater reward. And he took the body from its place of shame and laid it in a stone tomb that he had prepared for himself. I don't know what became of it after that. But I believe they've killed Joseph, my knight. So that's what I did: now judge whether I did wrong.'

Having heard all this, the messengers thought Pilate less guilty than before, and said: 'We don't know if what you say is true, but if it is, you may well absolve yourself of blame.'

'The Jews know the truth of it,' said Pilate. 'I'll have them confirm what I've said.'

'Call them,' the messengers replied, 'and let's hear what they say. Command all who were involved in the prophet's crucifixion to gather in this city a month from today.'

Pilate sent messengers throughout the land to summon all who had been present at Christ's death, and to let them know that the emperor's envoys wished to speak to them. While waiting for the month to pass, Pilate had people search the country for anything touched by Jesus Christ, but they could find nothing.

At the end of the month the Jews assembled at Arimathea. Pilate said to the emperor's messengers: 'Let me speak to them first: you'll hear my words and their replies, and when you've heard what both sides say, act accordingly.'

When they were all assembled, Pilate spoke as you will hear, saying: 'Sirs, here are the emperor's envoys, who wish to know who it was that you put to death, the one held to be King of the Jews.[5] For the emperor has heard he was a great healer, and has commanded that he go to him, if he can be found. But I've told his envoys he's dead, and that you yourselves, the powerful men of this land, put him to death because he said he was your king – and you did so without the emperor's leave.'

'Because you were so poor a governor,' the Jews replied, 'that you dared not punish him; instead you seemed grieved when we said we'd put him to

---

5 Literally 'lord of the Law'.

death, and that we wouldn't tolerate any man to be lord over us but would kill him if we could.'

'Sirs,' said Pilate to the messengers, 'now you've heard what they say and what sort of men they are: I have no power or control over them.'

One of the wisest of the emperor's men said: 'Pilate, we don't yet know the whole story.'

And the messengers addressed the Jews, saying: 'Sirs, this man who claimed to be a greater lord than the emperor, did Pilate then not sentence him to death?'

'No indeed,' they replied, 'we had to take it upon ourselves and our children, or Pilate would never have agreed.'

Realising that Pilate was less guilty than had been said, they asked the Jews: 'Who was this prophet of whom so much has been spoken?'

They replied that he performed the greatest miracles and wonders in the world; he was an enchanter. Then the messengers asked all those present to tell them if they knew of anything that had ever been touched by the prophet, but they replied that they knew of nothing, for everything he owned had been thrown away and anyone might have taken it. With that the assembly broke up, and Pilate was cleared of the envoys' suspicion.

Then, a while later, while they were still distressed at their failure to find anything that had touched the body of Our Lord Jesus, a man came to them saying that he knew a woman who had an image of Christ that she revered, but did not know how she had come by it. They summoned Pilate and told him what he had said. Pilate asked them the woman's name, and he sent for her and she came. And when Pilate saw her he rose to greet her, and embraced her and asked her name, and she told him her name was Veronica. But the good woman was baffled by Pilate's joyful welcome. He drew her aside, and said: 'Veronica, I hear you have the image of a man in your keeping; I beg you to show it to me.'

'I know nothing about this,' the woman said, greatly alarmed, and denied it vigorously. The messengers approached, and Pilate said: 'Sirs, here is the woman who you told me had the image of the prophet's face.'

They all embraced her and greeted her with joy, and told her why they had come to the land and about the illness of the emperor's son. 'We believe that if he was given the image, he'd be healed.' If she would sell it to them, they would pay whatever she asked.

Hearing the plight of the emperor's son, she realised she must reveal the truth, and said: 'Sirs, I could never sell the thing you seek, however much you paid me. But if you and your companions swear by all you believe in that you will not keep what I give you, I'll come with you to Rome.'

They were overjoyed at this and said: 'You'll be taken to Rome most gladly, and as you have asked, so we swear.' They made their vow all together, and then said: 'You'll be made a rich woman. Now show us the thing we seek.'

'Stay here and wait a while,' she replied, 'and I'll go and fetch it.'

So Veronica went back to her house and took the image of the face, all red, and returned to where they were waiting.

'Sit down,' she said when she arrived, and they did so, and she took out the image. When they saw it they were overjoyed and all rose to their feet.

'Why have you stood up?' she asked, and they replied: 'When we saw the face we couldn't help it. Ah, lady,' they said, 'tell us where you found it and how it came to be yours.'

'I'll tell you,' she said. 'I happened to have made a linen cloth and was carrying it to market where I hoped to sell it, when I met the people who were leading the prophet through the streets, his hands bound, followed by the Jews. And he asked me to wipe away the sweat that was running down his face. So I took one end of the cloth at once and wiped his face; then I went on my way and the Jews led him on, flogging him. And when I got home and looked at the cloth, I found this image of his face. That's exactly how it happened. And if,' she said, 'you think it would be of use to the emperor's son, I'll go with you and take it to him.'

'Many thanks,' they said, 'we believe it would indeed be of use to him.'

This image was the only thing they found which had touched Our Lord.

And so they returned across the sea, leaving Pilate to govern the land as before. The emperor was overjoyed when they arrived back in Rome, and asked them how they had fared on their journey, and whether the pilgrim had told the truth. They replied that every word he had said was true, and that Pilate had not acted as badly as they had thought. Then they told him all about their travels, and the emperor asked if the prophet was such a great man as was said, and they replied: 'Yes, and a good deal more!'

Then the emperor asked: 'Have you brought back anything that touched him?'

'Yes,' they said, 'and we'll tell you all about it.' And they told him how they had found the woman, and how she had long had the image of the face in her keeping. The emperor was filled with joy, and said: 'This is a very great thing you've brought; I've never heard of the like.'

'We're sure,' they said, 'that no-one could have known she had it.'

Then the emperor went to her and bade her a joyful welcome, and said he would make her a rich woman for what she had brought him. And Veronica showed him the face on the cloth; and when he saw it, the emperor, filled with wonder, made three deep bows and said: 'This is the most beautiful face I've ever seen.'

Then he took it in both hands and carried it into the chamber where his son was shut away. He was sleeping; so the emperor placed the cloth at the window, and called to his son and showed him the face. As soon as his son set eyes upon it he was healed, in better health than he had ever been in his life. And Vespasian said: 'Dear Lord God, whose face is this that has healed me of all sickness?' Then he said to his father: 'Sir, have this wall knocked down at once!'

And he did so with all possible speed, and when the wall was demolished, Vespasian left the chamber in perfect health and spirits, to the great joy of the emperor and everyone. Vespasian asked where the image of the face had been found, and whose it was, which had healed him as no man on Earth could do. And the emperor told him everything he had heard, and about the other miracles the pilgrim had seen. Then Vespasian asked the messengers: 'Sirs, did they truly put to death such a worthy man as he?'

'They did,' they said; and when he heard this he was deeply angry and said they had done a shameful deed, and that he would never be content until they had paid for it. And he said to his father: 'Sir, you are not our king or emperor: the true lord is the man who by his very image has healed me with his gracious power as neither you nor anyone else could do. He is the lord of men and women and of all things, and I beg you, my lord and father, to let me go and take revenge upon those who killed him.'

'Dear son,' the emperor replied, 'do exactly as you wish.'

And Vespasian was overjoyed.

Thus it was that Veronica's holy face of Christ was taken to Rome to heal the emperor's son.

Vespasian now prepared with Titus for their journey to the land of Judaea. After crossing the sea they ordered Pilate to come to them; and when he saw they had come with a great company he was filled with fear and said to Vespasian: 'Dear sir, I am at your command. Let me know your will.'

'I have come to avenge the death of Jesus Christ,' Vespasian replied, 'the prophet who healed me.'

Hearing this, Pilate was terrified, imagining Vespasian had been told he was responsible; and he said: 'Sir, would you like to find all those who were present at his death and know who was guilty and who was not?'

'Indeed I would,' said Vespasian.

'Then have me taken and imprisoned,' said Pilate, 'and say it's because I wouldn't sentence him. Pretend to despise me.'

Vespasian did as Pilate said, and summoned those involved from all parts of the land. When they had all assembled, Vespasian asked them about the prophet who was a higher lord than his father, and said: 'You committed treason, allowing him to make himself your lord.'

And they all replied: 'It was Pilate, your governor, who stood up for him! He said that even if the prophet claimed to be our king, it wasn't enough to merit death. But we said it was, and that we wouldn't allow him to be lord above our masters, but Pilate said the man was lord above all kings!'

'That's why I've thrown Pilate in prison,' Vespasian said, 'for I'd heard all about his actions, and how he loved the prophet more than us. Now I wish to know,' he said, 'which of you did the prophet most harm, and who was most offended at his claim to be king, and how you behaved towards him from the first day you saw him; why you felt such hatred for him, and which of you were involved in the plot against him. Tell me everything, exactly as it happened.'

When the Jews heard that Vespasian wished to learn the truth they were delighted, imagining it was for their benefit and Pilate's downfall. So they told him exactly what they had done: how he had made himself king of kings, and why they hated him, and how Judas had betrayed him; and they pointed out the one who had paid the thirty pence and the ones who had captured Christ. Each one of them bragged of the foul things they had said and done. Then they told him how they had led him before Pilate.

'But he wouldn't pass judgement, so we killed him without leave. We had to take his death upon ourselves and our children, otherwise Pilate wouldn't have allowed it. We pray you now, declare us relieved of this responsibility.'

When Vespasian heard their treachery and wickedness, he had them all seized and kept under guard;[6] and then he sent for Pilate.

When Pilate came before him, Vespasian said: 'You're not as guilty of wrongdoing as I thought. But I mean to destroy all who were involved in the killing of the Lord who has cured me of my sickness, for they've made it plain why they put him to death.'

Then Vespasian called for a great number of horses, and with four horses to each man he began to have the guilty torn to pieces. They were astounded to see him impose such justice and asked him why, and he said it was because they had killed Jesus Christ, and now they were all to suffer this death unless they delivered to him Christ's body.

'We gave it to Joseph,' they replied, 'and we don't know what he's done with it. But if Pilate gives us Joseph, we'll give you Jesus Christ.'

'You didn't trust Joseph at all,' said Pilate, 'but had the body watched by your own guards. And now Christ's disciples say they've seen him since, and that he is resurrected.'

'All these people must die,' said Vespasian, 'unless they return the body to me.'

He began to have more of them put to death – I cannot tell you the number – commanding them to deliver up either Jesus or Joseph. Then he had a great many more of them burnt. When the Jews saw they were all destined to die, one of them said: 'Would my children and I be spared if I told you where to find Joseph?'

'Yes,' replied Vespasian; and the man led him to the tower where Joseph had been immured, and said: 'I saw him imprisoned in this tower, sealed up under this great stone slab, for we feared Pilate would send people in search of him.'

'How long ago was this?' Vespasian asked.

'On the third day after the prophet was crucified,' he replied.

---

6   Literally 'placed in a strong house'.

'Why did you put him here?' said Vespasian. 'What wrong had he done you?'

'He'd taken the prophet from us and hidden him where we couldn't find him. We'd been robbed of the body and knew we'd be asked for it, so we decided to seize Joseph and lock him away to die, so that if we were asked for the prophet's body we could say: if you can give us Joseph, we'll give you Jesus's body! For we didn't think Joseph could survive. We heard the disciples saying Christ had risen from the dead: that's why we took Joseph captive.'

'Did you kill him before you threw him in prison?' Vespasian asked.

'No,' he replied, 'but we gave him a good beating for his crazy words!'

'Do you think he's dead now?'

'How could he possibly be alive,' he said, 'after so long in here?'

And Vespasian replied: 'He might well have been saved by the one who healed me of my sickness as no other man could do – the very one on whose account he was imprisoned. He healed me, even though I had never done anything for him and had never even seen him. It was that very man for whose sake Joseph was imprisoned, and whose body was given to him. I cannot believe he would let Joseph die so wretchedly.'

Then the stone slab was lifted, and Vespasian bent down and called to Joseph; but there was no reply. The others said: 'It's incredible, what you say. Do you really think this man could have survived so long?'

'I will not believe he's dead,' Vespasian replied, 'until I have seen him.'

And he took a rope and called to Joseph again. And when no reply came he clambered down. When he reached the bottom he looked all around, and in one corner of the dungeon he saw a brilliant light. He commanded that the rope be pulled back up, leaving him there in the dungeon. Then he moved towards the light. When Joseph saw him he stood to meet him and said: 'Welcome, Vespasian.'

Vespasian was astonished to hear his name, and said: 'Who are you who call my name, but wouldn't reply when I called to you?'

And he answered: 'I am Joseph of Arimathea.'

Vespasian was filled with joy, and said: 'Blessed be the Lord who has saved you, for none but he could have done so.'

They embraced each other with the greatest joy, and Vespasian asked Joseph: 'Who told you my name?'

And Joseph replied: 'The one who is omniscient.'

Then Vespasian asked if he knew the man who had healed him, and he replied: 'Of what sickness did he cure you?'

And Vespasian told him of his illness in every detail. Joseph was amazed by the story, and said: 'I know him very well. Do you want to know his name and who he is? If you do, I'll let you know what he commanded me to tell you.'

'Yes indeed,' said Vespasian, 'I'd be very glad to hear it.'

'Believe then,' said Joseph, 'that it is the Holy Spirit that created all things: Heaven and Earth, night and day and the four elements. The Holy Spirit created the angels, too; but the evil angels became full of pride and envy and wickedness – though as soon as they were so, Our Lord Jesus Christ knew it; and He cast them out of Heaven and for three days and three nights they fell like the heaviest rain that ever was; three generations of them fell to Hell and three to Earth and three into the air; and the three generations who fell to Hell undertook to torment souls, leading people into sin and then keeping records of their misdeeds: that is how they trick us. Those who are in the air [and on Earth[7]] are likewise bent upon deceiving us and bringing us to grief: they take many different forms to trick men and make them slaves of the Enemy. Thus it was that three times three generations fell; nine generations fell from Heaven, bringing to Earth evil deceit and wickedness. The angels who remain in Heaven strive to guide men, to keep them from sin – in the face of those who rebelled against Christ and turned from the spiritual state that He had willed to hatred, and whose reward was to lose, by His command, all spiritual joy. It was in contempt of them that Our Lord created man from the very basest mud. He made him just as it pleased Him, and gave him intelligence and light; and Our Lord declared that with this new creation He would fill the place vacated by the fallen angels. When the Devil realised that so base a being had risen to the glory from which he had fallen, he was filled with anger, and pondered deeply on how he could deceive him. After making man and placing him in paradise, Our Lord made woman out of man; and when the Devil knew this he strove with all his might to deceive him. First he tricked the woman, and the woman tricked the man. And when they had been led astray, Our Lord, who will not countenance sin, cast them out of paradise. And they conceived and gave birth to mankind; and the Devil wanted all mankind to be his, now that he had consented to do his bidding. But to save mankind, the Father, who is Lord of all things, sent His son to Earth to save His people, being born of the Virgin Mary. Since it was through woman that man had been delivered into the hands of the Devil, Our Lord, not wishing to do wrong, said it was through a woman that He would redeem all mankind. The Father fulfilled his promise to send His son Jesus Christ to Earth: He was born in Bethlehem of the Virgin Mary. He it was who walked the Earth for thirty-three years. He it was who performed the great miracles and wonderful deeds such as no other man has ever done. He it was that the Jews put to death on the cross. Because Eve committed sin with the apple, the Son had to die on a tree. And so it was that the Son came to Earth to die at the behest of His Father, and He was the son of the Virgin Mary, put to death by the Jews who would not recognise Him as Lord. It was He who

---

7   Arithmetic suggests an accidental omission.

healed you,[8] and on whose account I am imprisoned. It was He who suffered agony to save mankind from the pains of Hell. And thus it was that the Son fulfilled the purpose of the Father, Son and Holy Spirit – and you must believe that these three are one and the same being, whose power is manifest in the fact that He healed you and brought you here and saved me. Believe, too, the commandments of His disciples, whom He has sent into the world to glorify His name and to keep sinners from the clutches of the Enemy.'

'Joseph,' Vespasian replied, 'you have shown me clearly that He is Lord of all things, and that God is the Father and the Son and the Holy Spirit. Just as you have said, so I believe, and will do so all the days of my life.'

'As soon as you leave here,' said Joseph, 'seek Christ's disciples who work in His name and who carry the commandments that He gave them in this world. And know this for certain: He is risen again, and has returned to His Father in the same flesh in which He walked the Earth.'

Thus Joseph converted Vespasian to a firm belief in the true faith. Then Vespasian called to the people in the chamber above, and said he had found Joseph and wanted the tower destroyed. They were amazed, and said the man could not possibly be alive. But he commanded them to break down the tower quickly, and they did so at once. And as soon as it was done, Vespasian came out first and Joseph after. And when they saw him they were filled with wonder, and declared it was a mighty power indeed that had saved him.

And so Vespasian freed Joseph from prison, and led him to where the Jews were gathered. When the Jews saw him they were astounded; and Vespasian said to them: 'Will you deliver Jesus to me, if I give you Joseph?'

'We gave him to Joseph!' they replied. 'Let him tell you what he's done with him!'

'You know very well what I did,' said Joseph, 'and you set your own guards to watch the place where I laid his body. But know this now: He is risen again, as Lord and God.'

The Jews were horrified by his words; and Vespasian exacted such justice upon them as he pleased. As for the one who had told him where to find Joseph, Vespasian threw him and his children upon the mercy of Christ by putting them in a boat and casting them out to sea. Then he came to Joseph and asked him: 'Do you wish to save any of these people?'

And Joseph answered: 'Unless they believe in the Father, the Son, the Holy Spirit and the Trinity, and that the Son of God was born of the Virgin Mary, they will perish in body and in soul.'

Then Vespasian asked his retinue: 'Do any of you wish to buy any of these Jews?'

---

8 The manuscript reads 'me'.

'Very gladly,' they replied; and they did indeed buy some, Vespasian selling them at thirty for a penny.

Now Joseph had a sister named Enigeus whose husband's name was Bron, and Bron loved Joseph dearly. When Bron and his wife heard that Joseph had been found they were overjoyed and came to meet him and said: 'Sir, we have come for your blessing.'

Their words filled Joseph with joy, and he said to them: 'Not for my blessing, but for the blessing of the one who was born of the Virgin Mary and who kept me alive in prison, and in whom we shall believe for evermore.'

Then Joseph asked them if they could find more people who would be willing to believe in the Trinity and in God; and they went and spoke with others and found many who said they would believe in Joseph's words.

And so the Jews came before Joseph and said they would believe in Jesus. Hearing this, Joseph said: 'Don't tell me lies or you'll suffer for it, for Vespasian says you'll pay a more terrible price if you do.'

'We could never lie to you,' they said.

'If you wish to follow my belief,' said Joseph, 'you will not stay in your homes and estates, but will come with me into exile and give up everything for the sake of God and me.'

Then Vespasian pardoned them. And thus it was that he avenged the death of Christ.

*

Joseph often told his company of the good words of Our Lord, and he set them to work upon the land. For some time all went well; but later, as I shall explain, all their work and labour was fruitless. This was the case for a long while, until they could bear it no more. This misfortune and misery had befallen them because they had embarked upon a sinful course which cost them very dearly: it was the sin of unbridled lust. When they had reached the point where they could abide it no longer, they came to Bron, who was very dear to Joseph, and said to him:

'Sir, the good and plentiful harvests that we used to enjoy are failing us; no people ever suffered such hunger as we – we're close to eating our children!'

Bron was filled with pity when he heard their words of grief, and asked them: 'Have you suffered like this for a long while?'

'Yes, sir,' they replied, 'but we've kept it to ourselves for as long as we could. But now we beg you in God's name to talk to Joseph, and find out whether it's because of some sin of ours or his.'

'I'll gladly ask him,' said Bron, and he came to Joseph and told him of his people's misery. 'They want you to let them know whether it's because of your sin or theirs.'

'I pray to the one who was born of the Virgin Mary,' said Joseph, 'and to my heavenly Father, to tell me why this famine has befallen them.' Joseph was afraid that he had failed to fulfil one of Our Lord's commands, and he said to Bron: 'If I can find the answer, I'll tell you.'

And Joseph came, weeping, to his vessel, and knelt before it and said: 'Lord who was born of the Virgin, by your holy pity and gentleness, and to save your obedient servant; Lord, I saw you truly both alive and dead, and saw you again, in the tower where I was imprisoned, after you had suffered the agonies of death, and you bade that, whenever I needed you, I should come before this precious vessel which held your precious blood; so truly, Lord, I beg and pray you now to guide me in answering my people's plea, so that I may act according to your will.'

And when Joseph had thus prayed, the voice of the Holy Spirit descended and said: 'Joseph, do not be afraid, for you are not guilty of this sin.'

'Ah, Lord,' said Joseph, 'give me leave to remove from my company the sinners who have brought this terrible famine upon us.'

And the voice replied: 'Joseph, you will give your people a great sign, testing the power of my flesh and blood against those who have sinned. Remember, Joseph, that I was sold and betrayed on Earth, and knew that it would be so; but I did not speak of it until I was at Simon's house, when I said that eating and drinking with me was one who would betray me. Then the guilty man was ashamed, and withdrew from my company and was no longer my disciple. I reserved his place for another, and none shall fill it before you. As I sat at the table of the Last Supper at Simon's house,' said the voice, 'and foresaw my suffering to come, make another table in its name; and when you have made it, summon your brother-in-law Bron – he is a good man and more good will spring from him – and bid him go and fish on the water and bring you the first he catches. While he is fishing, lay the table and take your vessel and place it where you will be sitting, and cover it with the edge of the tablecloth. When you have done so, call your people and tell them they are about to see the cause of their distress. Then take Bron and sit in my place, just as I did at the Last Supper. Seat Bron at your right hand; and you will see him move one seat away, leaving an empty place between you. Know this: that seat will signify the place abandoned by Judas when he knew that he had betrayed me, and it cannot be filled until the son of Bron's son fills it. When you have seated Bron, call your people and, in the name of the three powers that are one and the same being, bid those who have true faith in the Trinity of Father, Son and Holy Spirit, and are willing to obey the commandments, to come forward and take their seats by the grace of God.'

With that the voice departed; and Joseph did as Our Lord had commanded, and a great number of his people sat down at the table; but there were many more who did not. The table was full except for the place that could not be filled. And when those who had sat down to eat sensed the sweetness and the fulfilment of their hearts, they very soon forgot the others. One who was seated at the table, whose name was Petrus, looked at those who were standing and said: 'Do you feel what we feel?'

'We feel nothing,' they replied; and Petrus said: 'Then you are guilty of the sin you discussed with Joseph, which has brought the famine upon us.'

Hearing Petrus' words, they were filled with shame and left the house. But one stayed behind, weeping. And when the service was over, they all rose from the table and went off with the others, but Joseph commanded them to return daily at terce.[9] And so it was that, by the will of God, Joseph came to discover who had sinned, and this was the first place in which the vessel was put to the test.

So things remained for a long time, until those who were excluded asked those who attended about the grace they were given, saying: 'What is it you receive when you go each day, and how do you feel when you sit in the presence of that grace?'

'Our hearts could not conceive,' they replied, 'the great joy and delight we feel while we are sitting at that table, and we remain in a state of grace until the following day at terce.'

'Where can such great grace come from, which so fills man's heart?'

And Petrus replied: 'It comes from the one who saved Joseph in prison.'

'And what of the vessel which we've seen, but of which we know nothing, for it has never been presented to us?'

'By that vessel,' he replied, 'we are separated, for it will allow no sinner in its presence – you can see that for yourselves.'

And then the one who had been granted grace said: 'Now you know who committed the sin which had deprived us of God's grace.'

And they replied: 'We shall go now, wretched, but tell us at least what we should say about the state in which we leave you.'

And Petrus and his company answered: 'Say that we enjoy the grace of the Father, Son and Holy Spirit, and follow the instruction and the faith of Joseph.'

'And what can we say about the vessel we have seen, which has so delighted us and delights us still, so that we forget all pain – what shall we call it?'

'Those who wish to name it rightly will call it the Grail, which gives such joy and delight to those who can stay in its presence that they feel as elated as a fish escaping from a man's hands into the wide water.'

And hearing this, they said: 'This vessel should indeed be called the Grail.'[10]

Both those who went and those who stayed named it so, and when Joseph heard the name it pleased him greatly. They all came each day at terce, and said they were going to the service of the Grail.

Now, among those who were excluded was a man named Moyse, and he

---

9 The third canonical hour: nine o'clock in the morning.

10 An untranslatable play on words runs through this passage, linking the name *graal* to the verb *agreer* ('to delight').

stayed when the others left. And every time he saw one of those who had been granted grace he would beg for mercy most piteously, with an apparently good heart and good intentions, saying: 'In the name of God, sir, ask Joseph to have mercy on me, that I may share in the grace that you enjoy.'

He made this entreaty many times and for a long, long while, desperate to join them, until one day, when all the company of the Grail were gathered together, they said they felt sorry for Moyse and would plead to Joseph on his behalf. They all came to him and fell at his feet and implored his mercy. Joseph was taken aback and asked them what they wanted.

'Most of the people who came have departed,' they replied, 'because we enjoy the grace bestowed by your vessel. But there's one, sir, named Moyse, who's stayed behind, and he seems to us to be full of penitence, and he says he won't leave, and is weeping most grievously, begging us to implore you to grant him the grace that God permits us to share when we're in your company.'

When Joseph heard this he replied: 'Grace is not mine to bestow. Our Lord has granted it as He pleases, and those He chooses shall have it. And this man Moyse may not be all he pretends and seems. He may well be tricking us – but if so, he'll be his own victim.'

'We'll never trust him,' they replied, 'if he's been deceiving us by his behaviour. But in God's name, if the man is worthy, invite him to join us if you can.'

And Joseph said: 'I'll pray for Our Lord's guidance on your behalf.'

And they all replied together: 'Many thanks.'

Then Joseph went alone and prayed, prostrate, before his vessel, that Jesus Christ Our Lord, by His goodness, strength and mercy, might reveal to him whether Moyse was truly as he seemed. And thereupon the voice of the Holy Spirit appeared to Joseph and said: 'Joseph, Joseph, now the time has come when you will see what I told you about the seat left empty between you and Bron. You pray for Moyse. You think, like those who spoke to you on his behalf, that he is as he pretends, and that he seeks the grace of the Holy Spirit. Let him come forward then, and sit in its presence, and you will see what becomes of him.'

Joseph did as the voice commanded, and returned to those who had pleaded for Moyse and told them: 'Say to Moyse that if he is as he claims and deserves to be granted grace, no man can deprive him of it. But if he is other than good, he should not come, for he could betray no-one so badly as himself.'

They went and told Moyse what Joseph had said, and he was delighted and said: 'My only fear was that Joseph would think me unworthy of being granted admission.'

'You have his leave to come,' they replied, 'if you share our faith.'

They welcomed him into their company most joyfully, and took him to the service, and when Joseph saw him he said: 'Moyse, Moyse, stay away from anything of which you're not worthy. No-one can deceive you so thoroughly as yourself.'

'As I am truly a good man,' he replied, 'may God permit me to remain in your company.'

'Then step forward,' said Joseph, 'if you're as you say. Be seated, and we'll clearly see your goodness.'

Then Joseph sat down, along with his brother-in-law Bron and all the others, each in his rightful place. And when they were all seated, Moyse, still standing, felt afraid. He went around the table, and did not know where to sit except beside Joseph. So he sat there. And the moment he did so he was swallowed up – it seemed as if he had never been. Those who were seated at the table were dismayed to see one of their number disappear.

When they rose from the service at the end of the day, Petrus spoke to Joseph, saying: 'We have never been so bewildered as now. By all the powers you believe in, we beg you, if you know,[11] to tell us what has become of Moyse.'

'I've no idea at all,' Joseph replied, 'but if it please the one who has revealed so much to us, we shall find out.'

And Joseph returned and knelt, weeping, before his vessel, and said: 'Dear Lord God, your powers are wonderful and your ways are wise. Lord God, you came to Earth and were born of the Virgin Mary and suffered earthly torments and death; you kept me alive in the prison where, by your will, Vespasian came to find me; you told me that whenever I was in trouble you would come to me; Lord, I beg and implore you to free me from doubt and tell me truly what has become of Moyse, so that I may tell those people to whom you grant your grace in my company.'

Then the voice of the Holy Spirit appeared to Joseph and said: 'Joseph, Joseph, now is revealed the significance of my words when you established this table, when I told you that the place left empty beside you would be a reminder of Judas – who lost his seat when I said he would betray me – and that it would remain empty until one of Bron's lineage came to fill it. The third man of Bron's line will fill that place – or another established in its name. As for the one who was swallowed up, whose fate you do not know, I will tell you what became of him. When he stayed behind after his fellows left, he did so only to deceive you, for he did not believe that those of your company could have such great grace as they did. And be assured that he has fallen into abysmal depths and will never be heard of again. Tell this to your disciples, and consider what you have gained in serving me.'

And so the voice of the Holy Spirit spoke to Joseph and told him of the wickedness of Moyse, and Joseph related it to Petrus and Bron and the other disciples. When they had heard the story, they said: 'The justice of Our Lord

---

[11] The manuscript reads 'dare' (*oses*) rather than the more likely 'know' (*ses*).

Jesus Christ is very fierce, and he is a fool indeed who earns His wrath by leading a wicked life.'

*

They remained a long while in this state of grace. And Bron and Enigeus had children – twelve fair sons – and they became a great burden, and Enigeus came to her husband Bron and said: 'Sir, let's ask my brother Joseph what to do with our children, for we should do nothing except by his leave.'

'I agree with you,' Bron replied, and he went to Joseph and said: 'Sir, I've come to remind you that your sister and I have twelve fair sons, but we wish to take no decision about their future except with God's advice and yours.'

'May God keep them in His company and direct them to good,' Joseph replied. 'I'll gladly pray for guidance on their behalf.'

They let the matter rest until the next day, when Joseph came in private before his vessel, and remembered his nephews. He wept, and begged Our Lord Jesus Christ for advice about their future. And when he had finished his prayer, an angel appeared to him and said:

'Joseph, Jesus Christ sends me to you in answer to your prayer. He wishes your nephews to be in your company, to be disciples with a leader at their head; those who so wish should take wives, but the one who does not take a wife shall have the others as his disciples. And when they are married, command the father and mother to bring the unmarried son to you. Then come before your vessel and you will hear the word of Jesus Christ who will speak to you and to him together.'

Once he had spoken and Joseph had heard his words the angel departed, leaving Joseph in great happiness about the joyful news of what lay in store for his nephews. He returned to Bron and said:

'Bron, you asked for advice about my nephews, your sons. I want you to prepare them for this earthly life and direct them to keep God's law and to take wives and have children as others do. But if there's one who doesn't wish to take a wife, send him to me.'

'Gladly,' Bron replied, 'just as God and you command.'

Then Bron came to his wife and told her what Joseph had said. She was filled with joy and said to her husband: 'Hurry, sir, and do as my brother commanded with all speed.'

And Bron came to his sons and said to them: 'Dear children, what sort of people do you wish to be?'

And most of them replied: 'Such as you would have us.'

'My desire,' he said, 'is that all who wish to take wives should do so, and keep them well and faithfully, as I have kept your mother.'

They were delighted by his words and said: 'Sir, we'll do as you command unfailingly.'

Then Bron searched far and wide to find them wives according to the command of Holy Church.

Now the twelfth of the sons was named Alain li Gros. He had no wish to
marry, and said he would take none of the women, even if he were to be
flayed alive. His father was amazed by this and said: 'Dear son, why won't
you marry like your brothers?'

'Sir,' he replied, 'I have no desire to do so; I'll take none of those wives.'

And so Bron saw eleven of his children married, and the twelfth he took to
Joseph and said: 'Sir, here is your nephew who will not take a wife either at
my bidding or his mother's.'

And Joseph said to Bron: 'Will you and my sister give him into my
keeping?'

And they replied: 'Yes, sir, most willingly.'

Joseph was overjoyed at this, and he took Alain in his arms and embraced
him and kissed him, and said to the father and mother: 'Go now, and leave
him with me.'

So Bron and his wife departed, and the child stayed with Joseph, who said
to him: 'My good, dear nephew, you should feel joy indeed, for Our Lord has
chosen you to serve Him and exalt His name. You, dear nephew, will be the
chief of all your brothers. Stay with me now, and you shall hear the mighty
words of Jesus Christ Our Saviour, if it please Him to speak to me.'

Then Joseph prayed to Our Lord to reveal the truth about his nephew's
future life. And when his prayer was done, he heard the voice saying:

'Joseph, your nephew is chaste and honest and good, and will believe your
words in all matters. Tell him of the love I have shown you, as I do still, and
why I came to Earth; and how you saw me bought and sold, and how I was
abused here on Earth and suffered death; and how my body was granted to
you, and how you washed me and placed me in a tomb; and how you came
to have my vessel and the blood from my body; and how it led to you being
left for dead, and how I served and comforted you; and of the gift I have
bestowed upon you and your people, and upon all who tell and understand
the story of that gift and of the love I bear you. Tell your nephew with
certainty that he will receive the fulfilment of the human heart in your
company; and to all who pass on the truth of our words I grant grace in this
world. I will protect the inheritance of the good and ensure that they are
never wrongfully deprived. And I will guard them from shame, along with
all that is rightfully theirs, so long as they make a sacrament in my name. And
when you have explained all this to him, show him your vessel and tell him
to read what is written about me inside, for it will confirm his faith. But warn
him that the Enemy is keen to deceive those who follow me; he must beware
of the Enemy, and never be so blinded by violent emotion that he fails to see
clearly; and bid him keep close to him the things that will guard him from sin
and wrath, and to cherish them above all else, for they will be of most use in
guarding him against the Enemy's wiles. He should beware of the pleasure
which causes the flesh to languish: pleasures which lead to suffering are of
little worth. When you have given him these instructions, tell him to pass

them on to whoever he wishes: those who are eager to hear them he should take to be worthy men. Let him speak of me and my works wherever he goes: if he truly loves me, the more he speaks the more pleasure it will give him. And tell him this: that from him will be born a male child to whom my vessel is to come – tell this also to your company. When you have done all this, entrust to him the guardianship of his brothers; then let him go to the West, to the most distant parts he can find, and wherever he goes let him do all he can to exalt my name, and pray to the Father to grant him grace.

'Tomorrow morning, when you are all assembled, a light will appear to you, bringing with it a letter. Give the letter to Petrus, and bid him go wherever he thinks best: I shall not forget him. Then ask him to tell you truly where his heart is directing him, and he will tell you that he intends to go into the West, to the vales of Avalon. Tell him that at his destination he should await the son of Alain, and that he cannot pass from life to death until the one has come who will read him the letter and explain the power of your vessel; and the one who comes will bring him news of you. When he has seen and heard these things, he will die and pass on to eternal glory. When you have told him all this, send for your other nephews and repeat it to them.'

With that the voice departed, and Joseph came to Alain and told him all that had been said. He was entirely convinced, and filled with the grace of the Holy Spirit. Then Joseph said to him: 'My dear, sweet nephew, you must be good indeed, for Our Lord to grant you so much grace.'

And Joseph took him back to his father and said: 'Bron, this son shall be guardian on Earth of his brothers and sisters. They must trust in him and take his advice in all matters that trouble them; if they believe in him, it will be to their advantage. Give him your blessing in their sight and they will trust him and love him the more; he will lead them well for as long as they are willing to believe in him.'

The next day they all came to the service, and the light did indeed appear to them and brought them the letter. When they saw it they rose, and Joseph took it and called to Petrus and said: 'Dear friend, Jesus Christ Our Father, who redeemed us from the pains of Hell, has chosen you as a messenger to carry this letter wherever you wish.'

Hearing this, Petrus said: 'I never thought I was such that He would entrust a message to me without instruction.'

'He knows you better than you know yourself,' said Joseph. 'But in the name of love and companionship, we beg you to tell us where your heart directs you to go.'

'I know very well,' he replied. 'You never saw a message more surely entrusted than this. I shall go to the vales of Avalon, a lonely place in the West. And there I shall await my Saviour's mercy. I beg you all now, pray to Our Lord to grant me neither the strength nor the desire to do anything against His will, and that the Enemy may never deceive me into losing His love.'

'May He guard you from it, Petrus,' they replied, 'as He truly can.'

Then they all went together to Bron's house and spoke to his children, and Bron summoned them and said: 'You are all my sons and my daughters in law. Unless we're obedient, neither you nor I can gain the joy of Paradise. So I want you to be obedient to one of our number. All I can give that is of worth or grace I bestow upon my son Alain, with my prayer that he keep you all in God's name. And I command you to obey him and take his advice in all your troubles, and he will give you guidance. Be sure to undertake nothing against his will.'

With that the children left their father's house, knowing they had a protector. And Alain led them into strange lands; and wherever he went, and to all the worthy men and women he met, he recounted the story of the death of Jesus Christ. Alain was blessed with so much of God's grace that no man could have more.

And so it was that they took their leave; but I do not wish to speak more about them until the right point in my story. When they were gone, Petrus summoned Joseph and all the other companions and said: 'Sirs, it is time for me to go at Christ's command.'

They were all of one mind, begging Petrus to stay, and he said: 'I have no desire to do so, but for love of you I shall stay today and until tomorrow's service is over.'

So Petrus stayed, and Our Lord, who had arranged how everything was to be, sent his messenger to Joseph saying:

'Joseph, do not be afraid. You must do the will of Jesus Christ: tell Petrus of the love there has been between you, and then let him go. Do you know why you all felt so eager to keep him here for another day? Our Lord willed it so, so that He could explain the reason for his going; for he will see that your vessel, and everything else you have, will have an end as well as a beginning. Our Lord knows that Bron is a worthy servant, and He wants him to be guardian of the vessel after you. Tell him how to behave as its keeper, and tell him of the love between you and Christ, and everything you have learned in your life of Christ's deeds, so that you confirm him in his faith. And tell him how Christ came to you in the dungeon and brought you His vessel. The words He taught you when He spoke to you there are the holy words of the sacrament of the Grail. When you have told Bron all this, commend the vessel into his keeping thenceforth; and all who hear tell of him will call him the rich Fisher King because of the fish he caught.[12] There is no other way than this: just as the world is and always will be moving towards night, so must Bron and his people move towards the setting sun – into the West. As soon as the Fisher King has the vessel and grace bestowed upon him, he must journey westward, wherever his heart leads him. And where he comes to rest, there

12 Above, page 35.

he must await the coming of his son's son, and when the time is right to do so, pass on to him the vessel and the grace that he will have received from you. Between you then you will have completed a sign of the Trinity, which is in three parts. As for the third of you, what befalls him will be determined by Jesus Christ, who is Lord of all.

'When you have bequeathed the vessel and grace to Bron and are relieved of them, Petrus will go and report that he has witnessed their bestowal upon the rich Fisher King. This is the reason for his staying until tomorrow. Petrus will go as soon as he has witnessed it. And the Rich Fisher, once he has received the vessel, will travel with it over land and sea, and the Keeper of all good things will watch over him. And you, Joseph, when you have done all this, will leave this earthly life and come to everlasting joy, while your sister's line will be exalted forever. And all those who tell of them will be loved and cherished by all worthy men and women.'

Joseph did as Christ's messenger commanded. The next day everyone gathered for the service, and Joseph related to Bron and Petrus everything he had learned from the Holy Spirit – except for the words given to him by Jesus Christ in prison, which he entrusted to the Rich Fisher privately,[13] in writing. When the others learned that Joseph would be leaving them, they were deeply dismayed. But once Petrus had heard that Joseph was relieved of the Grail, and had seen him bequeath his grace and entrust his commandments to Bron the rich Fisher King, he took his leave and, when everyone rose from the service, he departed. At his leave-taking there was much lamentation and sighing and shedding of humble tears; and they prayed for Petrus, that God might guide him according to his will and pleasure.

Joseph remained in the company of the rich Fisher King for three days and three nights. Then Bron said to Joseph: 'Sir, a great desire to leave has come upon me; is it your will that I should go?'

'It is indeed,' Joseph replied, 'since it is the will of Our Lord. You are well aware of what you will be taking with you, and who will be watching over you; no-one knows as well as you and I. Go when you will – and I will go too, as my heavenly Father commands.'

So departed the rich Fisher King – of whom many words have since been spoken – while Joseph stayed behind, and ended his days in the land and country of his birth.

And now anyone who wants to hear the full story will need to know what became of Alain, the son of Bron, and where he had gone and where he was to be found; and know, too, what can be truly told about the fate of Moyse; and where the Rich Fisher went; and how he was to be found by the one who was to come to him. These four parts need to be brought together. I will tie all

---

[13] The manuscript reads *premierement* ('firstly') rather than the more likely *priveement* suggested by the verse *Joseph* (v.3420).

four strands together again, as surely as I have drawn them apart. But in this, as in all things, God is all-powerful.

But now I must leave these four and tell of the fifth part, until I return to each of them in turn. Were I to do otherwise, you would not understand what became of them, or why I am dealing with them separately.

Merlin

THE Enemy was filled with rage when Our Lord descended into Hell and freed Adam and Eve and as many more as He pleased. When the demons realised what had happened they were bewildered, and gathered together and said:

'Who is this man who has broken into our fastness? Nothing we've hidden is safe from him: he does whatever he pleases! We thought any man of woman born would be ours; but this one is defeating and tormenting us! How was he born of woman without any involvement with earthly pleasure? He's outwitting us as we've outwitted other men and women!'

Then one of the demons replied, saying: 'Our own power has been turned against us. Do you remember how the prophets spoke and said that the son of God would come to Earth to save the sinners Eve and Adam and as many more as he pleased? We seized those who said this and tormented them more than the other sinners, but they seemed to be untroubled by our tortures, and comforted the other sinners, saying that the one who was coming to Earth would save them from the pains of Hell. And what the prophets predicted has now happened! He's robbed us of all we had – we can keep nothing from him! He's rescued all who believed in his nativity – though by what power we just don't know.'

'Don't you know, then,' said another, 'that he has them baptised in water in his name? They cleanse themselves in water in the name of the Father and of the Mother so that we can no longer take them as ours; it's infuriating – we used to take them wherever we found them! Now they're lost to us because of this washing! We have no power over them – until they return to us by their own sinful deeds. Thus our power diminishes while his increases. What's more, he's left ministers on Earth to save the people – however much they may have been inclined to our work – if they'll repent and abandon our ways and do as these ministers command. So we've lost them all! Great is the spiritual work of Our Lord, who to save mankind came to Earth and was born of woman and suffered earthly torments. And he came without our knowledge and without any involvement with human pleasure. We tested him with every possible temptation; but after we'd tempted him and found in him none of our works, he was willing to die to save mankind. He loves man dearly, willing as he is to endure such pain to rescue him from our bonds. Now we must strive to win man back! He's taken from us what should be ours! We must find a way to bring men back to doing our works, to such a degree that they could never repent or even speak to those who might grant them forgiveness.'

'We've lost everything,' they all cried together, 'for they can be forgiven even mortal sins! If Our Lord finds them willing to repent and turn to his ways, they're safe. So we've lost them all!'

Then the demons spoke amongst themselves, saying: 'Those who said so most are the prophets: they are the cause of all our troubles! The more they spoke of him, the more we tormented them, and now it seems he hurried to their aid, to rescue them from the tortures we were inflicting. So, then, how can we find a man who'd speak to others on our behalf and tell them of our total knowledge of all things past? If we had such a man, he could converse with the people on Earth and help us greatly to deceive men and women alike, just as the prophets worked against us when we had them here.' Then they said: 'It would be a great deed to create such a man, for they would all believe in him.'

Then one of them said: 'I can't make seed or conceive a child in a woman, but there's one among you who could, and I know a woman who's somewhat in my power. Let the one who can take the shape of a man do so in utmost secrecy.'

And so the demons plotted to conceive a man who would work to deceive others. They were foolish indeed to think Our Lord would not know of their plan! Then one of the demons said he would devote all his thought and wit to deceiving followers of Christ; you may clearly see the Devil's folly, if he imagines he can work such deception.

Their gathering broke up with this plan agreed. And the one who claimed to have the power to lie with a woman made no delay, but came straight to her and found her most amenable. She yielded entirely to the Enemy. She was the wife of a wealthy man, who owned great herds and fine estates and other riches, and she had a son and three daughters. The demon did not neglect his task but went into the fields and contemplated how he could deceive the woman. One day he came to her and asked her how he could trick her husband. And she replied that he would be mightily angry 'if you took our possessions'. So the demon went and slaughtered a great many of the good man's flocks. When the shepherds saw their sheep dying in the open fields they were amazed and said they would report it to their lord, and they went and told him that his animals were dying in the middle of the fields. He was shocked and enraged, and said: 'Is this true?'

'Yes,' they replied; and he wondered what could be wrong with them to make them die so.

'Do you know what could be causing their deaths?' he asked the shepherds; but they said they had no idea. So matters stayed that day. And when the demon saw the worthy man was angered by so little, he realised that if he did him greater harm he would make him enraged indeed, and by so doing, bring him into his power. So he returned to where the livestock was kept and came upon two beautiful horses in the rich man's stable; and he killed them both in the same night. When the good man saw the ill fortune that had befallen him he was filled with rage, and his fury drove him to a foolish utterance: that he gave everything that remained to him to the Devil.

The demon was delighted to hear of this gift, and began to assail the man mercilessly to cause him further misery, leaving him none of his animals at all. Such were the good man's grief and wrath that he shunned all human company. Seeing this, the demon knew for certain that the man was in his power. He came to the rich man's handsome son and strangled him in his bed. In the morning the child was found dead. And when the worthy man knew he had lost his son he gave way to despair and abandoned his faith. Knowing the man had lost his faith filled the demon with delight, and he went to the wife – thanks to whom he had achieved all this – and made her climb on to a box in her cellar and put a rope around her neck and then pushed her off and strangled her: she was found hanging there. When the worthy man realised he had lost his wife as well as his son in such a manner he was overcome with grief so great that he fell ill and died. This is how the Devil works with those he can bring into his power.

Having done all this the demon was elated, and pondered on how he could deceive the three daughters who remained. He knew he could not unless he worked in a way that would please them. There was a young man in the town who was much inclined towards him, so he took him to the girls and had him begin to court one of them. Such were the youth's deeds and words that she was utterly deceived, to the demon's delight; and he did not want his conquest kept secret: he wanted it known openly to cause the greater shame. So the demon ensured that word was spread until it was common knowledge. At this time it was the custom that if a woman was taken in adultery, she should either give herself to all men or be put to death. The Devil, ever eager to bring disgrace upon those who come to him, made the matter known to the judges: the young man fled, but the girl was seized and led before them.

When the judges saw her, they felt great pity for her worthy father, and said: 'It's amazing that so much ill has befallen him in so little time: only a short while ago he was one of the wealthiest men in the land.'

And they discussed what to do and what sentence to pass, and they all agreed to bury her alive one night; and that is what they did.

Now in that land there was a worthy man who was a good confessor, and hearing of these strange events he came to the other two sisters, the eldest and the youngest, and began to give them comfort, and asked them how this misfortune had befallen them.

'We don't know, sir,' they replied, 'but we think God must hate us, to let us suffer this torment.'

'You're wrong to say so,' said the good man. 'God hates no-one; rather, it grieves him deeply when a sinner hates himself. I'm certain your misfortune is the work of a demon. As for your sister, whom you've lost in such a shameful way, do you know the truth about what she did?'

'No, sir,' they replied.

'Beware of wicked deeds,' he said, 'for they lead sinners to a woeful end.'

The good man gave them fine advice, if they were willing to heed it. The eldest daughter listened well and delighted in the good man's words. He taught her all about his faith and the powers of Jesus Christ, and she listened diligently.

'If you believe my words,' he said, 'great good will come to you; and you shall be my God-daughter, and whenever a great task or need confronts you, if you ask for my support I'll give you aid and advice with the help of Our Lord. Never fear,' he said, 'for Our Lord will assist you if you're true to Him; and come to me often, for I shan't be far from here.'

So the good man gave the girls sound advice and set them on the right path. The elder believed him utterly and loved him for his good advice. This troubled the demon mightily; he feared they might be lost to him. He considered long how he might trick them.

Nearby lived a woman who had done his will and his works many times; the demon took her and led her to the two girls. She came to the younger sister, not daring to speak to the elder because she saw her modest countenance. She drew the younger sister aside and asked her all about her life and condition.

'How's your sister?' she asked. 'Does she love you and treat you well?'

'My sister's very troubled,' she replied, 'about the misfortunes that have befallen us, so she gives no kind attention to me or anyone. And a worthy man who speaks to her about God each day has converted her so wholly to his ways that she does only what he tells her.'

And the woman said: 'Dear girl, what a shame for your lovely body, which will never know joy as long as you're in your sister's company. Oh God! My dear friend, if you knew the joy that other women have, you'd count all others as nothing! Oh, we have such pleasure from the company of men! Compared with that, what joy does a woman have? My dear,' she said, 'I tell you for your own good, you'll never know joy or understand the pleasure of being with a man so long as you're with your sister, and I'll tell you why. She's older than you, and will in time have her share of pleasure with men, and won't allow you to enjoy it before her! And while she's experiencing that pleasure she'll have no thought for you! So you'll lose the joy that your poor, lovely body might have had.'

'How could I dare to do what you say?' said the girl. 'For my other sister's suffered a shameful death for just such a deed.'

'Your sister,' the woman replied, 'was too foolish, too ill-advised, in the way she went about it! If you'll trust in me, you'll never be found out and will enjoy all bodily pleasure.'

'I don't know how I'll do it,' the girl said, 'but I'll say no more now, on account of my sister.'

The demon was overjoyed at hearing this, certain now that he would have her in his power. He led his woman away, and when she was gone the girl thought long about what she had said. When the demon heard and saw how drawn she was towards doing his will, as she talked about it to herself, he fanned the flames with all his power. She said: 'That good woman told me the truth indeed when she said I'd lost all worldly pleasure.'

And the day finally came when she summoned the woman and said to her: 'Truly, lady, you were right the other day when you said my sister had no care for me.'

'I know, dear friend,' the woman replied, 'and she'll care even less if she finds pleasure herself. And we were made for no other purpose than to have pleasure with men!'

'I would very gladly have it,' said the girl, 'were I not afraid it would earn my death!'

'It would,' the woman replied, 'if you acted as foolishly as your other sister. But I'll teach you how to go about it.'

And the girl said: 'Tell me!'

'My dear,' said the woman, 'you will give yourself to all men! Leave your sister's house, saying you can't bear to be with her any longer. Then do as you like with your body – no accusation will be levelled against you: you'll be clear of all danger. When you've led that life as long as you please, some worthy man will be pleased to have you on account of your inheritance! If you do as I say, you can enjoy all worldly happiness.'

The girl agreed to do as she said, and left her sister's house and gave her body freely to men just as the woman had advised.

The demon was overjoyed at deceiving the younger sister. And when the elder knew that she had gone she went to the good confessor. Seeing her terrible sorrow he felt great pity for her and said: 'Dear friend, make the sign of the cross and commend yourself to God, for I can see you're most perturbed.'

'I'm right to be,' she answered, and she told him how her sister had left her and was giving herself freely to men. The good man was aghast and said: 'My dear girl, the Devil is still about you, and he'll never rest till he's deceived you all.'

'In God's name, sir,' she asked him, 'how can I protect myself? I fear nothing in the world so much as his trickery.'

'If you'll trust in my words,' he said, 'he'll not deceive you.'

'Sir,' she replied, 'I'll believe anything you say.'

Then the good man said to her: 'Do you believe in the Father, the Son and the Holy Spirit, and that these three beings are one in God; and that Our Lord came to Earth to save sinners who were willing to believe in baptism, and in the other commandments of Holy Church and of the ministers that He left on Earth to save those who would come in His name and follow the right path?'

'I do indeed,' she replied, 'and always will, and may He guard me from the Devil's wiles.'

'If you believe as you say,' said the good man, 'no evil being can deceive you. I beg and command you above all things to beware of giving way to excessive wrath, for I tell you truly, the Devil finds his way into men and women possessed by wrath more readily than by any other path. So beware of all misdeeds, and whenever you do become upset, my good dear friend, come to me and tell me so. And admit your wrongs to Our Lord and all the saints and all Christian men. And every time you wake or go to bed, raise your hand and make the sign of the cross on which the precious body of Christ was hung to redeem sinners from the pains of Hell, in the name of the Father, Son and Holy Spirit, so that no devil or demon can possess you. If you do as I say,' the good man said, 'the Devil cannot deceive you. And make sure there's always light where you lie down to sleep, for the Devil hates places where light shines.'

Such was the good man's lesson to the girl who so feared being tricked by the Devil. Then she returned home, full of trust and humility towards God and the good, worthy people of the land. The good men and women came to her and kept saying: 'Lady, you must be very troubled by the torments that have befallen you, losing your father and mother and sisters and brother in such a terrible way. But take comfort in your good heart now, and consider: you're a very rich woman with a handsome inheritance, and some worthy man would be delighted to have you as his wife and keep you safe and well.'

And she replied: 'Our Lord knows my needs and keeps me accordingly.'

In this state the girl remained for a long while. For fully two years or more the demon could conceive no way to trick her or find any wrongdoing in her. It annoyed him greatly, as he realised he could not deceive her or influence her behaviour; and so averse was she to doing his works, which held no appeal for her, that he began to think the only way to make her forget the good man's advice was through a fit of anger. So the demon went and fetched her sister, and brought her to her one Saturday night to incense her and to see if he could then deceive her. When the good maiden's sister arrived at her father's house it was well into the night and she was accompanied by a band of young men. They all came flocking in together, and when her sister saw them she was furious and said: 'My dear girl, as long as you lead this shameful life you've no right to enter this house. I shall be held to blame, which I can well do without!'

Hearing her say that she would cause her shame enraged the younger sister, who said she was more guilty still: she accused her of being sinfully loved by her confessor, and said that if people knew of it she would be burnt at the stake. When she heard this devilish accusation the elder girl was filled with rage, and told her sister to leave the house. The mad sister replied that it was her father's house as much as hers, and that she would not leave on her account. Hearing this refusal, the elder girl grabbed her by the shoulders and was about to fling her out; but she fought back, and the young men who had come with her seized the sister and beat her grievously until she let her go. When they had had their fill of beating her she ran to her chamber and shut the door behind her. She had only a maid and a manservant to care for her, but they were enough to stop the boys beating her more.

There in her chamber all alone she lay down on her bed fully clothed; she began to weep and lament most terribly, and her heart was filled with the deepest anger. In this woeful state she fell asleep. And the demon, knowing anger had erased all else, was overjoyed that she had forgotten the good man's lesson, and said: 'Now I can do whatever I want with her! She's outside her teacher's protection and her Lord's grace. Now we can put our man in her!'

This was the demon who had the power to have relations with women and to lie with them; he made himself ready, came to her chamber, lay with her, and conceived. When it was done, she awoke; and as she did so she remembered her worthy confessor's words and made the sign of the cross. Then she said: 'Holy Lady Mary, what's happened to me? I'm not the maiden I was when I lay down in my bed! Dear glorious mother of Christ, daughter and mother of God, implore your dear son to keep me from peril and protect my soul from the Enemy.'

Then she rose from her bed and began to look for the man who had done this to her, for she imagined she would be able to find him. But when she came to the door of her chamber she found it locked. She searched every corner of the room and found nothing. She knew for certain then that she had been deceived by the Enemy. She began to lament and appeal to Our Lord to have pity and save her from worldly shame.

Night passed and morning came. And as soon as it was light the demon led the younger sister away – she had thoroughly fulfilled his purpose – and when she and the young men were gone, the elder girl came from her chamber, weeping, in great distress, and called her servant and told him to fetch two women. He did so, and when they arrived she set out with them to see her confessor. She made her way there, and as soon as the good man saw her he said: 'My dear friend, you clearly need help: I can see you're in a state of fear and shock.'

'Sir,' she replied, 'something has happened to me that never befell a woman before. I've come to you for advice in God's name, for you told me that no matter how great a sin might be, if a person will confess and repent and do as the confessor says, the sin will be forgiven. Sir, I have sinned indeed, and have been deceived by the Enemy.'

And she told him how her sister had come to the house and of their argu-

ment, and how she and the young men had beaten her; and how she had
gone to her chamber in a rage and shut herself in, and because of the depth of
her grief and anger had forgotten to make the sign of the cross.

'So I forgot all the instructions you gave me. I lay down in my bed fully
dressed and fell asleep, still in a state of deep anger. And when I awoke, I
found I'd been shamed and was a maiden no more. Sir, I searched my
chamber from top to bottom, and the door was locked, but I found no human
soul. I didn't know who'd done this to me: I knew I'd been deceived. I beg
you in God's name, though my body may be in torment, let me not lose my
soul.'

The good man had listened to every word she said and was astounded;
but he did not believe it at all, for he had never heard of such a wonder, and
he said to her: 'Dear friend, you are possessed by the Devil, and the Devil is
speaking through you still. How can I confess you or give you penance when
I fear you're lying? No woman ever lost her virginity without knowing by
whom, or without at least seeing the man! Yet you expect me to believe this
wonder has befallen you.'

'May God keep me from torment, sir,' she replied, 'as surely as I am telling
you the truth!'

'If you are,' said the good man, 'you'll know it soon enough! You've
committed a great sin in disobeying my command, and for your disobedience
I charge you as a penance that for the rest of your life you eat only once on a
Friday; and in payment for your lustful act – about which I do not believe you
– I must give you another lifelong penance, if you're willing to do as I say.'

'I'll do anything you command, sir,' she said, and he replied: 'May God
ensure that you do. Assure me that you'll submit to the instruction of the
ministers of Holy Church and of God, who redeemed us at the dear price of
His precious blood and His death; and that you'll make true confession and
humble repentance fully confirmed in heart and body, and act and speak in
all ways according to Christ's commandments.'

'Sir,' she replied, 'I'll do all in my power to do exactly as you say.'

'I trust in God,' he said, 'that, if you're telling the truth, you'll have nothing
to fear.'

'May God guard me from all baseness and reproach, for my words are
true.'

'So you swear to me,' he said, 'to do your penance faithfully and to
renounce and abandon your sin?'

'Yes indeed, sir,' she replied, and he said:

'Then you have abjured lust. I forbid you to indulge in lustful ways for the
rest of your life – except for what befell you while you slept, which no-one
could have avoided. Are you willing and able to accept this?'

'Yes, sir,' she replied, 'if you can ensure that I'm not damned for this sin, as
God has installed you on Earth at His command.'

She accepted the penance with which the good man charged her, repenting very willingly and with a true heart. The good man blessed her with the sign of the cross, and did all he could to restore her to the faith of Jesus Christ; and he pondered deeply how her story could be true. After much thought he realised she had been deceived by some demon, and he called her to him and made her drink holy water in the name of the Father, Son and Holy Spirit, and sprinkled it over her, saying: 'Be sure that you never forget my commandments. And whenever you need me, come to me and make the sign of the cross and commend yourself to God.' And he committed her in penitence to do all the good deeds that she could.

And so she made her way home, and proceeded to lead a good and honest life. And when the demon realised he had lost her, and had no knowledge of anything she did or said – she might as well never have existed – he was enraged. She stayed at home and led an excellent life, until the seed she had in her body could hide itself no longer, and she grew fat and round until it was noticed by other women. They looked at her belly and said: 'Dear friend, are you with child?'

'Truly, ladies,' she replied, 'I am.'

'God!' they cried. 'Who was it made you so? You're round and full-bellied indeed!'

'I know I am, truly,' she said.

'Who is responsible?' they asked.

'May God comfort me,' she replied, 'I've no idea at all.'

'Have you had so many men?' they said.

'So help me God,' she answered, 'no man has ever done anything to me to cause me to be with child.'

'That's impossible, my dear!' they said. 'But perhaps you have a secret lover who's done this, and you don't want to accuse him? Well truly, your body's at terrible risk, for as soon as the judges know of this you'll be stoned to death.'

When she heard that she faced certain death she was filled with fear and said: 'May God protect my soul as surely as I never saw the man responsible!'

With that the women left; they thought her mad, and said how terribly sad it was about her great inheritance and fine estates, for now she would lose everything. She was appalled by this, and returned to her confessor and told him what the women had said. Then the good man saw she was great with child, and he was deeply shocked and asked her if she had done the penance he had laid upon her. And she replied: 'Yes, sir, unfailingly.'

'And this sin has befallen you only once?'

'Yes indeed, sir,' she said. 'At no other time, either before or since.'

The good man was perplexed by these events; and he wrote down the night and the hour of the conception according to her story, and said: 'Be assured that when the child inside you is born, I'll know whether you've told me the truth or lied. And I have utter faith in God that, if your story's true, you'll be in no danger of death. You may well fear it, though, for when the judges know of it they'll seize you to get their hands on your fine properties and land, and will threaten to put you to death. When you're arrested send me word, and I'll bring you counsel and comfort if I can, and God will help you if you're as innocent as you say. But if you're not, be assured that He'll not forget you! Go home now,' he said, 'and stay calm and lead a good life, for a good life helps bring about a good end.'

So she returned home that night, and proceeded to lead a peaceful, humble life, until such time as the judges came to those parts and heard about the lady who had conceived a child in this strange manner. They sent people to her house to find and fetch her. When she was arrested she sent word to the good man who had been such a faithful counsellor, and as soon as he heard he came with all possible speed. The judges welcomed him, but repeated the lady's story that she did not know who had made her pregnant, and said: 'Do you believe that any woman can conceive and become pregnant without male company?'

'I shan't tell you all I know,' the good man replied, 'but what I will say is this: if you want my advice you'll not put her to death while she's with child – it wouldn't be right, for the child doesn't deserve to die. He has committed no sin, and wasn't involved in the sin of his mother. If you put her to death you'll be guilty of the death of an innocent.'

And the judges said: 'Sir, we'll do as you advise.'

'Then keep her in a tower under close guard, so that she can do nothing foolish. And place two women with her who can help her when the time comes for the delivery, and make sure they can't slip away. So she'll be well guarded until she has the child. And then I advise you to let her feed the child until he can feed himself and make his own needs clear. Then do whatever else you feel necessary. But give them whatever they need: you can easily do so by drawing on her own wealth. This is my advice, and you'll follow it if you trust me – though if you wish to do otherwise I can't stop you.'

But the judges replied: 'We think you're right.'

And they did as the good man advised, locking her in a house of stone with all the ground floor doors walled up. And with her they installed two of the worthiest women they could find for the purpose. They left windows upstairs through which the things they needed could be hauled inside. After arranging this, the good man spoke to her at the window, saying: 'Once the child is born, have him baptised as soon as you can. And when they bring you out and prepare to pass judgement on you, send for me.'

She was kept in the tower for a long while, and the judges supplied her and her attendants with everything they needed. There she stayed until it pleased Lord God that she had the child. And when he was born, he had the power and the intelligence of the Devil – he was bound to, being conceived by him. But the Enemy had made a foolish mistake, for Our Lord redeemed by His death all who truly repent, and the Enemy had worked upon the child's mother through sheer trickery while she slept, and as soon as she was aware of the deception she had begged for forgiveness and submitted to the mercy and commandment of Holy Church and of God, and had obeyed all her confessor's instructions. God had no wish to deprive the Devil of what was rightfully his, and since the Devil wanted the child to inherit his power to know all things said and done in the past, he did indeed acquire that knowledge; but, in view of the mother's penitence and true confession and repentant heart, and of her unwillingness in the fatal deed, and of the power of her cleansing baptism in the font, Our Lord, who knows all things, did not wish to punish the child for his mother's sin, but gave him the power to know the future. And so it was that the child inherited knowledge of things past from the Enemy, and, in addition, knowledge of things to come was bequeathed to him by God. It was up to him which way he inclined. If he wished, he could answer the claims both of Our Lord and of the devils; for a demon had made his body, but Our Lord had given him the spirit to hear and understand. Indeed, he had given more to him than to other men because he would certainly be needing it. It remained to be seen which way the child would lean.

And so he was born, and the moment the women received him and set eyes on him they were filled with fear, for he had more and far longer hair than they had ever seen on other children. They showed him to his mother, who crossed herself and said: 'This child frightens me.'

'We hardly dare hold him,' said the women.

'Take him below,' the mother said, 'and give orders that he be baptised.'

'What name shall he be given?' they asked; and she replied: 'The same as my father, whose name was Merlin.'

So the child was baptised and named Merlin after his grandfather. He was given to his mother to be fed, and she fed him until he was nine months old – when he looked at least a year or more. And time passed and he reached eighteen months, and the women said to her: 'We want to be out of here and go back to our homes – we've been here so long!'

'Truly,' she replied, 'I can't bear to see you go!'

But they said: 'We can't stay here any more!'

She began to weep and begged for mercy in God's name, that they should endure it just a little longer. They went and leaned at a window, and the mother took her child in her arms and sat down and wept, saying: 'Dear son, I'm going to suffer death on your account, but I haven't deserved it. But I shall die, because no-one knows the truth about who fathered you and no-one believes a word I say. So die I must.'

And while the mother lamented to her son – and complained to God of her woes, declaring that He should never have let her be born – the child looked at her and said: 'Mother, have no fear, for you will not die on my account.'

When she heard the child speak her heart quite stopped in dismay; she dropped her arms, and the child bawled as he fell to the ground. And when the women at the window saw this they leapt forward and ran to him, thinking she was about to kill the child. But she said she had no such thought.

'I dropped him in astonishment at what he said; my heart and arms failed me! That's why he fell.'

'What did he say,' they asked, 'to give you such a shock?'

'That I wouldn't die because of him.'

'Let's see if he'll say more!' they said, and they took him and watched him with rapt attention, wondering if he would speak again. But he gave no sign at all of doing so; he uttered not a word. After a long while had passed the mother said to the two women: 'Give him to me and let's see if he'll speak.'

And she took him in her arms, desperate that he should speak in the women's presence. But the women said: 'What a shame it is for your lovely body, that you'll be burnt for the sake of this creature. It would have been better if he'd never been born.'

And the child replied: 'You lie! That's what my mother would have me tell you!'

When the women heard this they were stricken with fear and said: 'This is no child but a demon, who knows what we've said and done!'

They burst into excited babble, and he said to them: 'Leave me be! You're wilder sinners than my mother!'

They could not believe their ears, and said that this marvel could not be kept secret. 'We must let the whole world know!'

They went to the window and called to the people below and told them what the child had said. The people were astounded and said it was high time the mother was put to death. They sent letters to summon the judges, and her execution was fixed for forty days thence. When the mother heard that the day of her death had been decreed she was filled with fear and sent word to her confessor.

Time went by until there were only eight days left before her stoning, and the thought of that day terrified her. The child toddled around the tower and saw his mother weeping and began to laugh in apparent delight. The women said to him: 'You're sharing few of your mother's thoughts! In this coming week she's going to die because of you. Cursed be the hour of your birth! God cannot love her, letting her suffer death on your account.'

But the child replied: 'They're lying, mother. You'll never be brought to shame as long as I live, and no-one will dare touch you or determine your death but God.'

Hearing this, the mother and the two women were stricken with awe and said: 'This child has remarkable powers and will be a great man, if he can make such pronouncements!'

So matters stayed until the day decreed. And when the day came, the women were released from the tower, the mother carrying her child in her arms. The judges had arrived, and they took the women to one side and asked them if it was true that the child had made these utterances. The women reported everything they had heard him say, and the judges were astounded and said: 'He'll need a way with words indeed if he's to save her from death!'

Back they came; and the good man was there to give her counsel. One of the judges said: 'Young lady, is there anything more you wish to say or do? Prepare yourself now, for you're about to suffer death.'

'If you please, sir,' she replied, 'I'd like to speak to my confessor there.'

The judge gave her permission and she went into a chamber, leaving her child outside. Many people tried to get him to speak but without success. Meanwhile the mother talked to her confessor, weeping most piteously; and when she had said all she wished the good man asked her: 'Is it true that your child speaks?'

She heard his question, and replied: 'Yes, sir.'

Then they left the chamber and found her child crying outside, and she took him in her arms and came straight before the judges. When they saw her they said: 'Lady, tell us who is the father of this child. Beware of concealing the truth.'

'My lords,' she replied, 'I can see I'm doomed to die. But may God have no pity on my soul if I ever knew or saw the father, or if I ever willingly gave myself in such a way as to be with child.'

But one of the judges said: 'We don't believe that can be true. We'll ask other women if what you're telling us could possibly happen. No-one has ever heard such a tale before.'

And with that the judges withdrew and asked many women if the mother's story could be true. One of the judges spoke to the large gathering and said: 'All you ladies assembled here, has it happened to any of you, or to any woman you've ever heard of, that a child has been conceived without the carnal involvement of a man?'

And they replied that no woman could become pregnant and have a child without male company. Hearing this, the judges returned to Merlin's mother and repeated what the women had said.

'And now justice must be done, for there appears to be no truth whatever in this woman's story.'

Then Merlin leapt forward, incensed by their words to his mother, and said: 'She'll not be burnt so soon! If all men and women who committed adultery were put to death, more than a couple of the people here would be burnt, for I know the ways of these women as well as they do themselves! If I were to speak of them, I'd make them confess and admit the truth in front of this whole assembly. There are some who've done worse than my mother! She's not guilty of the charges made – and if she is, this good man has taken them upon himself. If you don't believe me, ask him yourselves.'

The judges summoned the good confessor and asked him if what the child said was true, and he recounted word for word what Merlin's mother had first told him.

'And I told her that if her story was true she need have no fear of God or the world, for she would receive fair treatment.'

Then she told them herself how she had been deceived, and of the marvellous conception of the child while she slept, without having any pleasure of a man; she did not know who had fathered him. 'And I've made confession and repented.'

Then Merlin said to the good man: 'You wrote down the night and the hour when it happened. You can tell whether my mother's speaking the truth. From your note you can prove part of what she's said and done.'

'That's true!' the good man said. 'I don't know where your wisdom comes from, for you've far more sense than any of us!'

Then the women who had been in the tower with Merlin's mother were summoned. They reported to the judges the time of the child's birth, and therefore his conception, and compared it with what the good man had written, and found that it was as he said. But one of the judges replied: 'This doesn't acquit her on its own: she must tell us who begat you.'

The child was furious and said: 'I know my father better than you ever knew yours! And your mother knows who fathered you better than mine knows who fathered me!'

The judge was enraged and said: 'Merlin, if you know something about my mother you've a duty to tell me.'

'I can say for sure,' Merlin replied, 'that your mother deserves death more than mine! And if I make her admit it, then acquit my mother, who's innocent of the charge you've laid upon her, for be assured that what she's said about me is true.'

The judge was incensed by this and said: 'If you're right, you'll have saved your mother from the fire. But I tell you this: if what you've said about my mother is false, yours will certainly burn.'

They adjourned for fifteen days, while the judge sent for his own mother and put Merlin and his mother under close guard: indeed, he stayed with the guards himself. The child was often encouraged to speak by his mother and by others, but they could not get a word from him.

The appointed day came and the judge appeared with his mother, and Merlin and his mother were taken from prison and led before the people. Then the judge said to Merlin: 'Here is my mother, about whom you must speak.'

'This is not wise,' Merlin replied. 'Go, and take her to a house in private and summon your closest counsellors. I shall summon my mother's – God omnipotent and her confessor.'

Those who heard his words were almost speechless with astonishment, but the judge knew that what he said was wise. And Merlin said to the other judges: 'If I can deliver my mother from this man, will she be acquitted?'

'If she escapes his condemnation,' they replied, 'nothing more will be asked of her.'

And so they retired to a chamber, the judge taking with him his mother and two of the worthiest friends he could find, while Merlin took his mother's confessor. When they were all assembled, the judge said: 'Merlin, now you may say what you wish to my mother, to earn your mother's acquittal.'

'I've no desire,' said Merlin, 'to defend my mother if she's done wrong, but I wish to protect God's truth and hers. Be assured she's not deserved the torment you intend for her, and if you'll take my advice you'll acquit my mother and cease to inquire about your own.'

'You're not going to wriggle round me like this!' the judge replied. 'You'll have to say more!'

'You've taken my mother,' said Merlin, 'and intend to burn her for giving birth to me without knowing who begat me. But I know who fathered me better than you know who fathered you, and your mother could say whose son you are better than my mother could say whose son I am.'

Then the judge said to his mother: 'Am I not the son of your lawful husband?'

'Oh God, dear son,' his mother replied, 'whose son would you be, if not your good father's, long dead?'

'Lady,' said the child Merlin, 'you must tell the truth if your son is to acquit my mother and me. I dearly wish he'd do so now, without more being said.'

'I most certainly will not!' the judge replied; and the child said: 'All you'll achieve by making your mother testify is to find that your father's still alive.'

Everyone present was astounded by this; and the child turned to the judge's mother and said: 'Lady, you must tell your son the truth.'

The lady crossed herself and cried: 'Devil Satan! Haven't I done so?'

'You know very well,' Merlin replied, 'that he's not the son of the man he thinks.'

The lady was appalled, and said: 'Whose is he, then?'

'You know,' replied the child, 'that he's your priest's son. By way of proof, the first time that you conjoined with him, you told him you were afraid of becoming pregnant; and he said you wouldn't be so on his account, and that he'd make a note of all the times when he lay with you, because he for his part was afraid you'd lie with another man, for at that time you were on bad terms with your husband. And when your son was conceived, you weren't slow in lamenting your misfortune, being with child by him. If I'm telling the truth, admit it. If you won't, I'll reveal more.'

The judge was terribly distressed, and asked his mother: 'Is this true?'

And his mother, in great alarm, replied: 'Do you believe this demon?'

'If you won't admit it,' said the child, 'I'll tell you something else which you know to be true.'

The lady went quiet, and the child said: 'There's no point in hiding it, for everything done is known to me. The truth is that when you knew you were pregnant you sought to make peace with your husband, so that he wouldn't realise the child was not his. The priest arranged your reconciliation and encouraged you to lie together once more, and so made your worthy husband imagine it was his child – as did everyone else. Your son himself was sure of it. You've lived this lie ever since, and do so still. Indeed, the night before you left to come here, you and the priest lay together; and when you set out in the morning he accompanied you a good part of the way, and said: 'My dear, make sure you do and say all my son wants to hear' – for he knew he was his son because of the notes he'd kept.'

When the judge's mother heard these words – which she knew to be entirely true – she sat down, devastated. She knew now that she had to tell the truth; and the judge looked at her and said: 'Dear mother, whoever your lover may have been, I am still your son, and as such I want you to tell me the truth. Are the child's words true?'

'May God have mercy on me, yes,' she replied. 'I can't hide it: it's all true, every word.'

The judge turned pale, and said: 'This child is wise indeed, saying he knew his father better than I knew mine. It would be wrong to put his mother to death without doing the same to my own. In the name of God and love,' he said to Merlin, 'and so that I may clear myself of blame in the eyes of these people, tell me who is your father.'

And Merlin replied: 'I will do so, but it may not be to your advantage. I would have you know that I am the son of a devil who deceived my mother. He was one of a kind of demon called Hequibedes, who inhabit the air. And he bequeathed to me the power and intelligence to know everything that has been said and done: that's how I know all about the life your mother has led. And Our Lord has granted me the knowledge of things to come, as you'll see by what I'm about to tell you.'

Then Merlin took him aside and said: 'Your mother will go now to the man who fathered you and tell him everything I've said. And when he hears that you know the truth his heart will be overcome by terror. He'll flee in fear of you, and the Devil – whose ways he's followed so long – will lead him to a river where he'll drown himself. You can use this to judge whether I have knowledge of the future.'

'If it proves to be true,' the judge replied, 'I'll never doubt you.'

With that they left their private talk and returned to the people, and the judge said: 'Sirs, this child has saved his mother from the stake. All who see him may be sure they've never seen one wiser.'

And they answered: 'God be praised!'

So Merlin's mother was set free and the judge's mother known to be guilty.

The judge sent two men after her to see if Merlin's prediction was true. And as soon as the lady reached home she spoke in private to the priest and told him of the wonders she had heard, and he was terrified. He went away and thought in his heart that the judges would hunt him down and kill him; so he left the town and came to a river, where he said to himself that he would rather drown than be killed by the judge and die a base and shameful death in public. And so the Devil – whose works he had done so long – drove him to leap into the river and drown; and this was witnessed by the two men sent by the judge. The story teaches that this is why a man in distress should beware of being alone, for in solitude a man is more open to the Devil's wiles than he is in human company.

After witnessing the priest's remarkable death the men returned to the judge and reported exactly what they had seen. He was astounded by the news, and went and told Merlin, who laughed and said: 'Now you can see I was telling the truth! I beg you, repeat exactly what I told you to Blaise.'

Blaise was his mother's confessor, and the judge told him the amazing story of the priest. Then Merlin set off with his mother and Blaise, while the judges went their own ways.

Now this Blaise was a very shrewd, bright man, and when he heard Merlin – no more than two-and-a-half years old – speaking so cleverly, he wondered where such intelligence could come from. He went to great lengths to test Merlin in many different ways, until Merlin said: 'Blaise, don't put me to the test, for the more you do, the more dumbfounded you'll be. Just do as I say, and trust in my advice, and I'll teach you how to gain the love of Christ and lasting joy.'

'I heard you say you were the son of a demon,' Blaise replied, 'so I fear you may deceive me.'

'Ill-disposed hearts,' said Merlin, 'always pay more attention to bad than to good. You heard me say I was fathered by a demon, but you also heard me say that Our Lord gave me knowledge of the future. If you were wise, this would be a sign to you of which way I would incline. Be assured that from the moment it pleased Our Lord to grant me this knowledge, I was lost to the Devil. But I haven't lost the demons' craft and cunning: I've inherited from them some useful things, but they won't be used for their benefit! It wasn't a wise move on their part to beget me in my mother: they chose a vessel which would never be theirs – my mother's good life did them great harm! Had they conceived me in my grandmother I'd have had no knowledge of God, for she led a wicked life, and it was because of her that such ills befell my mother – her father's death, I mean, and all the other things of which she's told you. But believe what I say about the faith of Jesus Christ, and I'll tell you something which no-one but God could reveal – and I'd like you to set it down in a book, for many people who hear my words will benefit from them and beware of sin. If you'd do this it would be a great service.'

'I will gladly make the book,' Blaise replied. 'But I beseech you, in the name of the Father, Son and Holy Spirit – which three I truly believe are one being in God – and in the name of the blessed Lady who bore God's son – her son and father both – and in the name of all the angels and archangels and apostles and all the saints and the prelates of Holy Church, promise me you'll never deceive me into doing anything displeasing to God.'

'May all those you have named,' said Merlin, 'bring me Christ's disfavour if I ever make you do anything against His will.'

'Then tell me what you wish,' said Blaise. And Merlin said:

'Fetch ink and plenty of parchment, for I'm going to tell you many things; you're going to write down what no man but I could tell you.'

Blaise went to find the things he needed, and when he had gathered them together Merlin began to tell him all about the love between Christ and Joseph of Arimathea and everything that had happened to him; and about Alain and his company and his father, and their departure; and how Petrus had set out on his journey and Joseph had bequeathed the vessel at his death; and how, after all this had happened, the demons came together and discussed how they had lost their former power over men, and complained of the harm the prophets had done them, and agreed to create a man of their own.

'And they made me. And you know from my mother and from others the trickery they employed in my making. But through my mother's repentance they lost me and everything else they desired.'

And so Merlin told the whole story for Blaise to set down in writing.[1] Blaise was often amazed by the wonders Merlin told him, but they always struck him as good and full of beauty, and he listened in delight. As Blaise set about the task of writing, Merlin said to him: 'This work will cause you suffering, but I shall suffer more.'

Blaise asked him what he meant, and he said: 'I shall be sent on a journey[2] into the West, and those who'll come in search of me will promise their lord to take him back my blood. But when they see me and hear me speak, they'll have no wish to do so. I shall go with them, and you will go to the company who keep the vessel called the Grail. For evermore men will tell of your work and your writings, though your book will have no authority, for you are not and cannot be an apostle; and the apostles wrote about Our Lord only what they'd seen and heard themselves, but you're writing nothing from experience – only what I've told you. Just as I am a figure of secrecy, and always shall be to those I do not choose to enlighten, so shall your whole book remain a mystery and few will recognise its wonders. You will take it with you when I leave with those who are to come in search of me; and Joseph and his book will be combined with yours, for when your work is done and you join that other company, your book will be attached to his, and the truth of our work will be revealed. They'll have pity on us – if it please them – and pray to Our Lord on our behalf. And when the two books are brought together there'll be one beautiful book, for the two are one entity – though I

---

[1] A miniature has been cut from the Modena manuscript, along with a short section of the text. The missing lines are replaced here by the corresponding passage from the Paris manuscript B.N.fr.747.

[2] The Modena text resumes.

don't wish to relate, and it would be wrong to do so, the words that passed in private between Joseph and Jesus Christ.'

[3]My lord Robert de Boron, who tells this story, says, like Merlin, that it is in two parts, for he could not know the story of the Grail.

*

Now at the time of these events, Christianity was newly arrived in England and there had as yet been few Christian kings, and of them there is no reason to tell you except where it relates to this story. There was a king in England named Constans, who reigned for a long while and had three sons: one was called Moine, another[4] Pendragon, and the third Uther, and they had a seneschal named Vortigern. This Vortigern was very clever and worldly-wise, and as good a knight as any then living. Constans passed from life to death, and when he died the barons wondered who they should declare king. Most agreed it should be their lord's son Moine, but as soon as he was made king, war broke out. The Saxons were ranged against King Moine, and many from the Roman Empire, too, came to fight against the Christians. And Vortigern, seneschal of the land, turned everything to his own advantage. The child who had been made king was not as wise or strong as he needed to be, and Vortigern made the most of the war and gained the hearts of the people, knowing they thought him good and able. His pride grew ever greater as he saw that no-one could match his abilities, and he declared he would have nothing more to do with the king's war and withdrew his services. The Saxons gathered and advanced in great numbers, and the king came to Vortigern and said: 'Help to defend my land, dear friend: we're all at your command!'

'Sire,' Vortigern replied, 'find help elsewhere. I don't care to be involved, for there are people in your land who resent my service. They can fight your battle for you: I'm taking no part.'

King Moine and his followers saw there was no love to be found in Vortigern, so they turned to do battle with the Saxons. They were defeated – and said they would not have suffered this great loss if Vortigern had been at the battle. So matters remained: the child-king could not keep his people's support as well as he should and many began to despise him, and as more time passed King Moine lost all respect and they said they would tolerate him no longer. They came to Vortigern and said: 'Sir, we're without a king: the one we have is worthless! We beg you in God's name to be our king and lord.'

'I can't,' Vortigern replied. 'It wouldn't be right, as long as my lord lives. But if he were dead, and you and the others wanted me king, I'd gladly be so. But as long as he lives it's neither possible nor proper.'

---

[3] More lines are lost because of the missing miniature: the Paris manuscript replaces them.
[4] The Modena text resumes.

They heard Vortigern's words and wondered what to do; they took their leave and departed. On their return they summoned their friends and spoke with them, and those who had been to Vortigern told of their conversation with him. Hearing what he had said, the others replied: 'It would be best if we killed King Moine! Then Vortigern will be king, and he'll know he had the kingship thanks to us and will do whatever we wish! That way we'll rule through him!'

And at once they arranged who would do the killing. They elected twelve; and these twelve set off to find King Moine while the others stayed in the town, ready to come to their aid if there was trouble. The twelve tracked the king down, and attacked him with swords and knives and killed him: it was quickly done, for he was very young. After they had killed him, it was a deed of which no-one spoke for a long time. They returned to Vortigern and told him: 'Vortigern, now you shall be king, for we have killed King Moine!'

Hearing they had murdered his master, Vortigern feigned fury, saying: 'You've committed a great crime, sirs, in killing your lord! I'd flee if I were you, for the good men of this land will kill you if they catch you – I wish you'd never come here!'

So they took to flight. Such was the death of King Moine. And the people of the kingdom assembled and declared Vortigern king, for as I have told you, he had the hearts of most people in the land. They all agreed he should be king and declared their allegiance to him.

At this assembly were two worthy men who were guardians of Pendragon and Uther – Constans' other two sons, the brothers of the dead King Moine. And when these good men heard that Vortigern was to be king, it was clear to them that he had arranged Moine's death. They spoke together and said: 'Vortigern has had Moine murdered, and as soon as he's king he'll do the same to our two wards Pendragon and Uther. We loved their father dearly – he was very good to us, and we owe everything we have to him. It would be very wrong to let these children be killed. Vortigern knows the kingdom should be theirs, and will want to kill them before they're of an age to claim their land.'

They agreed to send the children away to foreign parts in the East, from where their ancestors had come. So they led them away to safety, to make sure Vortigern could not kill them. I shall tell you no more about them until the right point in the story; but this tale clearly shows that it is best to trust in worthy men.

So then, as you have heard, Vortigern was declared king by the people of the land. And after he had been crowned and was lord of that country, King Moine's killers came to him; but Vortigern behaved as if he had never set eyes on them before. They rushed forward and began to yell at him that it was thanks to them he was king, for they had killed King Moine; but when he heard them say again that they had murdered their lord he ordered that they be seized, and said: 'You've passed sentence on yourselves, sirs, admitting

that you killed your former lord! You had no right to do such a thing! You'd
do the same to me if you could! But I'm more than able to stop you!'

They were aghast at this, and said to Vortigern: 'We did it for your benefit!
We thought we'd earn your gratitude!'

But Vortigern said: 'I'll show you the gratitude that people like you
deserve.'

And he had all twelve taken and bound to the tails of twelve horses, and
dragged along behind them until little of them remained. But they had many
kinsmen who came to Vortigern after the executions and said: 'You've
wronged us greatly, putting our relations to such a base and terrible death.
Don't imagine you'll ever have our service!'

Vortigern was shocked and enraged to hear them threaten him, and said
that if they ever spoke of it again he would do the same to them. But they
were scornful of his threats, too, and showing little fear they angrily replied:
'King Vortigern, you can threaten us as much as you like, but we can assure
you that for as long as we have the support of our friends you'll find yourself
embroiled in war! We defy you from this time forth, for you are not our lord
or the rightful ruler of this land: you hold the kingship against God and
justice. We tell you this: you will suffer the same death as you inflicted on our
kinsmen.'

They left without another word. Vortigern was furious, but did nothing
more for the time being. So began the strife between Vortigern and the
barons. They assembled a great force and advanced into Vortigern's land,
laying waste one part of it, but he joined battle with them over and over until
he drove them from his kingdom. But he became so cruel to his people that
they could stand it no longer and rose against him, and Vortigern feared they
would force him from the land. So he sent messengers to the Saxons to sue for
peace – much to the Saxons' joy. One of them, named Hengist, the fiercest of
them all, lent Vortigern his service for a long while until they gained the
upper hand in the war against the barons; and when the war was finally over
Hengist commented how deeply the people hated him.

Hengist did many deeds of which there is no need to tell you, but I can tell
you this much: Vortigern took one of his daughters as his wife – and all who
hear this tale may like to know that it was she who brought the word *wassail*
to this kingdom. I will not tell you about Hengist and his affairs, but the
Christians grieved deeply that Vortigern had married his daughter. They said
he had largely abandoned his faith in taking a wife who did not believe in
Christ. Vortigern realised he was not loved by his people, and knew that
Constans' exiled sons would return as soon as they could – and that if they
did so, they would be seeking his downfall. He decided to build a tower so
huge and strong that he would have no fear of anyone, and he summoned all
the finest masons in the land and ordered them to start work. But after they
had been building for three days it came tumbling down. Four times they
began again, and four times it collapsed. Vortigern was distraught at the

news, and said he would never rest until he knew why it kept falling. He summoned the worthiest men of the land and told them of the collapsing tower and how nothing could be done to make it stand, and they were amazed. They saw the pile of rubble and said: 'Only a learned clerk could explain this, sire. Because of the depth of their learning clerks know many things beyond our knowledge: you'll find the truth only through them. You must speak to them.'

'In faith, sirs,' said Vortigern, 'I think you're right.'

He immediately summoned all the learned clerks of the land, and when they were assembled he explained to them the mystery of the tower. They said to each other: 'What an amazing story the king has told us.'

The king asked which of them were the wisest, and then said: 'Can you explain why my tower falls, no matter what I do? I want you to stay and do all you can to find the reason, for I've been told that only you, or other clerks, can tell me.'

Hearing his request, they replied: 'We don't know, sire, but there are some clerks here who could explain, for this involves an art called astronomy, of which they happen to have knowledge. You must find out which of them are the most learned in this sphere.'

'You know the clerks better than I do,' said the king. 'Decide amongst yourselves who are the most skilled in this art. They mustn't hesitate to come forward and boldly declare themselves. I'll do anything they ask if they can tell me why my tower keeps falling.'

The clerks withdrew and asked each other if they had knowledge of this art. And two of them said: 'We know a fair amount.'

And the king declared: 'Go and find like-minded men and come to me.'

'Gladly,' they replied, and the two clerks made enquiries and soon there were seven – each of whom thought himself the finest – and they returned to the king who asked them: 'Can you explain, sirs, why my tower keeps falling?'

And they replied that if anyone could, they could, and he said he would give them whatever they wished if they could find the answer. With that Vortigern left the clerks, and the seven of them set about the task of discovering why the tower collapsed and how it could be made to stand. These seven were very skilled in their art and each on his own set to work diligently; but the harder they laboured, the less they found out. The only thing they did discover seemed to have nothing to do with the tower, and was very disconcerting. The king became impatient, and summoned them and said: 'Sir clerks, what can you tell me about the tower and why it falls?'

'You've set us a great problem, sire,' they replied. 'Give us another eleven days.'

'I'll grant you this respite,' said the king, 'but if you value your lives, make sure you give me the answer then.'

They swore they would do so without fail, and withdrew together and asked each other: 'What do you think about this business?'

'We've no idea,' they all replied. None of them would reveal what he knew, and so the wisest of them all said: 'Let each of you, one after the other, tell me privately what you've discovered so far. I'll do nothing as a result except with everyone's agreement.'

So they all spoke to him in private, one at a time, and he asked them what they thought about the tower. And they all said the same: they had no idea how the tower could be made to stand, but they had seen something else, something remarkable. They had seen a seven-year-old child, born of a woman but fathered by no earthly man. All seven clerks told him the same; and when he had listened to them all, he said: 'Come to me now, all together.' They did so, and when they had all gathered he said: 'Sirs, you've all told me the same thing, one after the other, but you've also kept something back.'

'Tell us then,' they replied, 'what we've told you and what we've hidden.'

'You've all said you don't know how the tower can be made to stand, but that you've seen a child born without a father, begotten by no earthly man. But there's something else that you've left unsaid, and you must believe me when I tell you this: you've all foreseen that you're going to die because of that child. I've seen the same as you, truly. That's what you hid from me: that you'd foreseen your deaths. We must talk about this urgently – it's a serious matter!' Then he – and he was the wisest of them all – said: 'If you'll trust in me, I'll protect you from this fate. You'll soon know if I'm telling the truth.'

'Well certainly, you've told us rightly what we'd seen,' they replied, 'so we beg you in God's name to advise us how to save our lives.'

'Only a fool could fail to see the solution!' he said. 'Do you know what we'll do? We'll all agree to say something else entirely: that his tower will never remain standing unless it's built with the blood of a child born without being fathered! But if such blood could be found, we'll say, the tower would stand, good and strong. Let each of us say so separately, so the king doesn't realise we've conferred. This way we can be avenged on the child we've seen in our visions. We must make sure the king doesn't see him or speak to him: whoever finds the child must kill him on the spot, and take his blood back to the king.'

They all agreed to say the same, and returned to Vortigern and said: 'We'll not give you our advice all together, but speak to you in private, one by one; then you can decide whose advice is best.'

So the clerks pretended they had not conferred, and each spoke his mind to the king and one of his counsellors, who were astounded – but convinced that it could work, if a child could truly be born without a father. The king was deeply grateful to the clerks, and thought them wise indeed, and said: 'Sir clerks, each of you separately has told me the same thing!'

'Tell us what it was,' they replied, and he repeated what each of them had said and they answered: 'That's right!'

'Sirs,' the king asked them, 'can a man truly be born without a father?'

'Oh yes,' they replied, 'and he's now seven years old.'

'I'm going to keep you under close guard,' the king said, 'and send men to fetch me this child's blood.'

'Sire,' they all replied together, 'by all means keep us under guard, but make sure you don't see the child or let him speak to you! Give orders that he be killed and his blood brought back to you, and then your tower will stand.'

The king had all the clerks taken to a chamber and provided with everything they needed. Then he chose twelve messengers and sent them off in pairs, making them swear upon holy relics not to return until they had found the child, and that whoever did so would kill him and bring back his blood.

So, as you have heard, King Vortigern sent men to find this child, his messengers setting off two by two. They scoured many lands in search of Merlin, until two pairs of messengers met and agreed to continue a while together. One day they were passing through a field outside a town where a group of children were playing a game with a stick and ball. Merlin, who knew everything that had been happening, was one of the players. When he saw Vortigern's messengers, he went up to one of the wealthiest children of the town and struck him across the leg with the stick, knowing he would react angrily. The child began to cry and hurl insults at Merlin, accusing him of being born without a father. The messengers went straight to the weeping child and asked him: 'Who was it that hit you?'

And he replied: 'The son of a woman who doesn't know who sired him: he never had a father!'

Hearing this, Merlin came up to them and said: 'Sirs, I'm the one you're looking for, whom you've promised to kill so that you can return his blood to Vortigern.'

The messengers were dumbfounded, and said: 'Who told you this?'

'I knew it,' Merlin replied, 'the moment you made the promise.'

'Will you come with us,' they asked, 'if we take you?'

'I fear you'd kill me, sirs,' Merlin answered. He knew they had no desire to do so, but said this to test them further. 'If you swear I've nothing to fear I'll go with you, and tell you about the collapsing tower and why you intended to kill me.'

The messengers were astounded by his words, and said to one another: 'This child speaks wonders! It would be a great sin to kill him.' And each of them said: 'I'd rather break my oath a hundred times than kill this child.'

Then Merlin said to them: 'Sirs, will you come and take lodging with me at my mother's house? For I couldn't go with you without the leave of my mother and the worthy man who's with her.'

'We'll gladly go,' they replied, 'wherever you care to lead us.'

So Merlin took them to lodge with his mother in a nunnery where he had installed her. When he arrived he commanded everyone to make King

Vortigern's messengers welcome. They dismounted, and Merlin took them to Blaise.

'Sir,' he said, 'here are the men I told you would be coming to kill me.' Then he turned to them and said: 'Please confirm the truth of my words to this worthy man; and if you lie, you may be sure I'll know.'

'We'll never lie,' they replied. 'But make sure you don't lie to us.'

'Listen to what we have to say,' said Merlin to Blaise; then he said to the messengers: 'Sirs, you serve a king named Vortigern. He wishes to erect a tower, but after three or four days of building it will stand no longer but comes tumbling down. Such is his frustration that he summoned learned clerks, but none of them could explain why the tower wouldn't stand or how to make it do so. So they turned to a study of the stars, but it gave them no answers about the tower: they still had nothing to say. But they did learn about my birth, and realised I was a great threat to them; and they all agreed to have me killed, telling the king that the tower would never stand without my blood. Vortigern was amazed by this and believed their words; but they insisted that the king should forbid his messengers to take me back to him, but should kill me as soon as they found me and take my blood to mix into the mortar of the tower's foundations. That way, they said, the tower would stand. At their command Vortigern chose twelve messengers and made them all swear on holy relics that whoever found me would kill me. Then he sent them off, two by two, and four of them met and were crossing a field where children were playing with stick and ball; and I, who knew they were hunting me, struck one of the children on the leg with my stick, knowing he would insult me in the worst possible way by saying I was born without a father. I did this because I wanted these gentlemen to find me. And that, good master Blaise, is how they did so. Now ask them if I've told the truth.'

Blaise asked the messengers if the child's amazing words were true, and they replied: 'They are indeed, exactly so.'

Blaise crossed himself in wonderment, and said: 'If this child is allowed to live he'll grow to be a wise man indeed; it would have been a grievous wrong to kill him.'

'Sir,' the messengers replied, 'we'd rather perjure ourselves for the rest of our lives and have the king seize our estates! And the child himself knows whether we've any desire to kill him.'

'True enough,' said Blaise, 'and I'll ask him – and other things, too – in private.'

So Blaise called Merlin, who had left the chamber so that they could speak together, and said to him: 'Merlin, they've confirmed every word of your story. But they've also said I should ask you if they have any desire to kill you.'

'I know very well they have not,' he replied.

'That's right,' said the messengers, 'so will you come with us?'

'Certainly,' he replied, 'if you promise faithfully to take me to King

Vortigern and allow no harm to be done to me until I've spoken to him – for once I've done so I know I'll have nothing to fear.'

They promised to do exactly as he asked. Then Blaise spoke to Merlin, saying: 'Merlin, I see now that you mean to leave me. So tell me: what do want me to do with this book you've set me to write?'

'I'll tell you, truly,' said Merlin. 'You can clearly see that Our Lord has given me so much wit and intelligence that the one who sought my downfall has failed. And Our Lord has chosen me to serve Him in a way that I alone could do, for no-one shares my knowledge. You can see, too, that I must go to the land from which these men have been sent to find me, and when I arrive there I'll do and say such things that no-one on Earth will have been so well believed, except God. And you'll come there, too, to complete the work you've begun. But not yet: first you'll go in search of a land called Northumberland, a land covered in great forests, a place strange even to its own inhabitants, for there are parts where no man has ever been. There you'll live, and I'll often visit you to tell you everything you need to know for the writing of your book. You must devote much effort to it, for[5] it will earn you a great reward – do you know what? I'll tell you: your heart's fulfilment in this life, and eternal joy hereafter. And your work will be retold and heard with gratitude for as long as this world lasts. And do you know the source of this grace? It comes from the grace bestowed by Our Lord upon Joseph – that Joseph to whom His body was[6] given when He was crucified. When you've done this great work for Joseph and his ancestors and descendants, and have earned the right to be in their company, I'll tell you where to find them, and you'll see the glorious rewards that Joseph enjoys because he was given the body of Christ. And to reassure you, I want you to know that God has given me such wit and intelligence that, in the kingdom to which I'm going now, I'll make all the worthy men obey me. And know, too, that your book will be much loved, and many worthy people will give it eager attention – but not until the reign of the fourth king from now. The name of that king will be Arthur. So you'll go to the land I've said, and I'll visit you often to tell you all the things I wish you to put in your book, and when you've completed it you'll take it to the company of good people who enjoy the glorious rewards of which I've spoken. And I tell you, the story of no king's life will ever have been heard so eagerly as that of King Arthur and his court.[7] When you've finished your work and told the story of their lives, you'll have earned a share in the rewards enjoyed by the company of the Grail. And[8] when they pass

---

5   Another miniature has been cut from the Modena manuscript. The missing lines are again supplied from the Paris manuscript B.N.fr.747.

6   The Modena text resumes.

7   Literally 'and those who at his time will reign'.

8   Another fragment is lost from the Modena manuscript because of the missing miniature. Lines from B.N.fr.747 again replace it.

from this world and go to the joyous presence of Jesus Christ – of which I mustn't speak – and you, too, die and leave this world, then your book, both what you've done so far and what you've yet to do, will for evermore, so long as the world shall last, be called *The Book of the Grail*, and will be[9] heard most gladly, for every word and deed therein will be good and beneficial.'

So said Merlin to his master Blaise, explaining what he had to do. Merlin called him 'master' because he had been such a support and guide to his mother. Blaise felt deeply happy at Merlin's words, and said: 'I'll do whatever you command.'

So Merlin returned to the messengers who had come in search of him, and said: 'Come with me, sirs; I want you to hear me take leave of my mother.' And he led them to her and said: 'Dear mother, these men have come from strange and distant lands to find me. I would like to go now by your leave, for I must do Christ the service for which he has given me the power, and I can do so only if I follow these gentlemen to where they wish to take me. Your master Blaise is leaving, too: you'll have to suffer on both our accounts.'

'Dear son,' she replied, 'I commend you to God, for I'm not clever enough to keep you here! But please, I dearly want Blaise to stay.'

'Mother,' said Merlin, 'that cannot be.'

So Merlin took his leave of her and set off with the messengers, while Blaise went his separate way to Northumberland as Merlin had directed. Merlin and the messengers rode and journeyed on until they passed through a town one market day; and as they left the town they saw a peasant who had bought a very good pair of shoes, along with spare leather to repair them if the need arose, for he was about to go on a pilgrimage. As he drew near the peasant Merlin laughed, and the messengers asked him why. And he said: 'Because of that peasant. If you ask him what he intends to do with his leather, he'll tell you he plans to mend those shoes when they wear out; but I tell you, he's going to die before he even reaches home.'

The messengers were amazed by this, and said: 'We'll find out straight away if this is true!'

So they rode up to the peasant and asked him what he meant to do with the shoes and leather he was carrying, and he said he was about to go on a pilgrimage and wanted to mend his shoes when they wore out. Hearing him say exactly the same as Merlin, the messengers were astonished and said: 'This man seems in perfect health. Two of us will find out what happens to him, while the others carry on and wait for us where they stop to sleep tonight, for we must know the truth about this wonder.'

So two of the messengers went after the man, and followed him until, after no more than half a league, they saw him collapse in the middle of the road and stretch out, dead, his shoes still in his arms. They had a good, clear look,

9 The Modena text resumes.

then turned back and rejoined their companions and reported the amazing sight they had seen. When they heard the news they all declared: 'The clerks were mad to tell us to kill such a wonderful fortune-teller!'

And they said they would rather suffer harm themselves than cause him to be a victim. All this was said in secret, for they did not want Merlin to hear. But Merlin came straight up to them and thanked them for their words.

'What have we said to earn your thanks?' they asked, and Merlin repeated their words exactly. They were astonished, and said: 'This child knows everything we say and do!'

They rode on day by day until they came to Vortigern's kingdom. And one day, as they were riding through a town, a child was being carried to his burial, with many mourners following, both men and women. Merlin saw the mourning, and the priest singing, and the diligent carrying of the body to burial, and he stopped in his tracks and burst out laughing. The messengers asked him what there was to laugh about, and he said: 'I can see something remarkable!' The messengers begged him to say what it was, and Merlin replied: 'Do you see the priest singing there at the head of the column? *He* should be the one grieving, not that gentleman. The dead boy is the son of the one singing! It strikes me as rather remarkable!'

'How can we prove that?' asked the messengers; and Merlin said: 'Go to the woman and ask her why her husband is grieving so, and she'll tell you it's for the death of his son. Then say to her: "Lady, you know very well he's not his son – we know he's the son of that priest who's singing! And the priest knows it himself, for he told you he'd calculated the date of the boy's conception." '

They went straight to the woman and told her what Merlin had said. She was aghast, and said: 'Before God, dear sirs, I know I can't hide it; you seem to be very worthy men, so I'll tell you the whole truth. It's just as you've said, but in God's name, don't tell my husband, for he'd kill me if he knew.'

Having heard this wonder, they returned to their companions, and all four of them agreed they had never known such a great seer as Merlin.

On they rode, until the day came when they neared Vortigern's tower. Then they said: 'Merlin, tell us how to deal with our lord Vortigern, for two of us ought to go and tell him we've found you. Advise us what to say. He may well abuse us for having not killed you.'

When he heard them say this, Merlin knew they meant him well, and he said: 'Sirs, do exactly as I say and you'll incur no blame.'

'We'll do whatever you command,' they replied, and he said: 'Go to Vortigern and say you've found me, and tell him the truth about what you've heard me say, and that I'll reveal why his tower won't stand if he'll promise to deal with the clerks who sought to have me killed exactly as he would have done with me. And tell him how and why the clerks had ordered my death.'

They agreed to this and went straight to Vortigern, who was overjoyed to see them, and told him how they had come together and found Merlin, and how the clerks knew nothing about the tower, and all about Merlin's exploits.

'Is he the child who was born without a father?' asked Vortigern.

'Yes,' they replied, and explained how they had left him in the custody of their companions. When Vortigern heard this he said to them: 'Sirs, if you'll pledge your lives on Merlin revealing why my tower falls, I will not seek his death.'

'We will indeed, most certainly,' they replied, and the king said: 'Go and fetch him, for I can't wait to speak to him.'

So the messengers went to get Merlin, and the king himself followed them. And when Merlin saw the messengers he laughed and said: 'Sirs, you've staked your lives on me!'

'We have indeed,' they replied. 'We'd rather be in danger of death ourselves than kill you. And we must do one or the other.'

'I'll make sure your pledge is safe,' he said.

Merlin and the messengers rode together to meet the king; and when Merlin saw him he saluted him and said: 'Vortigern, come and talk to me in private.'

And he took him to one side, telling the messengers to wait, and said: 'You sent men to find me because of your tower which won't stand, and ordered them to kill me and bring you back my blood. This was on the advice of the clerks, but I assure you, my blood[10] wouldn't make the tower stand. But if they'd said it would stand with the aid of my intelligence, they would have been quite right!'

'I'll take you to them,' said Vortigern, and Merlin was led into their presence, where he said: 'My dear clerks, you took your king for a fool, telling him the blood of a child born without a father would make his tower stand. You had no vision of a way to keep it standing; what your study of the stars revealed was that you'd die because of the child. You all agreed to tell a common story, and told King Vortigern to have me killed.'

When the clerks heard him utter what they thought no man could know, they were aghast and realised they were doomed. And Merlin said to the king: 'Sire, now you can see how these clerks wanted me killed on account of your tower, because they'd foreseen that I would bring about their deaths. Ask them the truth now, for they won't be so bold as to lie in my presence.'

And the king said: 'Tell me if this child's words are true.'

'Sire,' they replied, 'may God save us from our sins as surely as he has told the truth. But we don't understand how he got this amazing knowledge. We beg you, in God's name, let us live long enough to see if he can truly make the tower stand.'

'Sirs,' Merlin said to the clerks, 'you needn't fear dying till you've seen

---

[10] There is a play on words here, juxtaposing *sanc* ('blood') and *sens* ('intelligence').

why the tower falls.' The clerks thanked him deeply, and then Merlin said: 'Vortigern, do you want to know why your tower won't stand but keeps falling, and who it is that brings it down? If you'll do as I say I'll show you very clearly. Do you know what lies beneath the tower? A great body of water; and beneath it sit two great rocks, and beneath those rocks lie two dragons. One of them is red and the other white. They can see nothing down there but can feel each other, and they're huge and very strong. When they feel the weight of the water upon them they roll over, and create such a storm in the water that anything built above it is bound to fall. So there you have it: your tower collapses because of two dragons. Keep a close watch, and if you find I've lied have me dragged to death behind your horses, but if I'm right let my pledge be fulfilled and these clerks found guilty.'

'Merlin,' Vortigern replied, 'if what you say is true you are the wisest man in the world. So tell me now how I can clear the earth from above the water.'

'With horses and carts and men with yoked buckets. Have it moved well away.'

At once the king had men set to work to find everything needed for the task. The people of the land thought it a crazy scheme, but hardly dared show it for fear of Vortigern. Merlin commanded that the clerks be held under close guard. Then the labourers set to work. For a long while they toiled to shift the earth, until at last the water was revealed. They sent word to the king that they had uncovered the water, and he came in delight to see this wonder, bringing Merlin with him. The king saw the water and how immense it was, and he called two of his best advisers and said to them: 'This man is wise indeed, knowing this water to lie beneath the earth. And he said that two dragons lie under it. No matter what the cost I'm going to do as he says, for I want to see the dragons!'

'Vortigern,' said Merlin, 'you won't know the full truth of my story until you've seen them.'

And Vortigern said: 'Merlin, how can we clear away this water?'

And Merlin replied: 'We'll channel it far from here along great ditches.'

Orders were given at once for ditches to be dug to drain away the water. And Merlin said: 'Vortigern, as soon as the dragons under the water see each other they'll join in terrible battle. I command you to summon all the worthy men of your land to witness the contest.'

Vortigern willingly agreed, and sent word throughout the land; and when all the worthy men were assembled he told them the amazing things Merlin had said, and how the two dragons were about to do battle. They said to each other: 'This should be worth seeing!'

They asked the king if Merlin had predicted which dragon would win, the red or the white, but he said he had not revealed that yet. The workmen channelled the water across the fields, and when it had all drained away they saw the rocks that sat at the bottom, beneath which lay the dragons. When Merlin saw them he said to the king: 'Vortigern, do you see those great stones?'

'Yes, brother,' the king replied.

And Merlin said: 'Beneath those stones are the two dragons.'

'Merlin,' said the king, 'how can they be released?'

'Very easily,' Merlin replied. 'They won't move until they feel each other, but as soon as they do they'll join in a battle to the death.'

'Merlin,' said Vortigern, 'will you tell me which of them will be defeated?'

'Their battle,' Merlin said, 'will have great significance. What I can reveal must be in private, in the presence of just three or four of your barons.'

Then Vortigern called four of his most trusted barons and told them what Merlin had said. They encouraged him to ask privately which of the two dragons would be defeated, and Merlin said: 'Vortigern, are these four men completely trustworthy?'

'Yes,' he replied, and Merlin said: 'So I can safely reveal what you ask in their presence?'

'You can indeed,' the king replied.

'I tell you truly,' said Merlin, 'that the white dragon will kill the red, but not without a mighty struggle. And to those who understand, the killing of the red by the white will have great significance. But I'll tell you nothing more until the battle is done.'

Thereupon the people gathered, and the workmen shifted the rocks away and drew forth the white dragon. When the people beheld it, so fierce and hideous, they were filled with terror and drew back; but the workmen released the other dragon, the sight of which made the people even more aghast, for it was even bigger and more hideous than the white, more terrifying still. Vortigern was certain that the red would defeat the white. Merlin said to him: 'Vortigern, now my pledge is surely fulfilled.'

'It is,' the king replied.

At that moment one of the dragons moved so close to the other that their rumps touched; they swung round and assailed each other with teeth and claws. Never did two creatures fight so savagely: all day and all night the battle raged, and the next day until noon; and all the while everyone thought the red would defeat the white. On they fought until finally the white flung fire from its mouth and nose and consumed the red in flame; and when the red dragon was dead, the white drew back and lay down, and lived only three days more. The people declared it the greatest wonder ever seen; and Merlin said: 'Now, Vortigern, you can build your tower as tall as you like; however great and strong you care to make it, it will never fall.'

Then Vortigern gave orders for workmen to set about it, and he made it as tall and strong as it could possibly be. Then he asked Merlin to tell him the significance of the two dragons, and how the white had come to defeat the red when the red had so long had the better of it; and Merlin said: 'Everything that's happened – and is still to happen – has significance. If I told you the truth about what you ask, and you promised to do no harm to me or to anyone in your kingdom, I'd explain the significance of all these things to you and your closest advisers.'

Vortigern gave him these assurances, and Merlin said: 'First have the clerks brought to me.'

He did so, and Merlin told them: 'You were very foolish not to act with due goodness, sense and decency. Through your folly and dishonesty you failed to achieve your aims. By the power of the elemental arts you saw things of which you had no understanding, for you are not worthy to know them; but you saw very clearly that I had been born. And the one who showed you that vision of me gave you to believe that you were to die on my account. He did so because of his anguish at having lost me: for he was my father, and would have rejoiced had you killed me. But I have a Lord who'll protect me well, if it please Him, from the wiles of my father and his fellow demons. And I'll ensure that they lied to you, for I'll do nothing to bring about your deaths if you'll promise to do as I ask.'

When the clerks heard him offer a reprieve from death, they said: 'We'll do whatever you command if it's in our power, for it's clear you're the wisest man alive.'

'You must swear to me,' said Merlin, 'that you'll never again meddle in this art. For having done so, I command you to make confession and abandon sin, and subject your bodies to penance so that you do not lose your souls. If you promise what I ask, I'll let you go.'

And they gave their word to do as he commanded. So it was that Merlin set the clerks free; and the people, knowing Merlin had dealt with them so generously, admired him all the more. Then Vortigern and his counsellors came to him and said: 'Merlin, explain the significance of the two dragons.'

And Merlin replied: 'The red dragon signifies you, Vortigern, and the white signifies the sons of Constans.'

When Vortigern heard this he was downcast. Merlin saw this clearly and said: 'I'll say no more if you prefer. I've no wish to upset you.'

But Vortigern replied: 'Only my closest counsellors are here, and I want you to tell me: spare me nothing.'

And Merlin said: 'I told you what the red dragon signified; let me explain why. You're well aware that the sons of Constans were still young when their father died, and if you'd behaved as you should you'd have given them protection and advice and defended them against all men on Earth. You know, too, how you won the hearts of their people so that you could take over their land and their wealth; and when you were certain of the people's love you withdrew your services so that they'd be desperate for your help, until the people of the land came to you and said that Moine was unworthy to be king and you should take his place. You wickedly replied that you couldn't be king as long as Moine lived – a cunning answer, for they understood well enough that you wanted him killed, and kill him they did. Afterwards, the two remaining sons of Constans fled in fear of you, so you became king and have their inheritance still. But when Moine's killers came to you, you had them executed, to give the impression that his death grieved you. But nothing could have been further from the truth; you took their lands and hold them still. You built your tower to protect yourself from your enemies; but the tower can't save you – and you've no real wish to save yourself.'

Vortigern heard every word that Merlin said, and knew it to be true. And he said: 'Merlin, it's clear you're the wisest man in the world. I beg and entreat you to advise me in these matters, and to tell me what death I shall die.'

And Merlin replied: 'I can't tell you the significance of the two dragons without revealing how you'll die.'

Vortigern implored Merlin to tell him, and said how grateful he would be; and Merlin answered: 'Vortigern, I'd have you know that the red dragon signifies your wicked heart and mind, and his massive size your kingship and power. The other, the white, signifies the rightful inheritance of the children who fled in fear of your justice. The length of the dragons' combat denotes the long time you've held their inheritance. And when you saw the white dragon consume the red in flame, it signified that those children will destroy you with the fire of their power. Don't imagine that your tower or any other fortress can save you from certain death.'

Vortigern was appalled by Merlin's words, and asked him: 'Where are the children?'

'Crossing the sea,' he replied, 'with a great army. They're coming to their land to bring you to justice, declaring that you prompted their brother's death. And know this: they'll land in three months at the port of Winchester.'

Vortigern was deeply dismayed by the news of this advancing army, and he asked Merlin: 'Can this be avoided?'

'No,' was Merlin's reply. 'You're doomed to die by the fire of Constans' children, just as you saw the white dragon consume the red.'

So it was that Merlin told Vortigern the significance of the two dragons; and Vortigern, knowing that the children were advancing with a great army, called upon his people to muster at the time announced by Merlin, to confront them when they landed – though when they came and assembled, they did not know why their king had summoned them.

Meanwhile Merlin went to Northumberland to tell Blaise of these events, and Blaise wrote them down – and it is by his writings that we have knowledge of them still. Merlin stayed with his master for a long while, until Constans' sons sent men to find him.

So Vortigern was at the port of Winchester with all his army, and on the very day Merlin had predicted they saw sails on the sea: it was the fleet led by Constans' sons. As soon as Vortigern saw them he ordered his men to arm and prepare to defend themselves. But as Constans' children neared the shore, the people on land saw Constans' royal banner and were amazed; and when the ships drew in and Vortigern's people realised they were the sons of their lord Constans with a huge army, most of them went over to the children's side. Seeing his men defecting, Vortigern was terrified; and he fled to one of his castles with those retainers who could not desert him. Pendragon and his brother Uther followed him there and began a mighty siege. They hurled fire into the castle, and it caught and spread and engulfed the place, and in that fire Vortigern died.

*

So it was that Constans's children reclaimed their land, and their coming was proclaimed throughout the kingdom. The people were overjoyed at the news and acknowledged them as their lords. And so the two brothers returned to their inheritance, and Pendragon was made king. But the Saxons whom Vortigern had installed in the land held on to their castles and waged frequent war on Pendragon, sometimes defeated and sometimes victorious. The time came when Pendragon laid siege to Hengist in his castle. So long was the siege that he frittered away more than half a year, until he summoned his barons to a council of war. Five of them had been present when Merlin told Vortigern about the two dragons and his death, and they called Pendragon and Uther to one side and told them that Merlin was the greatest seer ever known, and that if he wanted he could say whether Hengist's castle would ever be taken. Hearing this, Pendragon said: 'Where is this great seer to be found?'

'We don't know,' they replied, 'but we can assure you, he'll already know we're talking about him! He'd come if he wished, and we know he's in this land.'

'If he is,' said Pendragon, 'I shall find him.'

And he sent men across the land in search of Merlin. And Merlin, knowing Pendragon had done this, set off immediately. After speaking with Blaise he headed for the town that Pendragon's messengers had reached. He came disguised as a woodcutter – a great axe on his shoulder, big boots laced on, and wearing a tattered jacket – with his hair lank and matted and his beard very long. He came to the house where the messengers were lodging, and when they set eyes on him they gazed at him in amazement and said to each other: 'What an awful-looking man!'

Merlin stepped forward and said: 'Sirs, you're not following your lord Pendragon's orders very well: he commanded you to find the seer named Merlin.'

Hearing this, they cried: 'What demons told this old wretch?' Then they asked him: 'Have you ever seen the man?'

'I have indeed,' Merlin replied, 'and I know where he lives. He's well aware you're looking for him, but you won't find him unless he wants you to. You're wasting your time, he'd have you know, because he wouldn't go with you even if you found him. You can tell the men who told Pendragon that the great seer was in this land that they were right. And when you get back, tell your lord that he'll never take the castle until Hengist is dead. And know this: there were five of the army who spoke privately about me to Pendragon, but you'll find only three on your return. Tell Pendragon that if he came to this country and scoured these forests he would find Merlin; but he must come in person: nobody will be able to fetch him and take him back.'

They heard what Merlin said and turned aside, and the moment they did so he was gone. They crossed themselves and said: 'We've been talking to a demon! What shall we do about what he told us?' They discussed this and decided: 'We'll go back and report the wonders we've seen and heard to our lord and those who sent us here. And we'll find out if those two men have died.'

So the messengers set off, and rode day after day until they arrived back at the king's army. As soon as he saw them he asked: 'Sirs, have you found the man you went to seek?'

'Sire,' they replied, 'something happened to us that we must report. Summon your counsellors and the men who first told you about the seer.'

The king did so, and when they arrived he took them aside to talk in private. The messengers told them all about their journey and their amazing encounter, and about the predicted deaths of the two men. They asked for news about this, and were told that the two men had indeed died. They were astonished, and said to the king: 'Sire, we think the man we spoke to was Merlin. And he said he'd never be found unless the king himself went in search of him.'

'Where was it you found him?' he asked, and they replied: 'In Northumberland.'

The king declared he would go in search of him, and he rode at once to Northumberland, where he enquired after Merlin but could find no-one with any information. So the king said he would seek him in the forests, and he and his party rode through the deep woods until one of his knights came upon a great flock of animals tended by an ugly, deformed herdsman. The knight asked him where he came from, and he said he was from Northumberland, so the knight said: 'Can you tell me anything about a man named Merlin?'

'No,' replied the herdsman, 'but a man passed by who said the king was looking for him here in these forests. Do you know anything about that?'

The knight said it was true that the king was seeking him, and asked: 'Can you put me on the right track?'

And the herdsman said: 'There's something I'd tell the king that I wouldn't tell you.'

'Come then,' said the knight, 'and I'll take you to him.'

'I'd hardly be a good herdsman if I did that – and it doesn't bother me whether I see him or not! If he comes here to me I'll tell him how to find Merlin.'

So the knight rode back to the king and told him what had happened, and the king said: 'Lead me to him!'

He did so, and said: 'Here! I bring you the king!'

'Pendragon,' said the herdsman, 'you're looking for Merlin, but you won't find him until he wants you to. Go to one of your towns nearby, and when he knows you're waiting for him he'll come to you.'

'How do I know you're telling the truth?' said the king.

'If you don't believe me,' he replied, 'ignore me! It's crazy to trust bad advice!'

'Are you saying your advice is bad?' said the king.

'No, but you are!' he answered. 'But I tell you, I know better than you.'

'I'll believe you,' said the king, and he rode to one of his towns, as close as possible to the forest; and there he stayed until there came to his lodging a very smart man, in fine clothes and shoes, who said to one of his knights: 'Sir, take me to the king.' And when he came into his presence he said: 'Sire, Merlin sends me to you with his greetings, and to tell you that he was the man you found in the woods tending the flock, who told you he'd come to you when he wished. That was true, but you don't need him yet. When you do, he'll gladly come.'

'I'm in permanent need of him!' the king replied. 'I've never been so eager to see anyone!'

'The moment you said that, he bade me give you some very good news.'

'What's that?' asked the king.

'Hengist is dead,' he replied. 'Your brother Uther killed him.'

The king was astounded and said: 'Can this be true?'

'He bids me say nothing more to you,' he replied, 'except that you're mad if you doubt it without checking! Send someone to see if I've told you the truth – and if I have, believe it!'

'Wise words,' said the king, and he chose a pair of messengers and mounted them on his two finest horses, and commanded them to ride without stopping – there or back – until they brought confirmation of the story of Hengist's death. The messengers set off and rode with all possible speed for a day and a night, until they met Uther's own messengers, on their way to tell the king that Hengist was dead. They all exchanged news and rode back to the king, but the man who had brought word from Merlin had gone. The messengers came before the king and told him privately how Uther had killed Hengist; and when he heard the news he forbade them, if they valued his love, to speak of it to anyone. So matters stayed, with the king wondering greatly how Merlin had known about Hengist's death. He waited to see if Merlin would come to him, and decided that as soon as he saw him he would ask him exactly how Hengist had died. He waited; and one day, as he was coming out of church, a handsome and well-dressed gentleman came up to him – very well presented he was; he seemed a worthy man indeed. He greeted the king and said: 'Why are you staying in this town?'

'I'm waiting for Merlin to come,' the king replied, and the gentleman said: 'Sire, you don't know him well enough to recognise him. Call those who ought to know him and ask them if I could be Merlin.'

The king was taken aback. He summoned those who had seen him before and said: 'Sirs, we're waiting for Merlin, but I don't think anyone here knows what he truly looks like. If you do, tell me.'

'Sire,' they replied, 'we'd recognise him, certainly.'

Then the gentleman said: 'How can a man know another when he doesn't really know himself?'

'We don't know him in all his forms,' they said, 'but we'd recognise him in the guise in which we saw him last.'

With that the gentleman turned and led the king into a chamber and told him: 'Sire, I am the Merlin whom you seek, and I wish to be a friend to you and your brother Uther. I am the Merlin whom you seek: tell me what you wish.'

And the king said: 'Merlin, if possible, I dearly crave your friendship.'

'Pendragon,' Merlin replied, 'I'll give you answers to anything you ask – if it's right to do so.'

'Then tell me, Merlin,' said the king, 'if I've spoken to you since I came to these parts to find you.'

'I am the herdsman you found, sire,' Merlin replied, 'tending his flock in the woods. And I am the one who told you Hengist had been killed.'

The king was amazed by this, and said: 'Merlin, how did you know of Hengist's death?'

'I knew of it when you first arrived here,' said Merlin. 'Hengist intended to kill your brother, and I went to him and warned him. And – thanks be to God and him – he believed me and took precautions. I told him of Hengist's strength and amazing resolve – for he planned to come all alone to your brother's battle lines, right to his own pavilion, to kill him! Your brother, I'm pleased to say, didn't doubt my words, but stayed up all night on his own – he told no-one – and armed himself in secret. He stayed in his tent all night, until Hengist came in, knife in hand, expecting to find your brother; but he couldn't see him; so he turned to leave the tent and came face to face with your brother, who attacked him and killed him in a moment, for your brother was armed and Hengist was not – he'd come intending to kill him as he slept in his bed and then to make a quick getaway.'

The king was overwhelmed by Merlin's extraordinary story, and asked him: 'Merlin, in what guise did you appear to my brother? I'm amazed that he believed you.'

And Merlin replied: 'I took the form of an old, white-haired man, and I told him in private that if he didn't take care he would die that night.'

'Did you tell him who you were?' asked the king.

'Your brother still has no idea who warned him,' said Merlin. 'Nor will he, until you tell him. And I beg you, tell no-one else. If our trust is ever broken our friendship will be over.'

'Merlin,' said the king, 'you can trust me in all things.'

Then Merlin said: 'Of this you may be certain, sire: I shall speak to your brother ten days after you and I have talked.'

So it was that Merlin made himself known to Pendragon; then he took his leave and went to his master Blaise to tell him of these events. Blaise recorded them in his book, thanks to which we have knowledge of them still. And Pendragon rode on day by day until he found Uther, who came to meet him and gave him a joyful welcome. The moment they met, Pendragon took him aside and told him of Hengist's death just as Merlin had related it, and asked him if it was true.

'Yes,' said Uther, 'but God help me, you've told me what I thought no-one but God Himself knew – and an old man who spoke to me in private. I didn't think anyone could know.'

'Well I do,' said Pendragon, 'as you've clearly heard!'

'In God's name,' said Uther, 'tell me who told you, for I don't know who the worthy soul was who spoke to me – though he seemed a good and wise man indeed, and I believed him, incredible though what he told me was. It was a bold act by Hengist, to be sure, coming into our own army and my own tent to kill me.'

'Would you know the man if you saw him again?' said Pendragon.

'Very well, I think,' Uther replied.

'I promise you,' Pendragon said, 'he'll speak to you within twelve days.' He specified the day that Merlin had mentioned, and then said: 'Uther, I beg you to stay by my side all that day, right until the day is over.'

Uther promised this, saying he would be only too glad of his company. And Merlin, aware of all that was happening, told Blaise how the two brothers were talking about him, and how the king was trying to test him.

'What are you going to do about it?' Blaise asked him.

'They're young men,' Merlin replied, 'and full of spirit, and there's no better way to secure their loyalty than by satisfying some of their whims! I know a lady whom Uther loves: I'll take him a letter from her. You must write it down as I tell you, and Uther will be wholly convinced! I'm going to let the eleventh day pass without them seeing or recognising me; the next day I'll reveal myself to the two young men together, and they'll be more impressed!'

Blaise did as Merlin said. Then Merlin appeared to Uther in the guise of his beloved's serving-boy and said: 'Your love sends you greetings – and this letter.'

Uther took it with great delight, never doubting it was from his beloved, and summoned a clerk to read it. The letter implored him to believe every-thing the boy said – and Merlin told him what he knew Uther would most want to hear. So it was that Uther spent the whole of the eleventh day with his brother, enjoying his company and in excellent spirits because of the good

news he had received from his love. But when evening came he was astonished that Merlin had failed to appear. Then, while Uther and Pendragon
talked together, Merlin took the form in which he had appeared to Uther to
warn him about Hengist, and Uther recognised him at once. Merlin told him
to fetch his brother, which he did, and said: 'Here he is!'

Pendragon asked Uther if this was the man who had saved him from
death, and he said it was, without a doubt. 'But tell me,' said Uther, 'do you
recognise him, too?'

'Not at all,' Pendragon replied.

Then Uther turned to Merlin and said: 'Sir, I bid you a hearty welcome,
and rightly so, for you saved my life; but one thing puzzles me: my brother
knew every word you'd said to me.'

'Then someone must have told him!' Merlin replied. 'Bring him back, and
ask him who it was!'

So Uther went to fetch the king, telling the guards outside his pavilion to
let no-one enter. As soon as Uther left the tent, Merlin took the form of the
boy who had brought him the letter, and when Uther returned with
Pendragon, expecting to find the old man, there before them stood the boy.
Uther was astounded, and said to the king: 'This is amazing! I left the old
man here, and now I find only this boy! Wait here: I'll ask my guards if they
saw him leave or the boy come in.'

So Uther left the tent, and the king began to laugh heartily, realising it was
Merlin. Uther asked his guards: 'Did you see anyone leave or enter while I'd
gone to fetch my brother?'

And they replied: 'The only people who've come in or out are you and the
king.'

And Uther returned to the boy and said: 'When did you get here?'

'I was here while you were talking to the old man.'

The king, knowing it was Merlin, began to laugh and said: 'Uther my dear
brother, I didn't think you were lying to me, but tell me now, could the one
who gave you the warning be this boy?'

'Impossible!' said Uther; and the king said: 'Let's go out, then come back in
and see if he's returned!'

In high spirits they walked among their army, and the king went up to a
knight and said: 'Go and see who's in my brother Uther's tent.'

The knight went and found the old man. He came back and told the king;
so he and Uther returned, and Uther was amazed to see the old man and said
to the king: 'This is the one who saved me from being killed by Hengist!'

Then the king whispered to Merlin: 'Do you want me to tell my brother
who you are?'

'I do indeed, sire,' Merlin replied, so the king said to Uther: 'Dear brother,
where's the boy who brought you the letter?'

'He was here a moment ago,' Uther said. 'What do you want with him?'

And Merlin and the king burst into peals of joyous laughter. Then Merlin took the king aside and told him the words he had given Uther from his beloved lady. 'Go now, and tell Uther!'

So the king went to him and said: 'Dear brother, you've lost the boy who brought you the letter from your love.'

'Why do you keep talking about that boy?' said Uther.

'Because he brought you such good news,' Pendragon replied. 'I'll tell you what I know about it in the presence of the old man.'

Uther agreed, thinking that nobody could know anything except the one who had told him first. But when he heard the king speak he was astounded and said: 'In God's name, tell me how you have this amazing knowledge – both of this and of the other matter!'

'I will tell you,' said Pendragon, 'if it please this good old man.'

'What has it to do with him?' said Uther.

'I will not tell you without his leave,' the king replied; and Uther said: 'Sir, please tell my brother to say!'

'Only too happy!' said Merlin, and when the king heard this he went up to Uther and said: 'Brother, I'd have you know that this is the wisest man in the world. No other boy than he brought you that letter or spoke the secret words from your love!'

Uther was astonished, and said to the king: 'How can I know if what you're telling me is true?'

So the king asked Merlin if he could give a demonstration.

'Well enough,' Merlin said. 'I'll show him the boy.'

With that he changed shape and became the boy, and Uther was speechless with amazement. The king said to him: 'You may be sure, Uther, that this is Merlin. Now make sure that he's your friend.'

Uther was overjoyed and said: 'If he were willing, I'd gladly have him on our side!'

'I'd be pleased to stay,' said Merlin, 'and to have you get to know my ways. You must understand that I sometimes need to be away from people; but wherever I may be, I shall be more mindful of your affairs than of any other's, and if you're in trouble I'll come to your aid. I beg you, however much you may desire my company, don't be upset when I leave you; and whenever I return, give me a joyful, public welcome. You may be sure that I'll never again change shape except privately, in your presence; each time I come I shall appear openly at your house, and those who've seen me before will run and tell you of my arrival; as soon as you have word, show your delight! They'll tell you I'm a great seer; you may ask me about whatever most concerns your people, and I'll advise you about anything you wish.'

Such was the arrangement Merlin made with Pendragon and his brother Uther, and they agreed he should go and appear to their people in the shape in which they would recognise him. When he arrived before those who had been privy to his meetings with Vortigern they were overjoyed to see him, and they ran to tell the king that Merlin had come. The king showed his delight at the news and went to meet him, and those who loved Merlin told him: 'Merlin, the king is coming to welcome you!'

The king greeted him joyfully and took him to his own lodging, where his counsellors assembled and said to him: 'Sire, ask Merlin to tell you how to take this castle, and what will be the outcome of our war with the Saxons. Truly, he could tell us if he wanted!'

The king replied that he would gladly ask. They let the matter rest for the present, for they wanted to pay Merlin all due respect. Then, three days after Merlin's arrival, all the king's counsellors assembled, and the king came to Merlin and said: 'Merlin, I pray you, tell me how I can capture this castle, and if there's any way of driving the Saxons from the land.'

'Sire,' Merlin replied, 'I can assure you that from the moment they lost Hengist, the Saxons had no other thought than to leave this land. Send your messengers to confirm this, and to seek a truce; they'll agree to yield the kingdom to you. Have them escorted from the land and provided with ships to carry them away.'

'Merlin,' said the king, 'you're a wise man indeed. First I'll seek a truce to see what they say.'

He entrusted his message to Ulfin – one of his counsellors – and two clerks, and they rode to the castle; and when the Saxons in the castle saw them coming they went to meet them and said: 'What do you want?'

And Ulfin replied: 'We seek a truce on behalf of the king.'

'We'll discuss it, gladly,' they answered, and withdrew a while and said: 'Hengist's death has severely weakened us. The king is seeking a three months' truce, but our supplies won't last that long! Let's send him word that we'll surrender this castle, and pay him a yearly tribute of ten knights, ten maidens, ten falcons, ten hounds, ten chargers and a hundred palfreys.'

Such was the decision they reached, and they told the messengers, who returned to the king and Merlin and the other barons. When the king heard their answer he asked Merlin what he should do.

'Reject it,' Merlin replied. 'Order them to leave the castle and the kingdom. Give them ships and boats to sail to other lands – I tell you, they'll be only too pleased, for they'll all have been expecting death!'

The king did exactly as Merlin said, sending messengers early next day; and the Saxons in the castle were overjoyed at the chance to escape with their lives, for they knew they were helpless after losing Hengist. The news was sent throughout the land, and the king had the Saxons escorted to the port where he found them vessels to carry them away. So, as you have heard, Merlin knew the Saxons' thoughts and had them driven from the land, and so it was that he became the king's chief counsellor.

*

He stayed with him for a long while, and one day he was with the king having just discussed an important matter, when one of the barons became very upset and came to the king and said:

'Sire, it's amazing that you trust this man so much, for you know all his knowledge comes from the Devil. Let me test him in such a way as to show that openly.'

'You have my leave to do so,' the king replied, 'but don't annoy him!'

'I'll say nothing offensive,' the baron said, but he was a cunning and wicked man, and powerful, wealthy and well connected.

One day Merlin arrived at court and the king gave him a joyful welcome. This baron invited Merlin to join their council, at which only five men were present; and he said to the king: 'Sire, here is one of the wisest men in the world. I've heard he predicted Vortigern's death, saying he would die in your fire, which he did. So I pray him to tell me how *I* shall die: I'm sure he could if he wanted.'

The king and the others asked Merlin to do so, and Merlin, well aware of the baron's wicked heart, replied: 'Know then, sir, that you'll die by falling from your horse and breaking your neck. That's how you'll leave this world.'

When he had heard this, the baron said to the king: 'Sire, you've heard what this man's said.' And he took the king aside on his own, and told him: 'Remember Merlin's words, sire, and I shall give him another test.'

And with that he went home and donned different clothes; and when he was ready he returned to the king's city as fast as he could. There he feigned illness, and sent a secret message to the king asking him to bring Merlin to him but not to let him know who he was. The king sent back word that he would gladly come, and would not tell Merlin his identity. So the king went to Merlin and said: 'Come with me to see a sick man in the town.'

Then he called for those he wished to accompany him and set off to see the invalid, who had prepared his wife to fall at the king's feet and say: 'In God's name, sire, ask your seer if he can cure my husband!'

The king looked deeply sympathetic, then turned to Merlin and asked him, and Merlin replied: 'You may be sure, sire, that this man is not on his deathbed!'

The sick man struggled to speak, and said to Merlin: 'In God's name, sir, how then shall I die?'

'The day you die,' Merlin replied, 'you'll be found hanging. You will hang the day you die.'

With that Merlin turned away from the sick man and looked very angry; and he left the king there in the house because he wanted the sick man to speak to him. When the invalid knew that Merlin was gone he said to the king: 'Sire, were you ever so sure of anything as that that man is a crazy liar? He's predicted two deaths for me, such that neither can be reconciled with the other! And I'll test him a third time in your presence: tomorrow I'm going to go to an abbey and pretend to be sick; I'll have the abbot send for you, saying I'm one of his monks and that he's very distressed and afraid that I may die. The abbot will beg you to come and bring your seer with you. It's the last time I'll test him.'

The king promised to go and to take Merlin with him. So the baron went to an abbey and did exactly as he had said. The abbot sent a messenger to the king, who duly set off, taking Merlin with him, and came to the abbey, where on arrival he went to hear mass. The abbot came to him and begged him to come and see the sick monk, and the king asked Merlin if he would accompany him.

'Willingly,' Merlin replied, but he wished to speak first to his brother Uther. The king called Uther and Merlin together before an altar, and there Merlin said to them: 'Sirs, the more I get to know you, the madder I find you. Do you think I don't know how this fool who's testing me is going to die? So help me God, I know very well, and I shall predict his death. And you'll be even more amazed by what I say than you were the two other times he asked me!'

'But Merlin,' said the king, 'is it really possible for any man to die such a death?'

'If he doesn't die so,' Merlin replied, 'don't believe anything else I say. But I know the nature of his death – and yours. I can assure your brother Uther that I'll see him king before I leave his company.'

With that Merlin, the king and his brother Uther went to see the baron; and the abbot said: 'In God's name, sire, ask your seer if this man can ever be cured.'

The king did so; and Merlin looked angry, saying to the abbot: 'Sir, he has no mortal sickness and is quite capable of getting up! He's wasting his time putting me to the test, for he will die in the two ways I've already described to him. But now I'll tell him the third, more surprising than either; for know this: on the day he dies he'll break his neck, and hang, and drown. Those who live will see him die this threefold death. Then they'll know for certain whether I've told the truth.'

'Sire,' the baron said to the king, 'you've heard this man say that on the day I die I'm going to break my neck and hang and drown! Surely this couldn't happen to me or anyone!'

'I won't be sure,' said the king, 'until I've seen how you die.'

The baron was furious when he heard that Merlin would not be expelled from court until after his death; and news of the death he had predicted spread throughout the land, and everyone longed to know how Merlin's words could be true. A little later, the baron who was due to die this death was out riding with a great company of men when he came to a river spanned by a wooden bridge. Suddenly his palfrey stumbled and fell to her knees; he was thrown forward and fell on his neck and broke it; and as his body tumbled into the river his gown snagged on an old, jagged bridge support, so that his legs and buttocks were up in the air and his shoulders and head in the water. So there he was: hanged, drowned, with a broken neck. He was pulled from the river, and the gentlemen who had been riding with him said: 'Sirs, see if his neck is broken.'

They looked and said it was, for certain. Meanwhile Merlin came to Uther, whom he dearly loved, and told him how the man had died and bade him tell his brother the king. Uther did so, and the king was amazed and said: 'Ask him when this happened.'

Uther came to Merlin and asked him, and he replied: 'Yesterday. Those who are to bring the news will arrive in six days. I'm going now: I don't want to be here when they arrive, for they'll bother me with all kinds of things I don't wish to hear, and I shan't speak in their presence except in riddles.'

So said Merlin to Uther, and then he departed. And Uther came to the king and told him what had happened, and Pendragon was most upset, thinking that Merlin was angry. Meanwhile Merlin returned to Northumberland and related these and other events to Blaise as further material for his book.

So matters stayed for six days, until the riders arrived and told the king the amazing news of the baron's death. Several people said they would write down everything Merlin said about the future: this was the beginning of the book of Merlin's prophecies about the kings of England and other matters.

*

A long while passed; and in this time Merlin had commanding influence over[11] Pendragon and his brother Uther. When he heard that his predictions were to be written down he told Blaise, and Blaise asked him: 'Merlin, will their books be similar to the one I'm writing?'

'Not at all,' Merlin replied. 'They will only record what has already happened.'

Then Merlin returned to the court, where they told him the news of the baron's death as if he knew nothing about it. It was then that Merlin began to make the mystical pronouncements of which the book of his prophecies[12] was composed. Then he came to Pendragon and his brother Uther and told them very openly that he loved them dearly and was eager that they should thrive. They were amazed to hear him speak so humbly, and asked him to tell them whatever he would, and to keep nothing secret that concerned them.

'I'll tell you nothing I should not,' Merlin replied, 'but I shall tell you something that will astound you. Do you remember the Saxons that you drove from the land after the death of Hengist? Well, Hengist was of a great family, and when they heard he was dead and his army driven from the land, they

---

[11] Literally 'Merlin was lord of . . .'.
[12] A reference to the work of Geoffrey of Monmouth.

spoke to their followers and said they'd never be happy until they'd avenged Hengist's death: they're intent upon conquering your kingdom.'

Pendragon and Uther were taken aback by this and asked him: 'Have they numbers great enough to match ours?'

And Merlin replied: 'For every one of your warriors they have two, and unless you act with great intelligence they'll destroy you and conquer your kingdom.'

'We'll do whatever you command, without fail,' they said; and they asked him: 'When do you think their army will arrive?'

'On the ninth day of June,' Merlin replied. 'But no-one in the kingdom will know but you. I forbid you to speak of this to anyone; just do as I say. Summon your people and welcome them with all possible celebration – it's wise to keep up men's spirits – and ask them and all their followers to assemble at the beginning of June at the gates of Salisbury. There your army will gather. Then let the enemy come and land unhindered, and when they've disembarked let one of you take half your army and set yourselves between the enemy and the river, so that they're forced to make camp away from their ships – even the boldest will be dismayed! I tell you, if you do this, you'll be victorious.'

Then the two brothers said: 'In God's name, Merlin, tell us: will we die in this battle?'

'Anything that has a beginning also has an end,' Merlin replied. 'No-one needs to fear death if he meets it as he should. Everyone must realise he's going to die, and you must know it, too.'

'You told me the other day,' said Pendragon, 'that you knew how I would die, just as you foresaw the death of the man who tested you. So I beg you, reveal it to me.'

And Merlin replied: 'I want you to send for the finest, most potent reliquaries and relics you possess. And give me your oath upon them that you'll do as I command – for your own benefit and honour. Afterwards I'll tell you with certainty what you want me to reveal.'

They did exactly as Merlin had described, and then said: 'Merlin, we've done as you commanded. Now tell us why you wanted this.'

And Merlin answered: 'King, you asked me a question about your death, and whether it would be in this battle. I'll tell you all you need to know and you must ask no more. Are you aware of the oaths you've made? If not, I'll tell you. You've sworn to behave as worthy knights in this battle, loyal to each other and to God. And I'll tell you how to be loyal and merciful and just. I command you to make confession: you've greater need to be confessed now than at any other time, for I have to tell you that one of you is about to leave this world. The one who is left must promise to follow my advice in ordering the creation of the richest, most beautiful cemetery possible. I shall ensure that it lasts until the world's end.'

Time passed and the day came. Their people gathered in great numbers beside the river at Salisbury, and many fine gifts and riches were exchanged and shared between them there. Then word came that a fleet of ships had arrived, and when the king and Uther heard the news they knew that Merlin had been right. The king ordered his prelates and the dignitaries of Holy Church to see that every man in the army made confession and forgave each other for any past ill-will. Meanwhile the enemy had disembarked and were now on land. For eight days they rested there, and on the ninth they took to their horses. Merlin told Pendragon to order his men to mount, and the king asked his advice on how to act. And Merlin replied: 'Tomorrow send Uther with a great body of men, and when they see that the enemy are well away from the shore, let your brother and his men advance so close that they're forced to make a fortified camp. Then Uther should draw back, but keep them so hemmed in that they're pinned down where they've camped. They'll all be desperate to return where they came from! For twelve days let it be so, and on the thirteenth – which will be a fine, clear day – order your men to arm. Then you will see a red dragon flying through the air between earth and heaven. When you see this symbol of your name,[13] you may join battle in the certain knowledge that your army will be victorious.'

They did as Merlin said, Uther leading a mighty force to pin the enemy down. They kept them so for twelve days, and on the thirteenth, when they saw all the signs appear, they were ready. Pendragon's men spurred their horses into a galloping charge against the Saxons, and when Uther saw the king's force massing he attacked with his men, too, just as fiercely if not more. So now you have heard how the battle of Salisbury began. And Pendragon was killed there, but Uther was victorious – though many died, both rich and poor. So many of the Saxons died that not a man escaped, for all were either killed or drowned. So ended the battle of Salisbury. Pendragon died but Uther survived and was king; and he had all the Christian bodies buried, each man burying his friend. But the bodies of his brother and his retinue were carried from the field, and each placed in a tomb with his name carved upon it; but Pendragon's was higher than the rest, and Uther said no name should be carved upon his, for only a fool could see that tomb and not recognise it as Pendragon's. When this was done he rode to London with his army and all the prelates of Holy Church, and there Uther was crowned.

On the fifteenth day after the coronation, Merlin came to court. The king gave him a joyful welcome, and Merlin said: 'I want you to tell your people what I predicted about the Saxons' invasion, and you must fulfil the oaths that you and Pendragon made.'

Then Merlin told Uther the significance of the dragon that had flown through the air, saying: 'The dragon came as a sign of King Pendragon's death and the accession of Uther.'

---

[13] i.e. Pendragon.

It was because of this that he was ever after named Utherpendragon.

So matters stayed for a long while, and Merlin was the closest friend and counsellor to Utherpendragon. A day finally came when Merlin said to the king: 'What are you going to do about Pendragon, who lies at Salisbury?'

'Whatever you wish,' Utherpendragon replied.

'You promised me you'd have a cemetery made,' said Merlin, 'and I vowed to ensure that it would last till the world's end. Fulfil your promise and I'll fulfil mine.'

'What should I do?' he asked.

'Undertake the building of something unheard of,' Merlin replied, 'and it will be talked of for evermore!'

'I'm at your command,' said the king.

'Listen, then,' said Merlin. 'Send men to fetch the great stones that are in Ireland. Send vessels there to bring them back. No matter how huge they may be, I'll lift them. I'll go there to show them which to bring.'

So Utherpendragon sent his biggest ships to Ireland with a great host of men. And when they arrived Merlin showed them an array of massive stones and said: 'Sirs, these are the stones you're to take back.'

When they saw the stones they thought him infantile, and said that all the people in the world together could not move one.

'We'll never put your stones in our ships, please God!'

'Then you've come for nothing,' said Merlin; and they returned to Utherpendragon and told him of Merlin's absurd command. And the king replied: 'Just you wait till Merlin comes.'

And when Merlin came, and the king told him what his people had said, Merlin replied: 'Since they've all let me down, I'll fulfil my oath by myself.'

Then, by magic, Merlin brought the stones from Ireland to the cemetery at Salisbury,[14] and there they are still. And when they arrived, Utherpendragon went to see them, taking with him a great number of his people; and when they beheld them they declared that no-one had ever seen such enormous stones, and did not believe that all the people in the world could have carried even one. They were baffled as to how Merlin could have brought them there, for no-one had witnessed it. Then Merlin said they should stand them up, for they would look better upright than lying down, but Utherpendragon replied: 'No-one could possibly do that, except God – or you.'

'Then go now,' said Merlin, 'and I shall erect them. Then I'll have fulfilled my oath to Pendragon – for I shall have made for him something inconceivable.'

And so Merlin erected the stones of the cemetery at Salisbury; and that was the end of the work.

---

[14] This is, of course, Stonehenge.

*

Merlin cared deeply for Utherpendragon and served him for a long while, until he knew he had the king's entire affection. Then Merlin spoke to him privately, saying: 'I ought to reveal to you some of my deepest secrets, now that this land is fully in your hands. Because of my love for you I shall conceal[15] nothing. Didn't I save you from death at Hengist's hands? That should have earned me your love in return.'

'I'll do all in my power,' Utherpendragon replied, 'to obey your every command.'

'If you do so,' said Merlin, 'it will be greatly to your benefit, for I'll teach you a simple way to win Christ's love.'

'Merlin,' replied the king, 'speak your mind openly.'

'You must understand, sire,' Merlin said, 'that I have knowledge of all things past, both word and deed, inherited from the Enemy. But Our Lord omnipotent gave me knowledge of things to come. Because of that the Enemy have lost me: I will never work on their behalf. Now you know the source of my power. Sire,' he said, 'I'll tell you what Our Lord wishes you to know; and make sure you use this knowledge to do His will. You must believe, sire, that Our Lord came to Earth to save the world, and sat at the Last Supper and said: "One of you has betrayed me." And the one who had done this wicked deed was severed from His company. After this, sire, God suffered death for us. There was a soldier who asked for the body from the one who had the power to grant it, and he took Jesus from the cross where He'd been hung. And then, sire, God came back to life. And after Christ's vengeful return, it happened that this soldier was in a desolate land with part of his family and many more people who were in his company, and a great famine beset them. They implored this knight, as their leader, to ask God why they were suffering such misfortune; and Our Lord bade him make a table in memory of the Last Supper. And on this table the knight placed a vessel which he covered with white cloths so that he alone could see it. This vessel separated the good people from the bad. Anyone who was able to sit at this table found the fulfilment of his heart's desires. But there was always an empty seat at the table, sire, signifying the place where Judas had sat at the Last Supper when he realised that Our Lord's words referred to him. This place was left symbolically empty at the knight's table, until such time as Our Lord should seat another man there to make up the number of the twelve apostles. And so Our Lord fulfilled men's hearts; and at the second table they called the vessel which bestowed this grace the Grail. If you'll trust in my advice, you'll establish a third table in the name of the Trinity, which these three tables will signify. And if you do this, I promise you it will greatly benefit your body and your soul, and such things will happen in your time as will astound you. If

---

15 The manuscript reads 'tell you nothing'. There appears to be a simple scribal error, writing *dire nule cose* rather than *celer nule cose*.

you're willing to do this I will lend you aid, and I assure you it will be a deed of high renown in this world. If you have faith you will do it, and I shall help you.'

So said Merlin to Utherpendragon, who replied: 'I would not have Our Lord suffer any loss on my account, but you should know I leave all decisions to you.'

'Consider, sire,' said Merlin, 'where you would most like the table to be.'

'Wherever you wish,' Utherpendragon replied.

'Then have it made at Carduel in Wales. Bid the people of your kingdom gather to meet you there at Pentecost. Be prepared to distribute great gifts; and provide me with men who'll do my bidding. And I'll decide who are fit to sit there.'

The king sent his decree throughout the land, and Merlin departed and ordered the making of the table. And when Pentecost came, the king set off to Carduel in Wales and asked Merlin how he had fared; and he replied: 'Very well, sire.'

So the people assembled at Carduel, and the king said: 'Merlin, who will you choose to sit at this table?'

'As for that,' Merlin replied, 'tomorrow you'll see something entirely unexpected. I shall choose fifty of the worthiest men of the land; and once they've sat at that table they'll have no desire to return to their homes or ever leave here. Then you'll see in your table the significance of the other two, and of the empty seat.'

'By God,' said the king, 'I'll be glad indeed to see it!'

Then Merlin came and made his selection and bade those men be seated. And once they had sat down, Merlin walked around them and showed the king the empty place. Many others saw it, too, but only the king and Merlin knew its significance. Then Merlin asked the king to be seated; but the king said he would not do so until he had seen everyone at the table served, and he ordered that they be served before he would move from where he stood. Only when that was done did the king go and take his place.

The court remained assembled for eight days, and the king bestowed many handsome gifts, and many beautiful jewels to ladies and damsels. Then he asked those who were seated at the table how they felt, and they answered: 'Sire, we've no wish ever to move from here. Rather will we call our wives and children to join us in this city, so that we can live at Our Lord's pleasure: such is our heart's desire.'

'Sirs,' said the king, 'do you all share this feeling?'

'Yes indeed,' they replied, 'and we wonder much how this can be, for some of us have never seen each other before, yet now we love one another as sons love their fathers – if not more! It seems as if death alone can part us!'

The king was astonished by their words, as were all who witnessed this. But he was delighted, too, and ordered that they should be as honoured in the city as he was himself.

When everyone had gone, the king came to Merlin and said: 'You told me the truth indeed. I now believe Our Lord wishes this table to be established. But I'm very puzzled about the empty place, and I beg you to tell me if you know who is to fill it.'

'I can tell you for certain,' Merlin replied, 'that it will not be filled in your time. The one who is destined to do so will be born of Alain li Gros, who is here now in this land. Alain sat at Joseph's precious table, but he has not yet taken a wife, and does not realise he is destined to father this child. The one who will fill the empty seat needs to have been in the presence of the Grail. The Grail's guardians have never seen what is due to be fulfilled, and it will not happen in your time but in the life of the king who will follow you. But I pray you, continue to hold your assemblies and great courts here in the city of Carduel, and attend yourself and hold annual feasts here.' Then Merlin said: 'I'm leaving now, and I shall not return for a long time.'

'Merlin,' said the king, 'where are you going? Won't you be here each time I hold court?'

'No,' Merlin replied, 'I can't be, for I want the people who are with you to believe what they're going to witness; I don't want them to say I've made it happen.'

So Merlin left Utherpendragon and returned to Blaise in Northumberland, and told him of these events and of the establishment of the table.

*

Some time later Utherpendragon held court, and his barons duly came – including the duke of Tintagel, who brought with him his son and his wife Igerne. As soon as Utherpendragon set eyes on Igerne his heart was filled with love for her – though he did not show it, except that he looked at her with more interest than he showed the other women. She noticed this herself; and when she realised he was paying her more attention than the others she avoided him immediately and was always slow to acknowledge him, for she was as worthy as she was beautiful, and very loyal towards her husband. The king, because of his love for her and to try to gain her attention, sent jewels to all the ladies, and to Igerne he sent the ones he thought she would most adore. She did not dare to refuse them, since the others all accepted; so she took them, but knew in her heart that the king had bestowed these gifts only on her account, and wanted her to have them. She hid her deeper feelings.

So Utherpendragon held court – and he was without a wife. He was so full of love for Igerne that he did not know what on earth to do. Finally the court departed, and the king summoned his barons to return at Pentecost. He said the same to the ladies and damsels, and they promised they would attend most gladly. The king saw the duke and duchess of Tintagel on their way, honouring them greatly; and he whispered to Igerne that she bore his heart away with her, but she pretended not to have heard. He took his leave and

Igerne departed, leaving Utherpendragon at Carduel. But wherever he was, his heart was always with Igerne.

And so the king suffered till Pentecost, when the barons and their ladies gathered once again, and he was overjoyed when Igerne arrived. At the feast he distributed many generous gifts to the knights and ladies; and when he sat down to dine he seated the duke and Igerne opposite him. Such were the king's looks and his countenance that Igerne could not help but know that he loved her. And afterwards, when the feast was done and everyone was about to return home, the king requested them to return when he summoned them, and they promised to do so without fail.

All that year the king was in torment, and confided in two of those closest to him, telling them of the anguish he suffered for Igerne. And they said: 'Sire, if it's in our power, we'll do anything you command.'

'But what can I do?' said the king.

'Summon all your men to Carduel,' they replied, 'and command them to bring their wives and to come prepared to stay for fifteen days. That way you'll be able to have Igerne's company for a while.'

The king's decree went out and the court assembled, and again the king bestowed great gifts upon knights and ladies alike; he was a happy man indeed that day. Then he spoke to one of his counsellors, named Ulfin, and asked him what he could do, for his love for Igerne was killing him. And Ulfin replied:

'What sort of a king would you be if you died of desire to lie with a woman! I'm poor compared with you, but if I loved her as much as you do I wouldn't be thinking about dying! Who ever heard of a woman being propositioned by a man with the power to bestow great gifts on all sides, who refused to do his will? And you're worried!'

'Good advice, Ulfin!' said the king. 'You understand how to handle this, so I beg you, help me in every way you can. Take whatever you like from my chamber and give it to all the people around her, and then speak to Igerne in the way you know my plight demands!'

'I'll do all I can,' said Ulfin, and as they ended their private talk he said to the king: 'Take care to stay on good terms with the duke, and I'll think about what to say to Igerne.'

So the king made a great fuss of the duke and his company, and gave him and his companions many beautiful gems. Meanwhile Ulfin spoke to Igerne, saying what he thought would please her most and plying her with magnificent jewels; but Igerne resisted, declining them all, and finally drew him aside and said: 'Ulfin, why do you want to give me these jewels and all these beautiful gifts?'

'Because of your great beauty and intelligence,' Ulfin replied, 'and your lovely face. But what can *I* give you, when everything the king possesses is at your disposal, to do with as you wish?'

'What?' said Igerne.

'You've captured the heart,' Ulfin replied, 'of the man to whom this whole city owes obedience. But his heart is now at your command, which is why this whole city is at your mercy!'

'Whose heart do you mean?' she asked.

'The king's!' replied Ulfin; and Igerne raised her hand and crossed herself and said: 'God, how treacherous the king is! He feigns friendship to the duke but means to shame him – and me likewise! Ulfin, make sure you never speak of this, for if you do, so help me God, I'll tell my husband – and if he ever hears of it you'll be sure to die. I'll keep silent this time, but never again, I promise you!'

'Lady,' Ulfin replied, 'it would be an honour to die for my lord! No lady before has ever resisted taking the king as her lover, and he loves you more than any mortal soul. But maybe this is all a tease! In God's name, lady, have pity on the king! And be sure of this: you cannot resist his wishes.'

'I will!' Igerne answered, weeping. 'I'll stay forever out of his sight!'

With that Ulfin and Igerne parted. And Ulfin came to the king and told him what Igerne had said, and the king replied that that was how a good lady should answer – 'but don't stop asking!'

A day later, the king sat down to dine with the duke beside him. Before him the king had a most beautiful golden cup, and Ulfin advised him to send it to Igerne. The king looked up and said: 'Sir duke, tell Igerne to take this cup and drink from it out of love for me. I'll send it to her by one of your knights, filled with fine wine.'

The duke, suspecting nothing untoward, replied: 'Many thanks, my lord; she will gladly take it.'

And he called to one of his knights, named Bretel, and said: 'Bretel, take this cup to your lady from the king, and tell her to drink from it out of love for him.'

So Bretel took the cup and came to where Igerne was seated, and said: 'Lady, the king sends you this cup, and the duke bids you accept the king's gesture and drink from it out of love for him.'

Hearing this, the lady was filled with shame and flushed red; but she took the cup and drank. She made to send it back, but Bretel said: 'My lord bids you keep it, lady.'

And he returned to the king and thanked him on Igerne's behalf, though she had said no such thing.

When they had eaten they rose, and Ulfin went to see what Igerne was doing. He found her deeply troubled, and she said to him: 'Ulfin, it was a treacherous act by the king to send me that cup of his. By God, I'm going to tell my lord of the shame the two of you mean to deal him!'

'You're not that foolish!' Ulfin replied. 'Your husband would never believe you!'

But Igerne said: 'Damn anyone who hides it from him!'

Meanwhile the king took the duke by the hand and said: 'Let's go and see the ladies!'

'Gladly,' said the duke, and they went to the ladies' chambers; but the only reason for going was to see Igerne, as she knew full well. So she suffered all day; and that night, when the duke went to his lodging, he found her in her chamber weeping. Seeing this, he took her in his arms and kissed her, for he loved her dearly, and said: 'Lady, why are you crying?'

'Sir,' she said, 'I'll not hide it from you: the king says he loves me. The only reason he summons all these ladies to all these courts he holds is because of me! And today he made me take his cup and commanded me to drink from it out of love for him. For that, I wish I were dead!'

When the duke heard his wife's words he was most distressed, for he loved her very deeply, and he summoned his knights and said to them: 'Prepare to leave, sirs – and don't ask why until I choose to tell you.'

They did as the duke commanded; and he mounted with all possible secrecy, and Igerne with him, and back he rode to his own land, taking with him his wife and all his knights.

His departure caused a great stir in the city next morning, and when the king was told that the duke was gone he was much aggrieved and said to his barons: 'Sirs, tell me what to do about the insult the duke has committed at my court.'

They all replied that he had acted crazily – 'and we don't know how he can make amends'. So they said, not knowing the reason for the duke's departure.

'If you so advise,' said the king, 'I'll summon him to make amends for the offence he committed in leaving here.'

They all agreed and advised him to do so; and two worthy men set out with his message, and rode on until they reached Tintagel. When they arrived they found the duke and delivered their message precisely; and hearing it, the duke, realising he would have to take his wife, told the messengers he would not return to court.

'The king has so abused me and mine that I've no cause to trust or love him. God will support me in this, for He knows well enough that the king's behaviour at court was such as to lose my love and trust.'

So the messengers returned from Tintagel to the king, while the duke called for his men and spoke to those he trusted most, and told them why he had left Carduel and how the king had tried to make his wife betray him. When they heard this they said that, God willing, that would never happen, and that the king deserved nothing but ill if he meant such harm to one of his liegemen. Then the duke said: 'In God's name, sirs, help me defend my land if the king attacks me.' They replied that they would do so most willingly.

Meanwhile the messengers returned to Carduel and found the king and delivered the duke's reply. The king was furious. He implored his barons to help him avenge the duke's insult, and they said they could not refuse, but asked him as a mark of loyalty to challenge the duke but with forty days' grace. The king agreed, and asked them then to be gathered at Tintagel ready for war.

'Willingly, sire,' they said, and the king sent messengers to challenge the duke with forty days' grace. The duke made ready to defend himself, and the men who had borne the king's challenge returned to tell him that the duke was preparing to resist. The king was incensed at the news, and summoned his barons and invaded the duke's lands with a great army. When word of this reached the duke he was most alarmed. Not daring to await the king's advance he took refuge in a strong castle and placed his wife in another. The king was advised to lay siege to the duke, and besiege him he did.

And so the king laid siege to the duke's castle; but he was there for a long while, for he could not take it. And he was tormented by his love for Igerne – so much so that one day, while he was in his pavilion, he began to weep; and all his men, seeing him cry, went out and left him alone. When Ulfin, who had been outside, heard this, he came to him and found him weeping. He was disturbed by this and asked him the reason for his tears.

'I weep for Igerne,' the king replied, 'and I can see it's going to be my death, for I can find no peace at all. I feel so sorry for myself – it's killing me!'

'My lord,' said Ulfin, 'you're being very weak-hearted, thinking you're going to die for a woman! If Merlin were here he'd give you good advice.'

'I fear I must have angered him,' the king replied. 'He's come nowhere near me for a long time. Or perhaps he disapproves of me loving the wife of my liegeman. But it's no good – my heart is lost; and I know he forbade me to send for him.'

'But I'm sure,' said Ulfin, 'that if he's in good health and cares for you, he'll come and give you guidance.'

So Ulfin comforted the king, and told him to put a good face to it and be of good cheer and to summon his men and be with them again: that would relieve a good deal of his sorrow. The king told Ulfin he would willingly do so; and so their talk ended. And the king besieged the castle for a great while longer and launched attacks against it, but capture it he could not.

Then one day, while Ulfin was riding amongst the army, he came across a man he did not recognise. And the man said to him: 'Sir Ulfin, I'd like to speak with you privately, away from here.'

'Very well,' Ulfin replied, and they drew away from the army, the man on foot and Ulfin riding. Then Ulfin dismounted to talk to the old man and asked him who he was, and he answered: 'I'm an old man, as you can see. But when I was young I was held to be wise. Sir Ulfin, I've just come from Tintagel, where a worthy man accosted me and told me that your king Utherpendragon is in love with the duke's wife, and is destroying the duke's land because he took her away from Carduel. But if you'll get me a good reward, I know a man who can guide the king in his love for Igerne and arrange for him to meet with her.'

Ulfin was amazed, wondering how the man could say these things, and begged him to direct him to the one who could give the king such help.

'First,' said the old man, 'I want to know how the king will repay him.'

'When I've spoken to the king,' Ulfin replied, 'I'll meet you back here.'

'You'll find either me or my messenger,' the old man said, 'on this path between here and the army.'

Then Ulfin left him and rode back to the king and told him what he had said. When the king heard his words he laughed, saying: 'Ulfin, will you know him tomorrow if you see him?'

'Why yes,' replied Ulfin, 'he's an old man, and he's going to meet me down there in the morning to find out what reward you'll give.'

And the king laughed again, guessing that it was Merlin. Next morning he followed Ulfin, and when they had ridden out beyond the army they came upon a crippled man, who cried out as the king rode past him: 'King! If God will grant your heart's dearest wish, give me a decent reward!'

The king roared with laughter, and said to Ulfin: 'Will you do something for me?'

'If it's in my power I'll do anything,' he said.

'Then go,' said the king, 'and give yourself to this cripple, and tell him I've nothing else to offer!'

And Ulfin went at once and sat beside him. Seeing him sit at his side the cripple said: 'What do you want?'

'The king has sent me to you,' Ulfin replied. 'He wants me to be yours.'

When the cripple heard this he laughed and said: 'The king has twigged, and knows me better than you! But go to him now, and tell him he's running a grave risk in the pursuit of his desires; but he's been very perceptive and will be duly rewarded.'

Ulfin remounted and went to tell the king what the cripple had said. Hearing his words, the king replied: 'Ulfin, do you realise who the cripple was that I gave you to? He was the man you spoke to yesterday!'

'My lord,' said Ulfin, 'can a man really change shape so?'

'It's Merlin playing games with us!' replied the king. 'When he wants you to know his identity, he'll let you know for sure!'

Just then Merlin arrived at the king's tent in his familiar shape and asked where the king was. A boy ran to tell him that Merlin was asking for him, and the king was speechless with delight. Then he said to Ulfin: 'Now you'll see what I meant about Merlin!'

'I'll see, my lord,' replied Ulfin, 'whether you'll gain by doing his will, for no-one is more able to help you in your love for Igerne.'

Then the king went to his pavilion and gave Merlin a joyful greeting. And Merlin asked him if he would swear to give him whatever he asked for, and the king replied: 'I will indeed, gladly.'

Then Merlin asked Ulfin if he would swear likewise, and Ulfin answered: 'I'm sorry I haven't already done so!'

Merlin laughed at this and said: 'When the oaths are made, I'll tell you how to fulfil your wish.'

Then the king called for holy relics to be brought upon a book, and he and Ulfin made their oaths as Merlin had requested, promising to give him whatever he craved. When the vows were made Merlin came to the king and said: 'Sire, you'll have to act very boldly if you're to get into Igerne's presence, for she's a wise lady and very loyal both to God and to her husband. But now you'll see what power I have to accomplish your desire.' Then he said: 'Sire, I'm going to give you the appearance of the duke: she won't be able to tell you apart. The duke has two knights specially close to him – one named Bretel and the other Jordan. I'm going to give Ulfin the appearance of Jordan and I'll take the shape of Bretel, and I'll have the gate of Igerne's castle opened and you shall lie with her. But you'll have to leave very early, for the morning will bring chilling news. And make sure you don't tell anyone where you're going.'

The king swore he would tell no-one, and Merlin said: 'Let's go; I'll give you your new guises on the way.'

The king prepared to do Merlin's bidding with all possible speed, and Merlin came to him and said: 'I've done my work – now get ready to do yours.'

They rode on till they neared Tintagel. Then Merlin said to the king: 'Wait here, sire; Ulfin and I will go on ahead.' Then he turned to the king with a herb and said: 'Rub this on your face.'

The king took the herb and did so, and thereupon he looked exactly like the duke. And Merlin took the shape of Bretel and gave Ulfin the appearance of Jordan. Then they rode to Tintagel and called for the gate to be opened, and people rushed to tell the duchess that the duke had arrived.

When the king entered the city Merlin led him into the palace and took him aside, and told him to put on his happiest face. Then all three of them went to Igerne's chamber. As soon as Igerne heard that the duke had come she had taken to her bed, and when Uther saw her lying there in all her beauty, the blood stirred throughout his body. Merlin and Ulfin removed their lord's boots as fast as they could, and saw him to bed.

Utherpendragon and Igerne lay together that night. And he begat an heir who was later to be called King Arthur.

In the morning news came that the duke was dead and his castle taken. When Merlin and Ulfin heard this they roused their lord from his bed with all possible speed. The king kissed Igerne at their parting. And when they were outside in the open fields Merlin said: 'I've kept my promise to you, my lord king; now keep yours to me. I want you to know that you've conceived an heir – make a written record of the night it happened. And I want to have the child.'

'I give him to you,' said the king, 'for I promised to grant whatever you asked.'

So Ulfin recorded the night of the child's conception. Then Merlin took the king aside and said: 'Sire, make sure Igerne never knows you lay with her or fathered the child. That way she is surer to turn to you, and it'll be easier for me to acquire the child.'

With that Merlin took his leave of the king, and the king returned to his army and Merlin to Blaise in Northumberland. The king asked his men to guide him in resolving the matter in hand, and they said: 'Sire, we advise you to make peace with the duchess and the duke's supporters: it will earn you great respect.'

The king commanded them to go to Tintagel and speak to the duchess – 'and tell her she cannot hold out against me' – and if her counsellors agreed, he would offer them peace on their terms. With that the barons rode to Tintagel, while the king took Ulfin aside and said: 'Ulfin, what do you think about this peace? I think it was your idea.'

'If it was,' Ulfin replied, 'you can say whether you like it.'

'I do,' said the king.

'Don't concern yourself with the business,' Ulfin said. 'Just agree to peace and I'll arrange it.'

The king was very grateful. Meanwhile his messengers arrived at Tintagel and found the duchess and the duke's supporters, and made it plain that the duke was dead – and through his own misdeeds – and that the king was very sorry and wished to make peace now with the lady and her friends. They realised they had no defence against him, and that the king was offering peace, and they said they would discuss it. So the duke's men withdrew to a chamber, taking the duchess with them, and advised her to make peace, saying that of two evils it was best to choose the lesser. And the lady replied: 'I'll take your advice, sirs, for I trust no-one as much as you.'

They returned from their council, and one of the worthiest spoke to the king's messengers, saying: 'Sirs, what reparation will the king make to our lady for the death of her husband?'

'Dear sir,' they replied, 'we don't know our lord's own will. But he said he would do as the duchess's men advised.'

'We cannot ask for more,' said her followers, and they agreed to make peace in fifteen days. So the date was set, and the king's messengers returned and reported what had happened. While the fifteen days passed the king spoke to Ulfin of many things. Then the lady asked safe conduct of the king to come into his army on the day set to make peace. The king assured her of the safest conduct, and sent his barons to escort her. When the lady arrived the king assembled all his barons, and asked her men what reparation she would like for her husband's death. Her friends replied: 'Sire, the lady hasn't come here to plead, but to know what amends you'd like to make.'

Then the king called his barons and said: 'Sirs, what peace terms should I offer this lady?'

And they replied: 'You know your own heart better than we do.'

'Then I'll tell you what I wish, and swiftly,' said the king. 'Sirs, you are all my liegemen and counsellors and I defer in this matter entirely to you. But be careful now in advising your lord, for I'll do whatever you say.'

'No-one could ask more of his lord,' they replied. 'But it's a very great responsibility: are you sure you'll bear us no ill-will?'

'Sirs!' said Ulfin. 'You seem to think your king's a fool! Don't you believe a word he says?'

'We do, Ulfin,' they replied, 'we do indeed, but we beg the king to send you to our council, and that you give us your soundest, best advice.'

When the king heard them ask for Ulfin's guidance he pretended to be angry; but to Ulfin he said: 'Go, Ulfin, and do your best to steer them to my will!'

And Ulfin answered: 'Gladly!'

Then they all withdrew and asked him: 'Ulfin, what do you advise?'

'I'll tell you what I think,' he replied. 'And what I say here I'd say anywhere. You know very well that the king has brought about the duke's death by force, and whatever wrong the duke might have done him it wasn't enough to deserve death. Isn't that the truth? And know this now: the lady has been left heavy with child, while the king has laid waste her land; and she's the finest lady in the world, the wisest and most beautiful. And I tell you, the duke's kin have suffered a great loss by his death, and if the king is to retain their friendship it's only right that he should compensate them for a large part of that loss. It seems to me he can make amends only by taking her as his wife. Not only will it make amends; it'll gain the admiration of all in the kingdom who hear the news. And he should marry the duke's daughter to King Lot of Orkney: then he'll be deemed a most loyal king. That's my advice,' said Ulfin. 'Now tell me yours, if you disagree with what I've said.'

'You've given the noblest advice,' they replied, 'that any man could conceive. If the king agrees, we do so heartily!'

'A brief answer,' said Ulfin. 'But if you all fully agree I'll report your decision to the king. But what of King Lot of Orkney here, on whom I've placed part of the peace terms?'

'Whatever you may have laid upon me,' said King Lot, 'I'll not stand in the way of peace.'

Hearing King Lot's approval, they all agreed wholeheartedly. They came before Utherpendragon, and Ulfin said: 'My lord, will you accept these worthy men's plan for peace?'

'I will,' he replied, 'if the lady and her supporters are in agreement.'

So Ulfin told him of the terms suggested, and the king said: 'If King Lot of Orkney accepts, then I accept also.'

'I do indeed,' said King Lot; so Ulfin came to the lady's messengers and said: 'Do you agree to these terms?'

And they replied: 'Never has a king made such fine reparations to a liegeman! We accept them fully.'

Then both parties exchanged vows of peace. And so it was that the king married Igerne. She had had three daughters by the duke: King Lot of Orkney took one of them as his wife, and from their marriage came Mordred and Sir Gawain and Guirret and Gariet. King Niautre of Garlerot took another of the daughters, whose name was Batarde. And the third daughter's name was Morgan; and by the advice of her friends she was sent away to study in a nunnery – and study she did, until she knew a good deal about the secret arts, and much about astronomy and physic; and she made use of her knowledge, until people were so amazed by her deeds that they called her Morgan the Fay. The upbringing of the other children was arranged by the king.

And so the king took Igerne as his wife. And at night while he was lying with her he asked her by whom she was with child, for it could not be by him or the duke, as the duke had not lain with her for a good while before his death. Then the queen began to cry, and said:

'If you promise to do me no harm, I'll tell you truly.'

And the king said to Igerne: 'You may tell.'

The queen was relieved to hear him grant her freedom to speak; and she told him how a man had lain with her in the semblance[16] of her lord – the story that the king knew so well. And when she had finished the king said: 'Make sure no-one learns of this, for it would bring you great shame. And since this child is rightly neither yours nor mine, I want you to give it to the person I choose, so that it stays forever secret.'

'Sir,' she replied, 'I and all I possess are at your command.'

Then the king came to Ulfin and told him of his conversation with the queen, and Ulfin said: 'Now you can see, my lord, what a wise and loyal lady she is, revealing such a great and dark secret. And you've arranged Merlin's business perfectly, for he would otherwise not have had the child!'

So matters stayed for six months, when Merlin had vowed to return. He duly did so, and spoke secretly to Ulfin to ask him the news he sought, and Ulfin told him truly all he knew. After they had spoken together the king sent Ulfin to fetch Merlin, and when all three were together the king told Merlin how he had arranged matters with the queen and married her when they had made peace.

'My lord,' Merlin replied, 'Ulfin is absolved of his sin in arranging the affair between you and the queen. But I'm not yet absolved of my part in helping you with my trickery and in the conception of the child she bears, whose fathering is a mystery to her.'

'But you're so clever,' said the king, 'that you'll know how to absolve yourself!'

'I'll need you to help me, my lord,' said Merlin.

16 The Modena manuscript reads *en cambre son segnor* ('in her lord's chamber'), rather than *en samblance son segnor* as in other texts. The latter phrase is probably necessary to make full sense of the situation.

The king said he would gladly do so, and Merlin said: 'Sire, in this town there's a worthy man with a very worthy wife who's about to have a son. But he's not at all wealthy. I want you to make a deal with him: such that he'll give his child to be nursed by another woman, while a child will be brought to him to be fed with his own wife's milk.'

'Very well,' said the king. Then Merlin went to Blaise in Northumberland, while the king summoned the worthy man, who was a knight, and welcomed him with great joy. The knight could not understand why the king made such a fuss of him. Then the king said: 'Dear friend, I've a secret to share with you, and you must keep it to yourself.'

'I'll do whatever you ask, my lord,' he replied, and the king said: 'In my sleep I had a marvellous dream in which your wife bore you a son.'

'That's true, my lord!' the knight said.

'Now,' said the king, 'I want you to send the child away and have him raised by any woman you choose, and have your wife nurse another child that will be brought to you. A man will deliver him, and you must give him to your wife to feed.'

'Very well,' the knight replied; and he returned home and persuaded his wife to send their son to be nursed elsewhere in the town, though she felt very ashamed.

The time then came for the queen to give birth. The day before the child was due Merlin came to court in secret and spoke to Ulfin, saying: 'I'm very pleased with the king, Ulfin: he's done exactly as I asked. Now bid him go to the queen and tell her that she'll have the child tomorrow after midnight, and to instruct her to give the child to the first man found outside the chamber. I must be gone.'

'Aren't you going to speak to the king?' said Ulfin.

'Not for now,' Merlin replied, and Ulfin went to the king and told him what Merlin had said. The king went to tell the queen, saying: 'Lady, you'll be delivered of the child tonight. Have one of your women carry him from the chamber, and tell her to give him to the first man she finds.'

'I will indeed,' Igerne replied, 'if God grants me life.'

That was the end of their conversation. And the queen gave birth at the time the king had said, and gave the child to a woman, saying: 'Take my child and carry him to the door, and give him to the man you find there.'

She did as her lady asked. She came to the door and gave the child to a most handsome man she found, though she did not know him. It was Merlin. And he went to the worthy knight who was to be his guardian, and said: 'I bring you a child, and I pray you raise him better than you would your own. I'd have you know that I am Merlin, and this is King Utherpendragon's child, who will in time be likewise king of this land. And you must have him baptised.'

'I will, sir, gladly,' said the knight. 'And what's to be his name?'

And Merlin replied: 'His name will be Arthur. I'm going now, for my business here is ended.'

With that they parted. The name of the knight who was to care for the child was Entor; and he came to his wife and said: 'My lady, this is the child I've asked you to take.'

'Has he been baptised?' she said.

'Yes,' he replied, 'and his name is Arthur.'

And she began to nurse him.

*

So matters stayed. And Utherpendragon ruled his land for a long time, until he fell very ill. Then the Saxons rose up in many parts of his land; and he summoned his barons, who said he should take revenge if he could. He told them to go and fight as worthy men should for their lord, and they replied: 'We'll go!'

And they did, and were routed, and the king lost many of his men. When the king heard the news he was most distressed. The remnants of his army returned, but the Saxons, having won the battle, gathered forces in ever greater numbers. Merlin knew all this, and came to Utherpendragon, who had little time left. The king was overjoyed at his coming, and Merlin said: 'You seem very afraid, my lord.'

'And with good cause, Merlin,' he replied. 'Those who should be my subjects have destroyed my kingdom and routed and killed my men. Tell me what I can do.'

'I will,' said Merlin. 'Summon your people and have them bear you in a litter and go and do battle with your enemies. And know that you will defeat them. When the battle is won, distribute all your wealth; then you will die.'

'Merlin,' the king replied, 'how is the child who was delivered to you?'

'I tell you,' said Merlin, 'he is fair and tall and well cared for.'

Then the king said: 'Merlin, will I ever see you again?'

And Merlin answered: 'Yes, once, but no more.'

With that the king and Merlin parted, and the king summoned his people and declared that he was going to do battle with his enemies. And he went, carried on a litter. And they confronted the Saxons and engaged them and defeated them, inspired by their lord, and killed a huge number. And so it was that he conquered his enemies and peace was restored to the king's land. He then returned to Logres[17] and, remembering what Merlin had said, distributed all his wealth under the guidance of the ministers of Holy Church, until none remained to him: thus he humbled himself before God. Then his illness worsened, and his people assembled at Logres, feeling great sorrow as they realised his death was near. He had become so ill that he was

---

[17] Logres is here thought of as a city rather than – as is more usual in Arthurian romance – a land.

losing the power of speech, and he did not speak for three days. Then Merlin, who knew all that had happened, made his way to the town, and the worthy men led him before the people and said: 'Merlin, the king whom you loved so dearly is dead.'

But Merlin answered: 'You're wrong. No-one will die as good a death as he, but he is not yet gone.'

'He is,' they replied. 'He hasn't spoken for three days, and he'll never speak again.'

'Yes, he will, if it please God,' said Merlin. 'Come now, and I'll make him speak.'

'That would be the greatest wonder in the world,' they said, and Merlin replied: 'Come; I shall make him speak.'

So they went to where the king lay, and opened all the windows. And the king looked at Merlin and turned towards him and seemed to recognise him. And Merlin said: 'If you wish to hear the king's words, come forward, and you will hear.'

'Merlin,' they said, 'do you think he can speak?'

'You'll see well enough,' Merlin answered; and he turned to the king and whispered softly in his ear: 'Utherpendragon, you have made a very good end, if you are inwardly as you outwardly seem. I can tell you that your son Arthur will be lord of this kingdom after you, and will complete the Round Table that you have begun.'

And Utherpendragon replied: 'Merlin, ask him to pray to Jesus Christ for my sake.'

Then Merlin said: 'Sirs, you heard the king's words. But he will never speak again.'

And so it was that the king died that night, and his death was marked with great honour.

But Utherpendragon left the land without an heir, and the next day the barons assembled to declare a new king, but could not reach agreement. 'Sirs,' said Merlin, 'if you'll trust in me, I'll give you good advice. You know the feast of Christ's birth is near; pray to Him that, as surely as He was born of the Virgin Mary, He may give you a sign to let the people know who He would choose to be king. I promise you that if you do this Our Lord will send you a true sign.'

'No man alive who trusts in God,' the barons replied, 'would disagree.'

So they all accepted Merlin's advice. And he took his leave of Ulfin, who asked him to return at Christmas to see if what he had said was true; but Merlin answered: 'I won't be back until after the choosing.'

And with that he returned to Blaise, leaving the others pledged to gather at Logres at Christmas to see Christ's choosing of the new king: so it was agreed. They waited for Christmas to come.

Meanwhile Entor had raised the child, nursed with no milk but his wife's, until he was a fine and handsome youth; and Entor did not know which he loved the more, his own son or the king's. Indeed, he had never called him anything but his son, which the child had no doubt he was. It so happened that at the feast of All Saints before that Christmas Entor had made his own son a knight, and at Christmas he came to Logres along with all the other knights.

On Christmas Eve all the clergy of the kingdom assembled with all the barons of any worth, having arranged matters exactly as Merlin commanded. And when they were all gathered they prepared themselves for prayer, and implored Our Lord to send them a man fit to uphold Christianity. So they held the first mass; and when it was done, some departed but others stayed in the minster; then one of the wisest men of the land stood up and spoke to the people before the next mass was sung, saying: 'My lords and ladies, pray to Our Lord to send you a king and leader to uphold Holy Church and to guard and save the people. We cannot agree upon the choice of a man – we're not wise enough – so now we pray to Our Lord to send us a sign by which we might know him today.'

The archbishop sang mass as far as the gospel; and then, just as they had made the offering, and day began to break, a great square block of stone and an anvil appeared, and in the anvil was fixed a sword. Those who beheld this wonder ran to the church to tell the people; and the archbishop came out bearing holy water and precious relics, and he went and saw the stone and sprinkled it with holy water. Then he noticed what was written on the sword: that whoever could draw the sword from the stone would be king by the choice of Jesus Christ. When the archbishop had read these words he announced them to the people; and they set a guard upon the stone and returned to the church singing 'Te Deum Laudamus.'

Then the worthy man who had spoken earlier said: 'My lords, God has answered our prayers with a miracle! Now I beg you, let no-one contradict the choice.'

The highest men in the land all declared that they would pull the sword out by force; but the archbishop spoke, saying: 'My lords, you're not as wise as I would wish! I assure you that in this matter wealth and nobility are worthless unless combined with the power of God. My faith in Him is such that I believe that, if the right man has not yet been born, the sword will not be drawn until he comes to draw it.'

The worthy men agreed and said he was right and they would abide by his wishes. The archbishop rejoiced to hear this, and said: 'My lords, I want a hundred of the worthiest men here to try and draw the sword.'

They did so; but for all their efforts, none could draw it. Then he commanded everyone present to try his hand, which they did; but they could not draw it. And when they had all made their attempts they returned to their lodgings to eat, and after eating they went into the fields to hold a tournament. After jousting a while they exchanged shields with their squires and began again, and the combat grew into a great mêlée, and the people of the town came running, fully armed. At the feast of All Saints Entor had made his elder son – whose name was Kay – a knight, and Kay sent his brother Arthur to their lodging to fetch his sword. But when Arthur came there he could not get it, for the chamber where it lay had been locked. But on his way back he passed the church, and took the sword that was fixed in the stone, slipped it under his coat and returned to his brother. And his brother said: 'Where's my sword?'

'I couldn't get it,' he replied, 'but I've brought you another.'

'Where from?'

'From the stone outside the church.'

And Kay took it, slipped it under his coat, and went to show his father. And his father said: 'Where did you get this?'

'From the stone outside the church,' said Kay.

And Entor said: 'Don't lie to me; I'll know if you are, and I'll never love you more.'

Then Kay said: 'Arthur gave it to me when I sent him for my sword. I don't know where he got it.'

When Entor heard this, he said to him: 'Give it to me, dear son, for you have no right to it.'

Then he called to Arthur, and said: 'Dear son, take this sword back where you found it.'

And Arthur took it and fixed it back in the stone. And Entor said to Kay: 'Go now, and draw it if you can.'

And he went, but he could not draw it. And Entor said to Arthur: 'What good will it do me, if I make you king?'

And Arthur answered: 'Such as befits my father.'

Then Entor said: 'I am not your father; I have only fostered you.'

When Arthur heard this, he wept. And Entor said to him that if he became king he should make Kay his seneschal; and that Kay should not lose that office no matter what wrong he might do.

'If he's ever wicked or foolish you must bear with him, for whatever faults he may have came to him only from the woman who nursed him – and it was on your account that his nature was changed.'

Arthur granted this request, making an oath upon holy relics. Then Entor came to the archbishop and said: 'Sir, here is a son of mine who is not yet a knight, but he has asked me to let him try to draw the sword.'

Then the archbishop and the barons went to the stone, and when they were all assembled Entor said: 'Arthur, give the sword to the archbishop.'

And Arthur took it and drew it from the stone and gave it to the archbishop. When the archbishop received it he took Arthur in his arms and sang out loud: 'Te Deum Laudamus'; and they carried Arthur into the church. But the barons who had seen this were deeply vexed, and said that no common boy was going to be their lord; and the archbishop said: 'My dear sirs, Our Lord knows each man's true nature better than you!'

But though Entor and his kin and many others sided with Arthur, the common people and the barons of the land were against him. Then the archbishop boldly declared: 'My lords, even if the whole world opposed this choice and Our Lord alone was for it, it would still stand. And I'll show you the sign that God has sent to prove it. Go, Arthur, dear brother, and put the sword back where you found it.'

And in view of them all Arthur carried it back and replaced it in the stone. When he had done so the archbishop said: 'No finer way of choosing was ever seen! Go, my lord barons, wealthy men, and try: see if you can draw the sword.'

But they could not. Then the archbishop said: 'He is a fool indeed who challenges the will of Jesus Christ.'

'That's not our intention,' they replied, 'but we can't accept a common boy as our lord. We pray you, leave the sword in the stone till Candlemas.'

The archbishop granted their request, and the sword remained in the stone. At Candlemas all the people assembled, and everyone who wished to try his hand did so. Then the archbishop came to Arthur and said: 'Go, my dear son Arthur, and fetch me the sword.'

And Arthur went up and brought it to him. When the people saw this they began to weep. Then the archbishop said: 'Sirs, is there anyone here who would challenge this choice?'

And the rich men said: 'We beg you to leave it till Easter. If no-one arrives who can draw the sword, we'll give obedience to this boy as you command. If you wish it to be otherwise, we'll do our best to agree.'

'If I wait until Easter,' said the archbishop, 'will you accept him as your lord?'

'Yes,' they answered; and the archbishop said to Arthur: 'Dear brother, put the sword back, for the honour God has promised you will not be denied.'

So Arthur went forward and put the sword back in the stone, where it stayed fixed as fast as ever. Then the archbishop, who had taken the child under his wing, said: 'Know, Arthur, that you will be king in all certainty. Now turn your thoughts to being a worthy man, and be determined from this time forward to be a good king.'

'Sir,' replied Arthur, 'I'll do as you advise.'

'You won't regret it!' said the archbishop. 'Now you must assign people to be your chief officers, and appoint your seneschal and chamberlains.'

'Sir,' said Arthur, 'summon my father Entor.'

And at Arthur's request Kay was appointed seneschal.

So matters stayed until Easter, when all the barons assembled at Logres. And when they were all gathered on the eve of Easter, the archbishop called them all into his palace to discuss the situation, and said to them: 'My lords, receive this child as your king.'

But the rich men replied: 'Sir, we don't mean to dispute the choice of Jesus Christ, but we're dismayed by the idea of a common boy as our lord.'

And thereupon the archbishop said: 'Sirs, you're not good Christians if you challenge the will of Our Lord!'

'That's not our wish,' they replied, 'but allow us some concession! Whatever test this child may have passed, we know next to nothing about him! We beg you, before this child is anointed king, let's find out what sort of man he means to be; for though we know little yet, when we see the way he acts there are some of us who'll be able to read his mind!'

'Would you like, then,' said the archbishop, 'to postpone his choosing and anointing till Pentecost?'

'We would indeed, sir,' they replied, 'in case he proves to be unfit to be our king.'

So it was left till the next day, when Arthur was led before the stone. And he drew forth the sword as he had done before; and they took him and raised him on high and accepted him as their lord. Then they asked him to put the sword back and speak with them. He replied that he would do so gladly, saying: 'Sirs, I'll do whatever you request.'

Then the barons said to him: 'Sir, it's clear that Our Lord would have you be our king, and since that is His wish it is our wish also. So we accept you as our lord and will hold our fiefs as your vassals. But we pray you as our lord to delay your anointing till Pentecost – without being any the less lord of us or the kingdom. Please give us your answer now, without debate.'

And Arthur replied: 'Sirs, what you say about accepting your homage and granting you your fiefs as my vassals, that I cannot and should not do until my kingship is clear. And when you say I should be lord of the kingdom, that cannot be until I am anointed and crowned and receive the true office of kingship. But I'll willingly grant the delay you request before my coronation. I need the blessing of both God and you.'

After hearing the child's words the barons said: 'If this child lives he'll be a wise man indeed; he has answered admirably. Sir,' they said, 'it would be good if you were crowned at Pentecost.'

And Arthur said he would gladly agree if that was their advice. So the day was postponed till Pentecost, and in the meantime they all obeyed Arthur as the archbishop commanded. And they had great riches and their finest jewels brought to him, and all the things a man might covet, to see if his heart might be open to greed. He asked his friends what each thing was worth, and did with it accordingly; for when he had received all these treasures he distributed them, so the book says. To good knights he gave fine horses and other wealth; to happy lovers he gave money and gold and silver; and to wise and worthy men he gave handsome gifts and the benefit of his company. He asked their retainers what it was they liked best, and gave them gifts accordingly. So he distributed all the wealth he was given: they could find no greed in him at all. Then they waited until Pentecost, when all the barons assembled at Logres and all who wished to do so tried to draw the sword. The archbishop had prepared the crown and the sacraments on the eve of Pentecost;

and before vespers on the Saturday evening, by the common advice and consent of almost all the barons, the archbishop made Arthur a knight.

That night he kept vigil in the cathedral until day broke next morning, when all the barons assembled there, and the archbishop addressed them, saying: 'Behold, sirs, a man whom Our Lord has chosen for us; you have all known of the choosing since Christmas; and all who have wished to try their hand at the sword have done so. If any man opposes the choice, let him speak.'

But the barons said: 'We all agree, and wish before God that he be anointed king.'

'And does he bear any of you ill-will for having opposed his consecration?'

At that, Arthur wept with pity and knelt before them and declared at the top of his voice: 'I pardon you all most sincerely, and I pray the Lord who has bestowed this sacred office upon me to pardon you all likewise.'

Then they all rose as one and led Arthur to where the royal vestments were kept, and dressed him. When they had done so the archbishop was ready to sing mass; but first he said to Arthur: 'My lord, go and fetch the sword, the mark of the justice with which you must defend Holy Church and safeguard Christianity in every way and with all your power.'

They went in procession to the stone, and when they came there the archbishop called to Arthur, saying: 'If you are willing to swear to God and my lady Holy Mary and my lord Saint Peter and all the saints to uphold Holy Church and keep peace and faith on Earth, and to give counsel to all men and women in need, and to guide the wayward and uphold all right with all your power, then go forward now and take the sword with which Our Lord has marked your choosing.'

When Arthur heard this he began to weep with emotion, and many others for him, and said: 'May Our Lord, as surely as He rules all living things, grant me the strength and power to do as you have said, which is truly my intention.'

Arthur, kneeling, took the sword in both hands and raised it from the anvil as easily as if nothing held it, and carried it back, held high. They led him to the altar, and he laid the sword upon it. And when he had done so they blessed him and anointed him and performed all the rites necessary for the making of a king. And when Arthur had been crowned and mass had been sung, all the barons left the church. But when they looked they saw no sign of the stone, and did not know what had become of it. And so it was that Arthur was the chosen king; and he ruled the land and kingdom of Logres in peace for a long time.

After his coronation and the singing of mass he returned to his palace along with all the barons who had seen him draw the sword from the stone. And once he had been made king Merlin arrived at court, and the barons who knew him were overjoyed to see him; and Merlin spoke to them, saying: 'Sirs, listen to me now. I want you to know that Arthur, whom you have accepted as your king, is the son of your liege lord Utherpendragon and Queen Igerne. When he was born the king commanded that he be given to me, and as soon as I received him I took him to Entor, for I knew him to be a worthy man, and he willingly became his guardian for I promised him a great reward. And Entor has now seen my promise fulfilled, for Arthur has made his son Kay his seneschal.'

'I have indeed,' said Arthur, 'and he will never be removed from that office as long as I live.'

This news was greeted with jubilation, and all the barons were delighted – notably Gawain, who was the son of Arthur's sister and King Lot. After this business the king gave orders for the tables to be set up at once, and throughout the hall they all sat down to dine: they were richly served with whatever they asked for. And when the barons had dined the boys and serving-men cleared the tables; and the barons rose, and those who knew Merlin and had served Utherpendragon came to the king and said:

'Sire, you must treat Merlin with much honour, for he was a great soothsayer to your father and dearly loved by all your family. He foretold Vortigern's death, and ordered the making of the Round Table. Be sure he is given all respect, for he will answer anything you ask him.'

'I will do as you say,' Arthur replied; and he took Merlin and seated him at his side and gave him a most joyful welcome. And Merlin said to him: 'Sire, I would like to speak to you privately, with the two barons you trust the most.'

'Merlin,' the king replied, 'I'll do whatever you advise if it's for the good.'

To which Merlin answered: 'I will never give you any advice contrary to Our Lord's will.'

Then the king summoned Kay the seneschal, whom he had long taken to be his brother, and King Lot of Orkney's son Sir Gawain, who was his nephew. The four of them gathered in private, and Merlin said to them: 'Arthur, you are king now, thanks be to God. Your father Uther was a most worthy man, and in his time the Round Table was established, which was made to symbolise the table at which Our Lord sat on the Thursday when He said that Judas would betray Him. It was made, too, as a reference to the table of Joseph of Arimathea, which was established for the Grail, when the good were separated from the wicked. I want you to know this, too: there have been two kings of Britain before you who have been king of France and emperor of Rome; and be assured of this: there will be a third king of Britain who'll be king and emperor likewise, and he will conquer the Romans by force of arms. And I tell you, as one to whom Our Lord gave the power to know the future, that two hundred years before you were born, your fate was fixed and prophesied. But first you must be sufficiently worthy and valiant to enhance the glory of the Round Table. I assure you that you will not be emperor until such time as the Round Table is exalted in the way I shall now say.

'Some while ago the Grail was given to Joseph while he was in prison: it was brought to him by Our Lord Himself. And when he was set free Joseph journeyed into the desert with a great many of the people of Judaea. For as long as they held to a good life Our Lord granted them grace, but when they ceased to do so, that grace was denied them. The people asked Joseph if it was through their sin or his that they had fallen from grace, and Joseph grieved deeply and went to his vessel and prayed to Our Lord to send him a sign to guide him. Then the voice of the Holy Spirit came to him and told him to have a table made, which he did, and when it was ready he placed his vessel upon it and ordered his people to be seated there. And the innocent sat at the table, but those who were guilty of sin all left, unable to stay in its presence. Now, at this table was an empty place, which suggested to Joseph that no-one could sit where Our Lord had sat; but a false disciple named Moyse, who had often misled them in many ways, came to Joseph and begged him in God's name to let him fill the empty seat, saying he felt so full of Our Lord's grace that he was clearly worthy to sit there. Joseph said to him: 'Moyse, if you're not as you seem, I advise you not to put yourself to the test.' But the disciple replied that God would grant him success in filling the empty place as surely as he was a good man. Then Joseph said that if he was truly so good he should go and sit in the seat. And Moyse sat there, and plunged into an abyss.

'Know, then, that Our Lord made the first table, and Joseph the second; and I in the time of your father Utherpendragon ordered the making of the third, which in time to come will be greatly exalted, and throughout the world people will speak of the fine chivalry which in your time will assemble there.

'Know this, too: when he died Joseph, who had been given the Grail, bequeathed it to his brother-in-law Bron. And this Bron has twelve sons, one of whom is named Alain li Gros. And Bron, the Fisher King, commanded Alain to be his brothers' guardian. By Our Lord's command Alain has come here from Judaea to these isles in the West, and he and his people have now arrived in these parts; the Fisher King himself lives in the isles of Ireland in one of the most beautiful places in the world. But I tell you, he is in a worse state than any man has ever known, and has fallen gravely ill; but however old or infirm he may be, he cannot die until a knight of the Round Table has performed enough feats of arms and chivalry – in tournaments and by seeking adventures – to become the most renowned knight in all the world. When that knight has attained such heights that he's worthy to come to the court of the rich Fisher King, and has asked what purpose the Grail served, and serves now, the Fisher King will at once be healed. Then he will tell him the secret words of Our Lord before passing from life to death. And that knight will have the blood of Jesus Christ in his keeping. With that the enchantments of the land of Britain will vanish, and the prophecy will be fulfilled. So know, then, that if you do as I've instructed, great good may come to you. But I must go now: I can be in this world no longer, for my Saviour will not grant me leave.'

The king said that if Merlin could stay with him he would have his deepest affection; but Merlin said it was impossible. And with that he left the king and made his way to Northumberland to Blaise, who had been his mother's confessor, and who had kept a written account of all these events at Merlin's instruction. Meanwhile Arthur remained with his barons, pondering deeply upon Merlin's words.

Perceval

AND KNOW THIS: no king ever held so great a court or so great a feast as did King Arthur. And no king ever earned such love from his barons as he; and Arthur himself was the fairest man and the finest knight known. And because he was such a valiant king, and bestowed such handsome gifts, he became so renowned that throughout the world no-one spoke of anyone but him, so that all knights made their way to his court to see him and to be in his company. No man's deeds of chivalry were held in any esteem until he had spent a year in Arthur's household and received a sleeve or pennon from the king.

Thus it was that his renown was universal, and reached the land where Alain li Gros was living; and he set his heart on sending his son Perceval to Arthur's court when the time came to give him arms. He often said to him: 'When you grow up, dear son, I shall take you with the greatest pride to the court of King Arthur!'

So he said many times, until it pleased Our Lord that Alain li Gros should pass from this world. And when he was dead, Perceval decided to go to Arthur's court; and one day he armed himself handsomely, mounted a hunting-horse and set off so quietly that his mother did not know. When she realised Perceval had gone she lamented terribly, and was sure the wild beasts of the forest would devour him. The thought of this so overwhelmed her with grief that she died.

Meanwhile Perceval rode on till he reached the court of the great King Arthur; and he came before him and greeted him most nobly in the presence of his barons, and said that if it pleased him he would gladly stay and join his household. The king accepted him and made him a knight; and there at court Perceval grew much in wisdom and courtesy – for you may be sure that when he left his mother's house he knew nothing. Indeed he proved his worth so much to the other barons that he later became a knight of the Round Table, and was much loved at court. Later there came Saigremor and Yvain, King Urien's son; and another Yvain, of the white hands; and Dodinial, son of the lady of Malehaut; and Mordred, Arthur's nephew, who was later to commit great treachery, as you will hear; and Guirres his brother, and Garries and

Gawain. These four were the sons of King Lot of Orkney, and King Arthur was their uncle. And after them came Lancelot of the Lake, a knight of the highest stature. So many more knights gathered there that I cannot name them all; but I can tell you that there were so many good knights at King Arthur's court that throughout the world men spoke only of the fine chivalry at the great King Arthur's Round Table.

The time came when Arthur remembered Merlin's words to him; and he came before his barons and knights and said: 'My lords, you must all return here at Pentecost, for on that day I shall hold the greatest feast ever held by any king in any land. And I want each man here to bring his wife, for I wish the highest honour to be paid to the Round Table, which Merlin established in the time of my father Utherpendragon. The twelve peers of my court will sit in the twelve seats; but I want you to know that all who attend my feast and wish to stay with me will be forever of the company of the Round Table, and as a mark of high honour wherever they may go, each will carry the Round Table's pennon or device.'

This announcement caused a great stir, and all the barons of the court were overjoyed, for they longed to be known as members of the Round Table. With that they departed, each to his own land, while Arthur remained at Logres, thinking deeply about how he could further enhance the Round Table's reputation.

At Pentecost every knight from every land gathered for King Arthur's feast; for I tell you, Arthur was held in such esteem that even those who were not his vassals would have considered themselves dishonoured and would not have dared show themselves at court or in the presence of worthy men if they failed to attend King Arthur's court at Pentecost. So many came from every land that no man could record them all.

Then the day of Pentecost arrived, and Arthur came to the Round Table and had mass sung in the presence of everyone. And when the mass was ended, the king took the twelve peers and bade them sit in the twelve seats; the thirteenth remained empty, symbolising the place where Judas had sat before he rose [to go and betray Christ].[1] Merlin had left it empty at Utherpendragon's table, and for that reason Arthur did not dare to fill it.

On that day of Pentecost the king's feast was great indeed; and the knights of the Round Table dressed him in royal robes and set the crown upon his head and honoured him as he deserved. With more than seven hundred censers of fine gold they censed the air wherever he walked, and scattered flowers[2] and mint before him: they paid him all possible respect. Then the king declared that everyone present at his feast should be clad in the same robes and devices, and as soon as the command was given it was done. And

[1] The manuscript simply reads *quant il se leva*.
[2] Literally 'gladioli'.

so many knights and damsels were there that the king presented five thousand four hundred robes and devices of the Round Table. With that the king summoned the water[3] with a fanfare of a hundred trumpets, and then all the knights sat down to dine.

And Arthur, with crown on head and robed in gold, was much admired by all who had not seen him before, and indeed, was wondrously esteemed by all who beheld him that day.

When the meal was done the king gave orders for the tables to be cleared, and everyone went out into the fields to tourney. You would then have seen ladies and damsels climb the towers and lean on the battlements to watch the knights jousting amid great festivity. That day the knights of the Round Table jousted against those from elsewhere; and they were closely watched by the ladies and damsels – and so fought all the harder, for there was scarcely a knight who did not have his sister or his wife or his lover present. And be assured, that day the knights of the Round Table carried off the prize, for Sir Gawain, son of King Lot, fought mightily, as did Kay the seneschal who was Entor's son, and Urgan, a very bold knight, and Saigremor and Lancelot of the Lake, and Erec who was a fine knight indeed. They jousted on until they vanquished the outsiders, and when evening came they had won the prize. All through the day the valiant King Arthur was mounted on a palfrey, baton in hand, and rode between the ranks to keep order and prevent any interference. With him was Perceval, the son of Alain li Gros, who was most upset that he had not taken part in the tournament, but he had wounded his hand and could not joust. Instead he accompanied Arthur all day, along with Guirres and Garries, who were brothers to Sir Gawain and sons of King Lot. All day these three were with the king, and they went to see the ladies and damsels as they watched the jousting; and the daughter of King Lot of Orkney, Sir Gawain's sister, whose name was Elainne, and who was the most beautiful damsel then alive, saw Perceval the Welshman and was smitten with the deepest love for him. How could she help it? For he was the most handsome knight in all King Arthur's company.

At evening the tournament broke up, and the knights and damsels turned to dancing and the most joyful festivities. But Sir Gawain's sister Elainne could think of nothing but Perceval the Welshman: she loved him desperately. And when night came the knights went to their lodgings or their tents, but Elainne could not rest. She called a boy and sent him to Perceval with the message that Elainne, Sir Gawain's sister, greeted him most nobly and much desired to see him joust against the Round Table. And she bade him, by the faith he owed, to joust in the morning before her in red arms which she would send him. Perceval was taken aback by this, but his heart was filled with joy that such a worthy damsel as King Lot's daughter should bid him

---

[3] i.e. the water for washing hands before eating.

take up arms for love of her and joust against the Round Table. He sent back word that, for love of her, he would do anything the damsel asked: 'I will joust tomorrow, most willingly.'

The messenger was delighted, and returned to the damsel with Perceval's reply. And the damsel, overjoyed, fetched the arms and sent them to Perceval, who was mightily pleased with them. You may be sure that he slept very little that night.

Next morning the king rose and went with his barons to hear mass. When mass had been said the twelve peers went to eat at the Round Table, where they were well served: Arthur did them all possible honour. He bade a fanfare be sounded as the water was brought, and then the knights sat down to dine throughout the hall, and they were well served indeed. The story does not tell of the dishes they ate, but I can assure you they had whatever they asked for; and when they had eaten the king called for the tables to be cleared, and the ladies and damsels went out to the fields to see the jousting and celebrations of the Round Table.

Sir Gawain's sister Elainne was there, desperate to see Perceval clad in the arms she had sent him. And the knights who wanted to joust and win the prize rode from Carduel and joined in combat with those of the Round Table. So the festivities began once more, and none so great had there ever been. And be assured that Lancelot of the Lake – along with Gawain and Sir Yvain, the son of King Urien – overcame all the outsiders. Then it was that Perceval the Welshman came, finely clad in the arms that the damsel had sent him, and he charged full tilt at Saigremor, aiming straight at his shield; and when Saigremor saw him he turned towards him, and with their horses at full gallop they dealt each other such blows on their shields that their lances flew into splinters. But Perceval the Welshman, who knew what jousting was about, smashed into horse and man together, so that Saigremor did not know what had hit him and was sent flying, crashing to the ground in the middle of the field so heavily that everyone who saw him thought he must be dead. And Perceval took his horse and presented it to Elainne, who received it with the utmost joy. And know this: Perceval performed so well that day that he outfought all the knights of the Round Table, defeating Kay the seneschal, Yvain the son of King Urien, and Lancelot of the Lake, and they all declared that he should fill the empty place at the Round Table. And the king, who was valiant and wise, came to Perceval and said to him: 'Sir knight, I wish you to reside with me from this time on, to be a knight of my household and of the Round Table. You may be sure I shall pay you the utmost honour.'

And Perceval replied: 'Many thanks, sire.'

And with that Perceval took off his helmet; and the king recognised him and was astonished, and asked him why he had not been armed the day before and why he was now in disguise. And Perceval said: 'Sire, I'd like you to keep it secret, but let's just say that I did it for love – and if I'd had a choice, I'd have done quite differently.'

When the king heard this he began to laugh, and pardoned him kindly, saying that things done for love should be freely forgiven. And Sir Gawain and Yvain and Lancelot and all the knights of the Round Table agreed. Then Perceval told the king that he was eager to see the Round Table and those who sat there.

'Dear friend,' the king replied, 'you may do so tomorrow.'

'It will give me great pleasure,' said Perceval.

With that their conversation ended. That night there was a great feast, and in the morning the barons assembled to hear mass; and when mass had been said they all came to the place where stood the Round Table. The king bade them be seated; and when they had done so, one place remained empty. Perceval asked the king what was special about the empty seat, and the king replied: 'My dear friend, it has great significance, for it is the place destined for the finest knight in the world.'

Perceval longed to sit there; and he said to the king: 'Sire, grant me permission to take that seat.'

But the king replied that he should not do so, for great misfortune might befall him; for a false disciple had once sat in the empty place and the earth had swallowed him in an instant.

'Even if I were to grant you permission, you ought not to sit there.'

But Perceval was aggrieved at this and said: 'So help me God, unless you give me leave, my lord king, I swear I shall no longer be a knight of your household.'

When Gawain heard this he was most upset, for he loved Perceval dearly, and he said to the king: 'Sire, give him leave to sit there.'

Lancelot made the same plea, and the twelve peers likewise, imploring him so fervently that the king – most reluctantly – agreed, saying: 'I grant your wish.'

Perceval was overjoyed; and he stepped forward, crossing himself in the name of the Holy Spirit, and sat in the empty seat. And the moment he did so the stone split beneath him, uttering such an anguished groan that it seemed to all those present that the earth itself was crumbling into an abyss. And with the earth's groan came so great a darkness that for a league and more no man could see his neighbour. And then a voice rang out, crying:

'King Arthur, you have committed the gravest wrong of any king who ever reigned in Britain, for you have disobeyed the command that Merlin gave you. And know that Perceval here has shown more audacity than any man who ever lived, and it will cost him and all the knights of the Round Table the greatest suffering in the world. Were it not for the goodness of his father Alain li Gros and his grandfather Bron, who is known as the Fisher King, he would have fallen into the abyss and died the terrible death that Moyse suffered when he wrongfully sat in the place that Joseph had forbidden him.

'But hear this, King Arthur: Our Lord sends you word that the vessel which He gave Joseph in prison is here in this land, and is called the Grail. And the Fisher King has fallen into a great sickness and infirmity, and will never be healed – nor will the stone be mended in the place where Perceval sat at the Round Table – until one of the knights seated here has performed enough feats of arms and goodness and prowess. When such a knight is exalted above all other men and is counted the finest knight in the world, when he has achieved so much, then God will guide him to the house of the rich Fisher King. And then, when he has asked what this Grail is for and who is served with it, then, when he has asked that question, the Fisher King will be healed, and the stone will mend beneath the place at the Round Table, and the enchantments which now lie upon the land of Britain will be cast out.'

When the king and those seated at the Round Table heard this they were filled with wonder, and all declared that they would never rest until they had found the house of the rich Fisher King and had asked what was done with the Grail. And Perceval the Welshman vowed that he would not sleep two nights in the same place until he had found it. So said Sir Gawain and Erec and Saigremor and all those seated at the Round Table. And Arthur, hearing this, was filled with sorrow, but nonetheless gave them leave to go.

So Arthur dismissed his court, and some returned to their own lands while others stayed in their lodgings and with the king. Perceval and those of the Round Table prepared to leave, arming themselves in their lodgings. And when they were ready they came, all mounted, before the king and his barons; and Sir Gawain, in the presence of them all, said: 'My lords, we must go now as the voice of Our Lord instructed, though we don't know where or in which direction until Our Lord gives us guidance.'

When the king and his barons heard this they began to weep, for they did not expect to see any one of them again. And with that the knights departed.

But they rode together all that day without encountering any adventure; and all the next they rode till the ninth hour,[4] when they came upon a cross. They halted there and worshipped the cross and prayed for God's mercy. Then Perceval said to his companions: 'Sirs, if we ride together we're not going to achieve much. Let's split up and each go our own way.'

'If we carry on like this,' said Gawain, 'we'll accomplish nothing. Let's follow Perceval's advice.'

And they all said: 'We agree.'

So they went their separate ways, each following the path he fancied most, and so embarked upon the quest of the Grail. But of Gawain and his companions, and the adventures that befell them and the hardships they endured, I can tell you nothing; I will tell you only what matters for the book.

---

4   The ninth canonical hour: three o'clock in the afternoon.

*

So know now that when Perceval left his companions he rode all day without encountering any adventure; nor could he find anywhere to take lodging, and he had to lie that night in the forest. He unharnessed his horse and left him to graze. Perceval did not sleep at all that night, but kept watch over his horse for fear of the wild beasts of the forest. At the crack of dawn next day he resaddled and harnessed his horse and mounted without delay, and rode through the forest all day until the first hour.[5] And as he rode he glanced to his left, and saw a knight who had been struck through the body with a lance: he was still impaled upon it; and a sword had cut through his helmet right down to his teeth. Nearby stood a tethered horse and a shield; and beside his body was the most beautiful damsel that Nature ever made. She was grieving more bitterly than any woman has ever done as she lamented the knight's death, beating her fists and tearing her hair and clawing at her face in such anguish that no man could have seen her without feeling the deepest pity. When Perceval saw her he felt pity indeed, and spurred his horse towards her.

When the damsel saw him she stopped her grieving for a moment and rose to meet him, saying: 'You are welcome, sir.'

'Damsel,' Perceval replied, 'may God give you greater joy than you have now.'

'Sir,' she said, 'joy will never be mine, for I have seen the man killed whom I loved so much, and who valued me so dearly that there was nothing he cherished as much as me.'

'Damsel,' Perceval asked her, 'how long have you been with him?'

'I'll tell you, dear sir,' she replied. 'It so happened that I was at my father's house in this forest, and a half day's journey away there lived a giant. Some while ago he asked my father for my hand but was rejected, so he waged war upon him for a long time, until he heard that my father had gone to the court of the great King Arthur, for the Round Table was to gather at Carduel at Pentecost. Knowing my father had gone to Arthur's court, he came to our manor house and tore down the door and marched into the hall – finding no-one there to bar his way – and burst into my mother's chamber and seized me and carried me off. He made me mount his horse – you can see him there – and brought me here and made me dismount, and was about to lie with me. I was terrified, and wept and screamed; and the knight you see here heard my cries and came galloping towards us. The giant didn't notice him till he was right beside him; then he was enraged and attacked him with all his might. The knight was noble and valiant and fought back as boldly as he could. I tell you, the giant responded fearsomely and dealt him terrible blows;

5 The first canonical hour: six o'clock in the morning. This must be a scribal error for 'vespers': it does not tally with the damsel's story that follows.

but the knight attacked him with his sword and cut off his head, and hung it over there on the branch of a tree. Then he came to me and helped me to mount, and said he wished me to be his love; I was overjoyed and gladly granted his wish, and said he would always be my lord and love since he'd saved me from an enemy who would have taken my honour and my life.

'We rode together all yesterday and all this morning till the third hour,[6] when we came upon a pavilion. We rode towards it to see the merrymaking, for such festivity as was taking place in the tent was never seen before. The tent-flap was open so we went inside; but the moment they saw us enter the pavilion their grief was as great as their joy had been! My love was bewildered by their grieving. Then a damsel came and said we should leave the tent at once and flee, for if he stayed a moment longer he'd be sure to die. But he, knowing nothing of their business, refused downright to go, and begged them: 'Damsels, in God's name stop this grieving and return to your merry-making!'

' "Dear sir," they replied, "how can we make merry when you'll die before our eyes? It's the Proud Knight of the Heath who's pitched his tent here, and he'll kill you – you may be sure he'll have no mercy. Take our advice and go before worse befalls you."

' "Sweet damsels," he said, "I fear no knight."

'When they heard this they began to weep. And at that moment a dwarf came riding up on a nag, a whip in his hand, and he was wicked and cruel. His only greeting was to say we were unwelcome! And so we were, judging by his behaviour, for he lashed me across the face with his whip, raising weals, and then pulled the tentpole out of the ground and brought it crashing down on us. My love was furious, but didn't deign to meddle with the dwarf, who rode away, beating his nag with the whip. Then we left, too, and set off on our way, for we had no more business there; but we hadn't gone half a league before we saw a knight approaching, heavily armed in red, and galloping at such a speed that the whole forest shook: such a thunderous noise he made that we thought there must be ten! And as he drew near he cried aloud: "By God, sir knight, you'll regret bringing down my tent and ruining the celebration!"

'When my love heard this he turned to face him and they charged at each other; and the knight, who was mighty indeed, struck my love through the body, and then drew his sword and struck him through the helm, as you can see. And when he'd killed him he rode away, without a glance at either me or my horse. I was left all alone in this forest, and no-one can blame me for grieving when I've lost the one who saved me from my enemy. There: I've given you a true answer to your question.'

And with that she began to weep and lament most bitterly. Perceval felt

---

6 The third canonical hour: nine o'clock in the morning.

deeply sorry for her, and said: 'Damsel, this grieving will do no good; climb on this mule and lead me to the knight's pavilion, for I won't be content till I've taken revenge.'

But the damsel replied: 'Sir, take my advice and don't go: the knight is huge and mighty, and if he gets the better of you he'll kill you. Though I can't deny he's the man I hate most in all the world.'

And Perceval declared that he would not rest until he had seen the knight. So he helped her to mount, and they made their way together to the pavilion where they heard the damsels' merrymaking. As soon as they caught sight of Perceval their celebrations ceased and they screamed at him to go, for their lord was coming and Perceval would be sure to die. But he cared little for their words, and rode up to the tent; and no sooner had he entered and begun to speak to them than the foul and hideous dwarf appeared on his nag, whip in hand and beating the nag on the head and crying: 'Get out of my lord's pavilion now!'

And he came up to the damsel and lashed her across the neck and hands, and took hold of her palfrey and was about to drive her out of the pavilion; but Perceval, outraged, gripped his lance by the head and dealt the dwarf a mighty blow across the shoulders, sending him crashing from his nag to the ground. But the dwarf jumped up and climbed back on his nag and cried: 'By God, sir knight, before the day's out you're going to suffer!'

And he left Perceval in the pavilion, most distressed about the dwarf's foul treatment of the damsel. And while they stood there they saw the knight approaching clad all in red arms, and the dwarf with him. When the damsel saw him she was terrified and said: 'Good sir, that's the one who killed my love!'

Hearing this, Perceval turned his horse and rode from the pavilion. When the knight saw him he cried: 'By God, sir knight, you'll be sorry you hit my dwarf!'

But Perceval, caring nothing for his arrogant words, turned his horse towards him, and they charged at each other full tilt and full of hatred; and the knight, who was strong and brash indeed, struck Perceval such a blow on the shield that he smashed clean through it and the lance-head flashed under his left armpit: had it found flesh it would have killed him. But Perceval, so full of knightly qualities, struck a lance-blow on his shield likewise, and with such ferocity that neither hauberk nor shield – nor anything else he might have worn – could have saved him from feeling the iron head pierce his flesh. And so agonisingly did they collide – bodies and heads and shields together – that they were knocked almost senseless, and their reins and shield-straps flew from their hands and they brought each other down with such a crash that you could have ridden a league before they came to. But as soon as they could they jumped up and took their shields by the straps and drew their swords and came at each other; and the knight, who was full of strength and might, clutched his naked sword and set his shield and attacked Perceval in a fury. Perceval thrust out his shield, and the knight struck it so fiercely that he split it right down to the boss; the blow was so mighty that it sent flowers and gemstones[7] flying to the ground: it would surely have wounded him, but the sword turned in his hand and was deflected. This inspired Perceval to greater strength and courage, and he came at the knight aiming a blow at his helm; the knight thrust out his shield to parry it, but such was Perceval's rage and hatred that he smashed clean through and gave him a terrible wound in the left shoulder, the force of the blow nearly bringing him to the ground. He attacked him again, and mightily, but the knight fought back like a man who believed himself invincible. But Perceval pressed him so hard that he had to retreat across the field, unable to stand his ground, until Perceval had his helmet off and was about to cut off his head. Then the knight begged for mercy in God's name, that he might spare his life, and he would accept imprisonment wherever Perceval might decree. When Perceval heard his plea for mercy he did not deign to touch him further but drew back, and told him that he must swear upon holy relics that he and his damsels would declare themselves the prisoners of King Arthur. He made him promise also to take the damsel whose sweetheart he had killed to Arthur's court and give her into the keeping of the king's nephew Gawain – who would be sure to treat her as she would wish – or at least take her back to her father's house.

'I'll do so willingly, sir,' the knight replied. 'But tell me now, in whose name shall I declare myself a prisoner when I come to the court of the great King Arthur?'

'In the name of Perceval the Welshman,' he replied, 'who has embarked upon the quest of the Grail. But I forgot to say that if you don't find Sir Gawain, give the damsel to the queen, for indeed, I don't think Gawain will be there.'

'Sir,' said the knight, 'I'll do exactly as you wish. But before we go our ways, please come and eat with me: then I'll be all the happier to go where you ask.'

Perceval was famished and said he would gladly do so, and so they returned to the pavilion, where the knight commanded the damsels to give their guest a kind welcome. They did exactly as he asked, and dressed him in a rich mantle. Then the tables were set and they sat down to dine, and there was plenty to eat indeed. When dinner was done they rose, and Perceval called for his arms; they were brought to him and he armed and mounted. The knight did likewise, and bade his damsels mount and the damsel, too, whom Perceval had brought there. And I tell you, she grieved deeply when she took her leave of Perceval, and gave the impression that she would have preferred his company to the knight's; but that could not be, for Perceval had his mind fixed on other matters.

---

7 Enamel and other decorations, usually on a knight's helmet.

And so they parted; and the knight rode on until he came to the court of the great King Arthur. Arthur was in his main hall; and with him was his queen, who was most beautiful, and many fine knights who had come to his court. The knight sent by Perceval came into the hall and greeted the king and queen and all the barons, and said:

'Sire, I surrender to you as your prisoner – and these damsels likewise – and submit to your will in the name of Perceval the Welshman. And he entrusts the damsel you see here to Sir Gawain; if he's not here he wishes the queen to receive her – she's of very noble parentage. And for himself, he sends greetings to you all.'

King Arthur was overjoyed at this; and he made the knight a member of his household and declared him no longer a prisoner. And the queen took the damsel, welcoming her with honour on behalf of her cousin Sir Gawain. And so it was that the knight stayed with King Arthur, and he came to be much loved at the court.

*

Meanwhile Perceval, after leaving the knight, rode on all day without encountering any adventure; evening was near, and he prayed to Our Lord to send him somewhere to lodge, for he had had poor lodging the night before. Then he looked ahead, and through the tangled forest he saw the tip of a tall and handsome tower appear: he was filled with joy and rode swiftly towards it. And when he arrived he saw that it was the most beautiful castle in the world, and the drawbridge was down and the gate wide open: he rode straight in. He came to the mounting-block outside the hall, dismounted, tethered his horse to a ring and climbed the hall steps, fully armed, sword at his side. But when he entered the hall he looked high and low and saw neither man nor woman; he came to a chamber and went inside and looked everywhere, but there was no-one to be seen.

He returned to the hall, very puzzled, and said: 'By God, this is strange: by the way the hall is strewn with rushes I can tell it's not long since people were here, but now I can see no-one.'

But then, as he came to the middle of the hall, he noticed, underneath the windows, a chessboard of fine silver, and chessmen upon it of white and black ivory, set up ready for a game. Seeing these handsome chessmen, Perceval walked up and gazed at them for a long while. After looking at them closely he began to handle them, and moved one of them forward on the board. And a piece made a move in reply. Perceval was amazed, and moved another man. Again a piece responded. When Perceval saw this he sat down and began to play; he played, indeed, until the board had checkmated him three times. Perceval was taken aback, and said: 'By the faith I owe Our Lord, this is amazing! I thought I was fairly good at this game, but it's checkmated me three times! I'm damned if it's ever going to mate and disgrace me or any other knight again!'

And he swept the chessmen into the skirt of his mailcoat and strode up to the window, intending to throw them into the water that ran below. But just as he was about to let them go, a damsel cried out from a window above him, saying: 'Knight, your heart has stirred you to great wickedness if you mean to throw those chessmen in the water! Don't do it: it would be very wrong.'

'Damsel,' Perceval replied, 'come down here and I won't throw any.'

'I shan't come,' she said. 'Just do the courteous thing and put them back on the board.'

'What do you mean, damsel?' said Perceval. 'You want me to do you a favour, but you won't do one for me? By Saint Nicholas, unless you come down I'm throwing them out!'

Hearing this, the damsel said: 'Put the chessmen back, sir knight: I'll come down rather than have you throw them.'

Perceval was delighted, and returned to the board and put the pieces back; and they set themselves in place again more perfectly than any man could ever have done. Then the damsel entered through a chamber door, and fully ten girls with her; and four servants, too, who were well trained, for as soon as they saw Perceval they ran forward to help him from his armour: they took his helmet from his head, his boots from his feet and his mailcoat from his back, leaving him entirely undressed – and I tell you, he was the most handsome knight ever known. And two boys ran and stabled his horse, while a damsel brought him a short mantle of rich scarlet cloth and dressed him, and then led him to the chamber with the young lady of the house who seemed very happy to welcome him – and I assure you, she was the most beautiful damsel in the world. Perceval fell deeply in love with her at first sight, and said to himself that he would be mad not to seek her love, being alone with her as he was. And so he did, wooing her passionately in many ways, until the damsel said:

'Before God, sir, if I thought you meant what you said I'd lend a favourable ear! But indeed, I don't doubt your words, and if you do as I ask I'll grant you my love and make you lord of this castle.'

Perceval was overjoyed at this, and said: 'Damsel, ask me anything in the world and I'll do it! Tell me what you wish.'

And she replied: 'If you can catch the white hart that lives in this forest and bring me back its head, I'll be your love for evermore. And I'll give you a good and faithful hound who'll lead you straight to the hart as soon as you let him go. Follow him fast, cut off the hart's head and bring it to me.'

'Gladly, lady,' Perceval replied. 'I promise you, if God grants me life, I'll do exactly as you ask.'

With that the damsel's servants came forward and set up the tables, and they sat down to dine and were well satisfied. After eating they rose, and Perceval and the damsel walked together in the courtyard until it was time to go to bed. Then the servants came to Perceval and took off his shoes and led him to a beautiful bed they had prepared for him, and Perceval lay down; but

I tell you, he slept very little that night, for he could not stop thinking about the damsel and the task she had set him.

At the crack of dawn next day Perceval rose and armed himself, and two boys brought him his horse and he mounted. Then the damsel came and gave him her hound, and charged him for love of her to take good care of him.

'Before God, damsel,' Perceval replied, 'there's nothing I'd less like to lose than your dog.'

And he sat the hound across his horse's neck in front of him and took his leave of the damsel, and rode away swiftly until he came to the forest, when he put the dog down and let him go. The hound set off on the trail of the hart until he came to a thicket where he started it; and the hart, great, antlered and white as snow, took to flight; and when Perceval caught sight of it he was elated and spurred his horse forward: the whole forest echoed to the sound of its hooves. Why should I make a long story of this? The hound pursued the hart until it gave in, and pinned it down by its legs. Then Perceval, overjoyed, swiftly dismounted and cut off its head, and thought he would hang it from his saddle. But just as he was about to tie it on, an old woman came galloping up on a palfrey, seized the hound and rode off with it. Perceval was furious, and jumped on his horse and spurred after her; when he caught up with her he grabbed her by the shoulders and made her stop, saying: 'Give me back my dog, lady – it's very wrong of you to take off like this.'

When the wicked old woman heard his words she said: 'May you be damned for stopping me, sir knight, and saying this hound was yours: I think you've stolen it! I'm going to give it to the one it belongs to, for you've no right to it.'

'Lady,' said Perceval in reply, 'if you don't give it to me kindly I'll get angry and you'll not take it away – and it'll be the worse for you!'

'Dear sir,' she said, 'you can use force upon me, but force is not right. If you'll do as I say, I'll give the hound back without a fuss.'

'Tell me what it is,' said Perceval, 'and I'll do it if I can, for I've no wish to start a fight with you.'

'Ahead of us on this path,' she replied, 'you'll find a tomb with a knight painted on it. Go up and say that the one who painted it was a false rogue! When you've done so, come back to me and I'll give you the hound.'

'I'm not going to lose him for want of this!' said Perceval; and he came to the tomb and said: 'Sir knight, the one who painted you was a false rogue!'

But when he had said this and was on his way back he heard a terrible noise behind him; and looking round he saw a knight galloping towards him on a black horse of amazing size, and he was fully armed in armour blacker than any ink. Perceval was terrified at the sight of him, and crossed himself at once – for indeed, he was frighteningly huge. But as soon as he had made the sign of the true cross he grew in strength and courage; he turned his horse's head towards him and they came charging at each other full tilt. They struck one another such awesome blows that they shattered lances and shields, and

collided, bodies and chests and helms together, so violently that their hearts
erupted inside them and their eyes spun so wildly that they had no idea what
had happened. They lost their reins and shield-straps and plummeted to the
ground with such a crash that their hearts nearly burst: you could have
ridden two leagues before they came to or knew where each other had gone.
But when they recovered their wits and senses they stood up, drew their
swords, clutched their shields and came at each other once again. The knight
of the tomb attacked Perceval in a fury, and dealt him a sword-blow full on
the helm; but it was strong enough to withstand it, and Perceval attacked him
vigorously in his turn, pressing him so hard that he sent him staggering back;
and he struck one blow so mighty that the blade cut through both the helmet
and the hood of the mailcoat, wounding the knight on the left side of his head
and sending him reeling: had the sword not turned in his hand, I tell you, it
would have killed him. But the knight clutched his shield once more and
returned to a fearsome attack, and Perceval again defended; and while they
fought in the middle of the field, a fully armed knight rode up, took the hart's
head and the dog that the old woman was holding, and rode off again
without saying a word. When Perceval saw this he was most distressed, but
he could not go after him because of the knight's mighty attack. Then Perceval's strength and courage grew, and he assailed the knight ferociously. The
knight could take no more and, overawed, ran swiftly back to his tomb; it
opened for him and he dived back in. Perceval was about to dive after him,
but he could not, for the tomb slammed shut behind the knight – with such
force that the earth shook beneath Perceval's feet. He was astounded by what
he had seen, and came up to the tomb and called to the knight three times;
but there was no reply. Perceval, realising he would get no word from him,
returned to his horse and mounted, and rode swiftly after the knight who had
stolen the head and the hound, swearing that he would not rest till he tracked
him down. As he rode he saw the old woman who had sent him to the tomb,
and he spurred towards her and asked her who the knight of the tomb was,
and whether she knew the one who had stolen his dog.

'Sir knight, that's a damnably pointless question,' she replied. 'If you've
lost it, go and find it – it's your business; it's none of mine.'

Hearing she had no intention of helping, Perceval commended her to the
devil and set off again after the knight who had stolen the head and hound.
But he rode and rode for most of that season and heard no news of him.

*

Through the forests and woods he rode and encountered many adventures.
Chance led him one day to the wild forest where his mother and father had
lived, their castle now left to a damsel who was Perceval's sister. When he
came to the forest he did not recognise it at all, for he had not been there for a
very long time. But he made his way as chance led him and came riding up to
the house. When the damsel his sister saw him she ran to his stirrup and said:

'Dismount, sir knight, for you'll have good lodging if you'll care to stay here for the night.'

'Damsel,' Perceval replied, 'I came for no other reason.'

And he dismounted, graciously helped by his sister and two other damsels who were her nieces. They helped him to disarm, too; and when he was out of his armour his sister brought him a most beautiful silken tunic. Then she seated him beside her, and looked long at him and began to weep. Perceval was most upset to see her cry, and asked her the reason for her tears.

'I'll tell you, sir,' she replied. 'I had a brother, a noble young man – I was his full sister: we shared the same father and mother. Our father died when it pleased God – and I tell you, Christ sent the voice of the Holy Spirit to him at his passing – and after his death my brother went off to the court of the great King Arthur. He was very young, sir, and knew nothing of the ways of the world, and my mother was so distressed at his leaving that she fell sick and died of grief. I'm sure he must be burdened by the sin of causing her death.'

And Perceval, hearing this, said: 'Dear sister, know that I am Perceval your brother who left for the court of the great King Arthur.'

When the damsel heard this she was filled with joy and jumped up, weeping, and hugged him and kissed him a hundred times and more, and Perceval kissed her likewise as they rejoiced at their meeting. Then she asked him if he had been to the court of his grandfather, the rich Fisher King.

'Dear sister,' said Perceval, 'I've not been there yet, but I've been seeking it for a long time – for more than three years. And I promise you, I shan't rest until I find it.'

'Dear brother,' she replied, 'may God grant that you earn His favour.'

While they were talking together and delighting in each other's company, the damsel's young servants came into the house, and when they saw her kissing Perceval so passionately they were most distressed, and said she must be mad thus to kiss a stranger. But the damsel called them forward and said: 'Dear servants, know that this is Perceval my brother, who left here when he was very young.'

When the boys heard this they were overjoyed and greeted him with delight.

Later, after they had dined, the damsel called to Perceval and said: 'Dear brother, I'm very worried about you: you're so young, and the knights who roam these parts are very wicked and cruel; they'll kill you if they can to get your horse. Take my advice, dear brother, and leave this weighty task you've undertaken and stay here with me, for it's a great sin to kill another knight, and you're in great danger each day of being killed yourself.'

'Truly, dear sister,' said Perceval, 'I assure you I'd be glad to stay if I'd accomplished the quest I've begun, and as soon as I've done so I'll come back and do all I can to aid and guide you. But until it's accomplished I shan't stay.'

The damsel wept tenderly at his words and said: 'Then I beg you, Perceval, my dear sweet brother, do me the favour I shall ask.'

'Dear sister,' he replied, 'tell me what you wish and I'll do it.'

'I want you to come with me,' she said, 'to the house of an uncle of yours; he's a hermit, and a most worthy man, and he lives here in the forest half a league away. Make confession to him, and take penance for your mother's sake who died because of you, and you may be sure he'll give you the best guidance that he can. And be sure you do as he commands, for he's a most holy man, and came to this land from Jerusalem in the land of Judaea, and was one of the brothers of your father Alain li Gros. And know this: if he prays to Christ that God may guide you to your goal, his prayers may well direct you there; for he told me the most wonderful things about your ancestor, and about Joseph and Enigeus – his mother, Joseph's sister – and about his father Bron, who is known as the Fisher King. And he told me that Bron – your grandfather – has the vessel in which the blood of Our Lord was gathered. This vessel is called the Grail, and he said that Our Lord declared that it should come to you, and that you must search until you find it.'

When Perceval heard his sister's words he was filled with joy, and said he would gladly go to his uncle. He armed at once and mounted, and bade his sister mount a hunting horse that was kept at the house, and they set off together and rode to the hermit's dwelling. When they arrived at his door they rapped the knocker on the wicket gate, and the hermit, who was a most holy old man, came hobbling on his crutch to open it. Perceval and his sister dismounted and entered the hermit's house. But their horses remained outside: they could not come in, for the door was so low that Perceval had to stoop as he entered. The holy man was very surprised to see his niece arrive with a knight, and asked her why she had come with him, and whether he had seized or abducted her. And she replied:

'Dear uncle, this is my brother Perceval – the son of your brother Alain li Gros – who went away to the court of the great King Arthur to receive arms. He did so, thanks be to God, and has them now.'

The worthy man was delighted by her words and said: 'Tell me, dear nephew, have you yet been to the house of the rich Fisher King, who is my father and your grandfather?'

And Perceval replied that he had been in search of it for a long while but had not yet been there.

'Dear nephew,' said the hermit, 'know this: once, when we were seated together at supper, we heard the voice of the Holy Spirit commanding us to go to far-off lands in the West; and it commanded my father Bron to come to these parts, towards the setting sun, and said that to Alain li Gros would be born an heir who would have the Grail in his keeping, and that the Fisher King could not die until you had been to his court – and when you had done so, he would be healed and would bestow his grace and the vessel upon you, and you would be lord of the blood of Our Lord Jesus Christ. Now be sure to behave with all honour, and I beg you, have no thoughts of killing other knights, but spare them and bear with them in all kinds of ways for the sake of your mother's soul. And pray to Our Lord to have mercy on you, for it was the grief your mother suffered on your account that killed her. And I beg you, be mindful and ever careful to guard against sin and all misdeeds, for you are of a line devoted to Our Lord, and He has so exalted them that He has given His flesh and His blood into their keeping.'

'Sir,' replied Perceval, 'may God grant that I serve Him always according to His will.'

And the worthy hermit echoed this prayer to Our Lord. Then he told Perceval many good things which I cannot relate, but I can tell you that Perceval stayed with him all that night till morning, when he heard him say mass in his chapel. And when he had heard mass and the hermit had taken off the armour of Our Lord,[8] Perceval came and bowed to him most humbly and took his leave, saying that he wished to resume the quest he had undertaken. The worthy man prayed to Our Lord to grant that he would soon find his father's house; then Perceval left the hermit's cell, went to his horse and mounted, and bade his sister mount likewise; then he set off, leaving the hermit in tears. And Perceval rode swiftly away with his sister, who rejoiced in her brother's company.

As they rode along and were nearing their castle, Perceval stopped beside a cross where he had often played while a boy at his mother's house. And he saw a fully armed knight riding towards him, and as he came he cried at the top of his voice:

'By God, sir knight, you'll not take this damsel away with you unless you fight me for her first!'

Perceval heard him well enough but said not a word in reply, for he was so absorbed in his business that he had no thought for the knight's cries. The knight was deeply angered, and came galloping towards him, lance lowered. He would have struck Perceval if his sister had not cried out to him: 'Perceval dear brother, look out or this knight will kill you!'

Perceval was startled, so preoccupied by thoughts of the damsel who had given him the hound that he had not noticed the knight. But as soon as he did, he turned his horse's head and spurred him straight towards his attacker; the knight did likewise: both were intent upon doing each other harm. The knight struck Perceval's shield with his lance and smashed clean through it; but the mailcoat was strong enough to withstand it, and the shaft of the lance flew into splinters. Perceval returned a blow to the shield with all his strength: neither shield nor mailcoat could stop the lance plunging into the knight's chest. Such was the fury of the blow that he was sent flying full

[8] i.e. his vestments.

length to the ground; and such was the fall that his heart burst within him
and he died instantly: neither foot nor hand moved again.

'By God, sir knight,' said Perceval, 'you've brought this upon yourself:
you'd have done better to keep quiet than to come after me like this. But I'm
sorry I've killed you: I'd rather simply have defeated you, for it's a great sin
to kill another knight.'

Then he took the knight's horse and turned away, and rode back to his
sister and gave the horse to her. They set off swiftly and returned to their
manor and dismounted at once. The damsel's servants came to meet them
and took their horses and stabled them: they were very pleased to see them
return, but most surprised about the horse that Perceval had brought back.
They came to him then and very graciously helped him from his armour, and
once he was disarmed the servants set up the table and Perceval dined with
his sister. When he had eaten he lay down to sleep for a while, for he had
stayed up all the previous night; and after a short sleep he rose and called for
his arms and swiftly armed once more. When his sister saw this her heart was
filled with sorrow, and she came to him and said: 'What's this, dear brother
Perceval? What do you mean to do? Are you going to go without me and
leave me alone here in the forest?'

'Dear sister,' he replied, 'if there's any way I can return to you I'll do so,
and then I'll do all in my power to help you as a brother should. But for the
time being I can't stay.'

The damsel was very distressed at this, and wept most tenderly. Perceval
did what he could to comfort her, promising to return as soon as he could; but
then he called for his horse at once and quickly mounted, having no desire to
stay. Then he and his sister commended each other to God; she was weeping
and filled with grief, but there was nothing more she could do.

*

After leaving his sister, Perceval rode on all day without encountering any
adventure; nor did he find anywhere to take lodging. He had to lie that night
in the forest; he took off his horse's harness and let him graze all night on the
grass which was sweet and heavy with dew. Perceval watched over him all
night without sleeping.

At the crack of dawn next morning he rose and harnessed his horse once
more, took up his arms and mounted and rode all day. He greatly enjoyed
that morning: the forest was huge and bursting with green, and he listened
with delight to the birds' joyful dawn chorus. And then, as he rode along, he
looked ahead and saw a knight approaching on a horse, with a damsel beside
him of the most startling appearance ever seen: her neck and face and hands
were blacker than iron, her legs all bent, and her eyes redder than any fire –
and truly, a full hand's width apart. And I promise you, no more than a foot
of her peeped over the saddle-bow, and her feet and legs were so twisted that
she could not keep them in the stirrups. Her hair was tied in a single tress,

which was short and black, looking more like a rat's tail than anything else. But she was riding along most proudly, with whip in hand and one leg cocked elegantly over her palfrey's neck! And as she rode beside the knight she hugged and kissed him sweetly from time to time, as he did her.

When Perceval saw this he stopped and crossed himself in astonishment; then he began to roar with laughter. And when the knight saw him laughing at his sweetheart he was most upset, and rode up to Perceval and asked him what he was laughing about and why he had crossed himself three times.

'I'll tell you,' Perceval replied. 'When I saw that demon riding beside you I crossed myself in fear. And then when I saw her hugging and kissing you I began to laugh at the incongruity! But tell me now – kindly, and don't be angry – where you found her and whether she's a woman or a demon. For truly, I wouldn't spend three days in her company for the whole kingdom of Logres: I'd be afraid she'd strangle or murder me!'

When the knight heard this he turned red with anger, and furiously answered: 'I tell you, knight, nothing could have enraged me more than to hear you mock and laugh at the one I love with all my heart: she's so fair in my eyes that no lady or damsel in the world can match her for beauty. I swear I'll never eat again until I've taken revenge upon you! And if your insult was in her hearing I think she'd die of shame, she's so sensitive – and if she died I'd kill myself for love of her. So I challenge you here and now.'

'I think I can defend myself,' said Perceval, 'if it please God.'

They drew apart, putting the range of two bowshots[9] between them, took their shields by the straps and levelled their lances, then let their horses go and struck each other so mightily that both were sent flying from their saddles. But they leapt to their feet as soon as they could and attacked each other with vigour, exchanging terrible blows with their swords, full on their helms; I tell you, there was little left of their shields: they dealt such sword-blows that it was a wonder they did not kill each other – indeed, they would have done so if they had been as fresh as they were at the outset, but they were so tired that their blows were greatly weakened. But then Perceval gathered new strength and, ashamed that the knight had held out so long, launched such a mighty attack that he wore him down and overpowered him; he brought him down in the middle of the field, and pulled his helmet from his head and hurled it thirty feet and more; he was about to cut off his head, but the knight cried for mercy in God's name and to spare his life. And when Perceval heard him beg for mercy he did not deign to touch him more; he put his sword back in its scabbard and asked the knight his name. He replied that he was called the Handsome Coward.

'By my life, sir,' said Perceval, 'there's truth and falsehood in your name:

---

9   The reference to a bowshot is not strictly accurate, but is an attempt to translate *arpens*, a vague medieval term of measurement implying a distance of a couple of hundred yards. An *arpent* later came to be a measurement of area approximating to an acre.

you're not a handsome bad knight but a handsome good one, so help me God!'

Then Perceval looked at the damsel and could not help but laugh; and he asked the knight what her name was. He replied that she was called Rosete the Fair.

'And I tell you, she's the loveliest damsel known to man, for in addition to her beauty she has the sweetest disposition. I'd sooner lose an eye than lose her, such is the depth of my love.'

'By my faith, knight, then it would be very unkind to deprive you of her. But you must solemnly swear to me that you'll go to the court of the great King Arthur and surrender to him as my prisoner. Take this damsel with you and present her to the queen.'

'I'll do so gladly, sir,' the knight replied, 'for I'd take her to any good court in the world and present her as a noble and worthy lady. But tell me on whose behalf I'm to declare myself prisoner.'

'In the name of Perceval the Welshman,' he said.

'Certainly, sir,' replied the knight. 'Both she and I will do as you wish.'

And with that the knight left Perceval and made his way to Carduel in Wales. Many knights and barons and ladies and damsels were there with the queen, who treated them with great honour. The king had just heard mass with the queen and his barons and returned to the hall, the queen accompanied by Kay the seneschal. She had gone to her chamber; and Kay was leaning at a window when he saw the knight approaching, bringing his sweetheart with him to the court: they were riding very proudly. When he caught sight of the damsel Kay's heart jumped for joy; he leapt down from the window and came running to the queen's chamber, crying:

'Lady! Come and see this! A knight's on his way here, bringing with him the most beautiful damsel ever beheld by man! None of the ladies at your court can remotely match her beauty! In God's name, prepare to honour her and have her stay with you; so help me God, I wish all the ladies of Logres were as lovely as her!'

'I don't, good sir Kay!' the queen replied. 'It would put me in a terrible position! For you and the other knights here would want to take them all away from me!' Then she said to her attendants: 'Let's go and see if this damsel is as beautiful as Kay would have us believe.'

So they came to the windows of the hall; and when they saw the knight and the damsel approaching they were astonished and crossed themselves fervently and began to laugh. The queen called to her maids and, amidst her laughter, said: 'Damsels, Kay obviously loves you dearly, wishing you blessed with such beauty!'

And Kay went to the king and the barons and told them to come and look; and they joined the queen at the windows and began to laugh and joke. And when the queen told them what Kay had wished, they all burst into peals of delighted laughter.

Just then the knight arrived and dismounted outside the hall, and he took the damsel in his arms and gently helped her from her palfrey. Into the hall they came together, hand in hand, and walked towards King Arthur; and the knight stopped in the middle of the hall and greeted the king and all his barons on behalf of Perceval the Welshman and declared himself a prisoner in his name.

'And my sweetheart Rosete with her shining face, whom I love more than my own life, he has sent to the queen to stay with her in her chambers.'

When Kay the seneschal heard this he could not contain himself, and said to the queen: 'Thank him, lady, on bended knees! What a gift he's given you today! It'll bring you and the damsels of your chambers eternal honour! Mind you, if you keep her with you I'm afraid the king might love her as much as you!'

Then he begged the king, by the faith he owed him, to ask the knight where he had found her, and if there were more like her that he could have if he went there. The king was angered by Kay's words and said: 'By the faith you owe God, Kay, stop this now: it's very wrong to mock a stranger. It does you no good at all – it earns only hatred.'

'Sire,' Kay replied, 'I don't mean any harm: I'm saying it for the knight's own good, for truly, if I were to take her to some other court I'd be afraid they'd abduct her!'

The king was furious at this, and said: 'Kay, if only you realised the effect of your words. I forbid you to say more.'

And he walked up to the knight and embraced him and declared him free from imprisonment, and said he wished him to be a member of his household from that time on, and that the damsel should join the queen in her chambers.

Kay the seneschal could not restrain himself; he said: 'Sire, you'd better declare her out of bounds to the barons! They'll all be after her for her beauty! And if she were mistreated I'm sure that knight would sue you! And I'm damned if I'd defend you!'

When Arthur heard this he was filled with rage and said: 'Kay, you have a cruel and biting tongue. By the faith I owe God and the soul of my father Utherpendragon, were it not for the promise I made to your father Entor, you wouldn't be my seneschal.' Then he bowed his head and said to himself: 'But I must bear with him, for whatever faults he has came from the woman who nursed him when he was taken from his mother for my sake.'

Then Kay came up, looking very angry, and said: 'I'm damned if I'll ever look after him – it's up to you.'

And so, as you have heard, the damsel stayed at the court of the great King Arthur. And know this: she became thereafter the most beautiful damsel anywhere.

Now the book says that when Perceval left the knight, he wandered for a very long while from land to land and castle to castle, but could never find the house of his grandfather. He encountered many adventures, however, and one day, as he was riding through a great forest, he looked ahead and saw one of the most beautiful meadows in the world. Beside this meadow was a pleasant ford, and beyond the ford stood a pavilion. Perceval rode swiftly towards it, and came to the ford and was about to ride in; but just as he was about to let his horse drink, a magnificently armed knight came from the pavilion and galloped towards Perceval, crying:

'By God, sir knight, you'll be sorry you entered that ford: you'll have to pay for your passage!'

And with that he came charging at Perceval, aiming to strike him with his lance; but when he saw that he had neither lance nor shield – for Perceval had been in combat with a knight who had smashed his shield to pieces – he turned back to a damsel who was standing at the door of the tent and told her to bring the knight the lance and shield which were hanging inside, for he felt it would be shameful to joust against a shieldless knight. She did as he commanded and presented them to Perceval – who was very glad to have them. Then the knight called to him to defend himself, for he had done wrong in entering the ford without leave, and to be on his mettle, for he would make him pay if he could. Then they charged furiously at each other and exchanged mighty blows; their lances shattered, and Perceval's blow was so formidable that he sent the knight flying from his horse: he lay stretched out in the middle of the field. The laces of his helmet were broken, and as he fell it flew from his head. Perceval stepped down and dismounted, thinking it dishonourable to fight an unhorsed man; and he attacked him with his sword and dealt him such blows that he vanquished him; and the knight begged for mercy and declared himself his prisoner. But Perceval said he would have no mercy unless he first explained why he forbade men to water a horse at the ford and attacked and abused knights for doing so.

'Sir,' he replied, 'I'll tell you. My name, sir, is Urbain. I'm the son of the Queen of the Black Thorn, and King Arthur knighted me in his hall at Carduel. After he had made me a knight I wandered the country and encountered many knights and did battle with them – and I promise you, I outfought every knight I met. I was riding along one night as chance led me, when it began to rain with all the force God could muster: thunder crashed and the sky was riven by lightning bolts so frightening that I didn't know what to do – I rode as if demons were after me! My horse was so terrified that I couldn't control him – he bore me on, helpless. And then, I tell you, behind me came a tumult so terrible that it seemed as if the trees were being torn from the ground. But in the midst of my despair I saw a damsel ahead of me on a mule, the finest I'd ever seen; she was riding swiftly, but as soon as I saw her I headed after her and tried desperately to catch up, but it was so pitch dark that I could only see her in the lightning flashes that split the sky. I followed her until she rode into one of the most beautiful castles in the world; I spurred after her, and caught up with her just as she entered the castle hall. And when she saw me beside her she came and embraced me, and made me lay aside my arms and gave me the finest lodging that night. I fell in love with her, and plucked up the courage to ask for her love; and she said she would gladly grant it on one condition. I replied that I'd do exactly as she asked, no matter what. And she said that if I'd stay there with her and venture abroad no more, she would be my love. I agreed to this, but said it would grieve me to abandon deeds of chivalry. And she said:

' "Dear friend, you see that ford? Pitch a pavilion there, and prevent any knight who passes this way from seeing the castle beyond, and joust with any who try to water their horses at the ford. That way you can take your pleasure with me and continue to perform knightly deeds."

'I agreed to this, and I've spent almost a year here at the ford with my sweetheart and all the while have had all I could wish. The castle stands just beyond the pavilion, but no man has been able to set eyes upon it except me and my love and the girls who accompany her. In just eight days I'd have completed a year: if those eight days had passed I'd have been the greatest knight in the world; but God has not granted me that honour. And now I'm at your mercy, either to kill me or to let me live; and you can stay here and guard the ford for a year if you wish: if you do stay for a year without being defeated you'll achieve worldly fame.'

'My friend,' Perceval replied, 'I've no intention of staying, but I want you to give up this defence of the ford and stop troubling knights who pass this way.'

'Sir,' said the knight, 'I'll do whatever you wish, for you've clearly got the better of me.'

But while Perceval was speaking to the knight and forbidding him to guard the Perilous Ford, he heard a tumult so great that it sounded as if the whole forest were crumbling into an abyss; and the deafening noise was accompanied by smoke and a darkness so dense that for half a league around no man could have seen his neighbour. And out of the darkness came a mighty, anguished voice that said:

'Perceval the Welshman, we ladies curse you with all our power, for today you've inflicted the deepest woe upon us that we've ever endured. And be sure of this: you'll suffer greatly for it!' Then the voice cried to the knight beside Perceval: 'Be quick!' – meaning he should not linger, and said: 'If you stay longer you'll lose me!'

When the knight heard the voice he was most distressed, and came to Perceval and begged for mercy a hundred times and more; Perceval was bewildered, and asked him why he was so desperate for mercy; and the knight replied: 'Oh, sir knight, in God's name give me leave and let me go!'

Perceval said nothing, filled with wonder at the voice. The knight ran to his horse and was about to mount, but Perceval grabbed him by the skirt of his mailcoat and said: 'By my life, knight, you're not going to escape me like this!'

The knight was distraught, and turned to him and cried for mercy a hundred times more, begging him in God's name not to stop him, for if he stayed longer he would kill himself. Once again the voice rang out, saying: 'Urbain, hurry, or you'll lose me forever!'

When the knight heard this he fainted, and Perceval was dumbfounded and gazed at him in amazement. Then suddenly he found himself surrounded by a vast flock of birds, filling all the air about him; they were blacker than anything he had ever seen, and came flying at his helmet, trying to claw the eyes from his head. Perceval was horrified. Then the knight came out of his swoon, and seeing Perceval surrounded by the birds he leapt up, rejoicing and roaring with laughter, and cried: 'I'm damned if I'm going to help you!'

And he gripped his shield and clutched his sword and attacked Perceval once more; Perceval was enraged and cried: 'So, sir knight, you want to do battle again?'

'I defy you!' said the knight; and they launched themselves at each other in a fury with naked swords. But Perceval had the worst of it, for the birds were pressing so hard upon him that they almost beat him to the ground. It filled Perceval with anger, and clutching his sword in his right hand he struck a bird that was attacking him most fiercely clean through the body, spilling its entrails and bringing it plummeting to the ground. And the moment it fell it turned into a dead woman – and she was the loveliest he had ever seen: Perceval was most distressed when he realised she was dead. The birds that surrounded him drew back and then flew to the body and bore it away into the air. Then Perceval, seeing that he was rid of them, ran towards the knight, who begged him to have mercy in God's name and to spare his life. And Perceval replied: 'Then explain to me the marvel I've just seen.'

'Gladly, sir,' he said. 'Know then that the great noise and tumult you heard was the sound of my damsel destroying her castle out of love for me; and the voice was hers, crying out to me. And when she saw that I couldn't escape you, she turned herself and her damsels into the shape of birds and came here to attack you and rescue me. When I saw them I couldn't help but run to their aid; and we'd have killed you – but I see now that none can harm you: you're a worthy, godly man and one of the finest knights in the world. The one you wounded was my sweetheart's sister – but she's in no danger: she'll now be in Avalon. But I beg you, in God's name, let me go to my damsel: she's waiting for me still.'

At this Perceval began to laugh, and graciously gave him leave. The knight was overjoyed and rushed away – on foot: he forgot all about his horse in his delight at being released. And he had not gone two bowshots[10] before Perceval saw him being led away with the greatest jubilation in the world. Then Perceval came to his horse and mounted, intending to catch up with them, but he was hardly in the saddle before he realised that the damsels and the knight – and even the horse that had been standing beside him – had disappeared. Perceval was astounded; he turned back, saying to himself that it would be madness to go after them.

*

So he left that place and rode on, thinking deeply about his quest – and a good deal about the amazing adventure he had just encountered. He rode all that day without anything to eat or drink, and again he had to spend the night in the forest as he had done the night before.

Next morning he set off again and rode as chance led him; but all that day he journeyed on without finding any adventure or any house where he could lodge. He was most displeased, you may be sure, at finding nothing but hedges and bushes and woods, and he became very downhearted; and as he rode on, deep in troubled thought, it was well past the ninth hour[11] when he looked ahead and saw one of the loveliest trees he had ever beheld: it stood beside a beautiful cross at the meeting of four roads. He headed that way and halted there for a good while. And while he sat gazing at the tree in delight, he saw two naked children climbing from branch to branch, each, he thought, about six years old, and they were hugging each other and playing together. After watching them for a while he called to them, entreating them in the name of the Father, Son and Holy Spirit to speak to him, if they were creatures of God. At that, one of the children stopped and sat down, and said to him:

'Know, enquiring knight, that we are indeed God's creatures; and from the earthly paradise from which Adam was exiled we have been sent by the Holy Spirit to speak to you. You have embarked upon the quest for the Grail, which is in the keeping of your grandfather Bron, known in many lands as the Fisher King. Take the path to your right, and before you leave it, be assured, you will see something that will bring you to the end of your quest – if you are worthy to achieve it.'

When Perceval heard this amazing utterance he paused to think for a moment; and when he looked up again, he could see neither the tree nor the two children – nor the cross that had been there before. It seemed to him the greatest marvel in the world and his heart was filled with wonder; and then he was stricken with fear that they might have been phantoms.

And as he sat there, unsure of what to do and whether to go the way the

[10] See previous note, p. 133.
[11] See note 4 above, p. 120.

children had pointed, he saw an immense shadow coming and going before him: it passed four times or more in a row. Perceval's horse was very alarmed, and snorted and stamped; and Perceval, too, was deeply afraid, and made the sign of the true cross over himself and his horse. And then, out of the shadow, came a voice that said:

'Perceval! Merlin – of whom you have heard so much – sends you word that you should not reject what the children told you, for their advice comes from Our Saviour Jesus Christ. If you are worthy, before you leave the right-hand path to which you have been directed by Our Lord's will, you will fulfil the prophecy that Our Lord made to Joseph.'

When Perceval heard the voice he was filled with joy, and called out to it three times, wanting to speak further. But no answer came; and realising it would say no more, Perceval set off along the path the two children had shown him. The way was clear and open. And I tell you, while it remained so Perceval was most ill at ease, preferring to ride through the forest than along an open road. As he rode along he came upon a glorious stretch of meadow-land, and on the far side lay a beautiful river with handsome mills along its bank. He headed that way, and in the middle of the river he saw three men aboard a boat. As he drew nearer he saw, in the middle of the boat, a very old man lying on rich drapes. This worthy man was his grandfather, the Fisher King. He hailed Perceval and asked him to stay the night with him, and Perceval thanked him deeply. Then the Fisher King said:

'Good sir knight, go upriver and my castle will come into view. I'll head that way myself now: I'd like to be there to greet you.'

So Perceval set off and followed the line of the river, but he looked high and low and could see no sign of the house of the Fisher King. When he failed to find it he was most upset and cursed the fisherman who had sent him that way, saying:

'Damn you, fisherman, for mocking me and telling me tall stories!'

He rode on, troubled and annoyed, until suddenly he saw the tip of a tower peeping between two peaks on the edge of the forest he had crossed that morning. His spirits soared at the sight and he rode towards it, repenting deeply for having cursed the king – though he did not realise who he was. He rode on until he reached the fortress, and saw the river that ran around it, as beautiful as anyone could wish, and the hall and its outbuildings handsomely appointed. Seeing all this, he realised it was the home of a most noble man: it seemed more like the castle of a king than a fisherman, and the closer he came the more splendid it seemed. He came to the gate and found it open and the drawbridge lowered; so he rode in and dismounted at the mounting-block outside the hall. As soon as the boys in the courtyard saw him they ran to meet him, and held his stirrup while he dismounted and helped him to disarm; and they took his arms into the hall while two boys led his horse away and stabled him most handsomely. Then Perceval climbed up to the hall, where a boy dressed him in a mantle of scarlet and took him to be seated

on a splendid bed. Then four of the servants went off into the chamber where
the Fisher King had the Grail in his keeping. And I tell you, the Fisher King
was so old and frail and beset by sickness that he could not move his hands or
feet. He asked the servants if the knight had arrived, and they replied: 'Yes,
sire.'

And Bron said: 'I wish to go to him.'

And the four servants lifted him in their arms and carried him into the hall
where Perceval his grandson was; and when Perceval saw him coming he
rose to meet him and said: 'I'm sorry to put you to such trouble, sir.'

But the king replied: 'I mean to honour you as highly as I can.'

And they sat together on the bed and spoke of several things; and the lord
asked where he had come from that day and where he had lain the night
before.

'So help me God, sir,' said Perceval, 'I lay last night in the forest where I
had very poor lodging: I was uncomfortable indeed – though I was more
concerned for my horse than for myself.'

'I don't imagine,' said the lord, 'that you'd have had quite all you needed!'

Then he called two servants and asked if they could eat, and they replied:
'Yes, in just a moment.'

And they had the tables set at once and the lord and Perceval sat down to
dine.

And as they were sitting there and the first course was being served, they
saw a damsel, most richly dressed, come out of a chamber: she had a cloth
about her neck, and in her hands she carried two small silver platters. After
her came a boy carrying a lance, which shed from its head three drops of
blood. They passed before Perceval and into another chamber. After this
came a boy bearing the vessel that Our Lord had given Joseph in prison: he
carried it in his hands with great reverence. When the lord saw it he bowed
and said the *mea culpa*, as did all the others in the house. And when Perceval
saw it he was filled with wonder and would gladly have asked the question –
but he was afraid of upsetting his host. He kept thinking about it all that
night, but kept remembering how his mother had told him not to talk too
much or to ask too many questions. And so he refrained from asking. The
lord kept turning the conversation in such a way as to prompt the question,
but Perceval said nothing: he was so exhausted from his two sleepless nights
before that he was near to collapsing on the table. Then the boy returned
carrying the Grail, and passed back into the chamber from which he had first
come; and the boy bearing the lance did likewise; and the damsel followed
after – but still Perceval asked nothing. When Bron the Fisher King realised
no question was going to come he was most distressed. He had had the Grail
presented to all the knights who had lodged there, because Our Lord Jesus
Christ had told him he would never be healed until a knight asked what it
was for, and that knight had to be the finest in the world. Perceval himself

was destined to accomplish the task, and if he had asked the question, the king would have been healed.

When the Fisher King saw that Perceval wanted to sleep, he gave orders for the table to be cleared and for a fine bed to be made for his guest. Then he called four servants and said he would go to sleep and rest in his chamber, and took his leave of Perceval, saying he hoped he did not mind but he was an old man and could stay up no longer. Perceval replied that he did not mind at all, and commended him to God. So the Fisher King went to his chamber while Perceval stayed in the hall, his thoughts still fixed on the vessel that he had seen carried with such respect, to which the lord had bowed so deeply along with all the other people of the house. He was even more amazed by the lance which had shed three drops of blood from its head, and he decided he would ask the boys about it in the morning before he left. He had been pondering on this for a long while when three servants came and helped him from his shoes, and put him to bed most graciously. When he lay down he felt very tired, and slept till morning.

When morning came he rose, and when he was dressed and ready he went through the house and into the courtyard – but saw neither man nor woman. He returned to the house – and still found no-one. He was most disturbed. Then he looked up and saw his arms; so he armed and went out to the stable; he found it open, and his horse freshly groomed and harnessed and saddled. He was very puzzled, and mounted swiftly and rode from the stable, and when he looked ahead he saw that the gate was open. It occurred to him that the boys might have gone into the wood to gather herbs and other things they needed; so he decided to go after them, and if he found one of them he would ask the significance of the vessel he had seen carried through the hall, and why people had bowed so deeply to it, and by what marvel the lance bled from the tip of its head.

So off he went, and kept riding through the forest until prime;[12] but he found neither man nor woman to speak to, and was most distressed. On and on he rode, so burdened with troubled thought that he almost fell from his horse. He went on riding until, deep in the heart of the forest, he caught sight of a damsel who was the most beautiful woman any man could find; and she was weeping most tenderly and grieving bitterly. And as soon as she saw Perceval she cried at the top of her voice:

'Perceval the wretched! Damn you! You don't deserve an ounce of luck! You were at the house of your grandfather the rich Fisher King, and saw pass before you the vessel that contains Our Lord's blood, which is called the Grail. Three times you saw it pass, but still you didn't have the wit to ask about it! I tell you God hates you: it's a wonder He doesn't strike you dead!'

Hearing this, Perceval came riding towards her, begging her in God's

---

12 The first canonical hour: six o'clock in the morning.

name to tell him the truth about what he had seen. And she said: 'Didn't you lie last night at the house of your grandfather Bron, that man of such high lineage? And didn't you see the Grail and the other relics pass before you? Know then that if you'd asked what the Grail was for, your grandfather the king would have been healed of his infirmity and restored to health, and the prophecy that Our Lord made to Joseph would have been fulfilled. And you would have had your grandfather's blessing and your heart's deepest desire – and the blood of Christ in your keeping. After your death you would have joined the company of Christ's chosen ones, and the enchantments and evils which now beset the land of Britain would have been cast out. But I know why you've lost all this. It's because you're not wise or worthy enough, and have done too few deeds of arms and prowess and too few acts of goodness to have the precious vessel in your keeping.'

Perceval was astounded by the damsel's words, and so distressed that he began to weep; and he said he would not rest until he had found his grandfather's house and asked everything just as the damsel had said. With that he left her, commending her to God; and she, in tears, did likewise. And he rode back along the path that he thought would take him to the house of his grandfather the Fisher King; but he was way off the track, and rode on in great dejection. Two days and nights he rode, with nothing to eat except apples and other fruit he found in the forest, and he prayed to Our Lord for guidance.

*

After riding a whole day without encountering any adventure, he looked ahead and saw one of the loveliest damsels in the world, and beside her was tethered the most beautiful palfrey. And above the palfrey, tied to the branch of a tree, was the head he had cut from the white hart. Perceval was filled with joy; he galloped up and, without a word to the damsel, seized the head and pulled it from the tree. She was furious at this and cried: 'Knight, put down my lord's head – I tell you, if you take it away it'll be the worse for you!'

But Perceval began to laugh and said: 'Damsel, I've no intention of putting it down! I'm taking it to the one to whom I've pledged it.'

But while he was speaking to her he saw a doe running towards him in great alarm, and his hound behind her in hot pursuit; it caught her by the legs, and the doe was so terrified that she came to Perceval and the damsel as if begging for mercy. Perceval was overjoyed to see his hound, and took him on to his horse and stroked him with the greatest affection. As he was doing so, he saw the knight who had stolen him riding his way. As soon as he caught sight of Perceval he cried in anger: 'By God, you worthless knight, you'll be sorry you took my dog!'

Perceval thought him mad and said: 'You're crazy to call him yours: you wickedly stole him from me.'

At this the knight challenged him, and Perceval did likewise; and they drew apart and then spurred into such a furious charge that the whole wood resounded; and they struck each other such mighty blows that neither could save himself from crashing to the ground. But they leapt up instantly and drew their swords in a fury. They did combat for a long while, from noon till none.[13] I tell you, Perceval was exhausted, and so was the knight; but Perceval found new strength and, ashamed that the knight had resisted so long, raised his sword and brought it down from on high with such force that he split his shield in two, right down to the boss: such a great and fearsome blow it was that it crashed down on his helmet; it could not pierce the steel, but went plummeting down, stripping more than a hundred rings from the mailcoat, smashing off a spur and plunging two feet into the earth. The blow filled the knight with the utmost terror, and he realised that if Perceval dealt him another like it he would kill him. He drew back and begged him for mercy in God's name, and to spare his life whatever he might have done. And Perceval said: 'Then tell me why you stole my hound, and who the knight was I was fighting when you took him, and whether you know the old woman who sent me to the tomb.'

'I will indeed,' said the knight. 'I'll tell you everything.'

'If you do,' said Perceval, 'you needn't fear death.'

'Know then,' the knight replied, 'that the one who came from the tomb was my brother, and he was one of the finest knights to be found anywhere, until a beautiful fairy fell in love with him, smitten by his obvious prowess. And the moment my brother set eyes on her he was so love-stricken that he almost lost his senses whenever he was with her. The time came when she told him there was somewhere she wished to take him, and he agreed to go with her, provided it wouldn't cost him his knighthood. She promised it was a place where he could engage more in deeds of arms than any man, for it was frequented by all the knights of Arthur's court. And she led him to this forest where, beside the path you saw when you passed the tomb, they found one of the most beautiful meadows in the world. They dismounted, and spread cloths on the grass and ate together with great pleasure. When they had eaten my brother lay down to sleep; and after sleeping as long as he wished he awoke, and found himself in a magnificent castle with knights and ladies and damsels all ready to serve him. This castle stands beside the tomb, but it's invisible; and it was from there that the knight rode when he came to do battle with you. As for the old woman who directed you to the tomb, I tell you, when she wishes she's the most beautiful damsel you ever saw: it was she who placed the tomb there, and she's the very one who led my brother into the forest. I promise you, everything I've told you is true.'

[13] See note 4 above, p. 120.

Perceval was thrilled by the story, and said: 'By God, it's the most amazing thing I've ever heard!'

Then he asked the knight if he could direct him to the house of the rich Fisher King, but he replied: 'I've no idea where it is, truly, and I've never heard of any knight finding it – though I've seen plenty searching!'

Then Perceval asked him if he knew who the damsel was who had given him the hound, and the knight replied that he knew her well.

'She's the sister of the damsel that my brother loves. That's why she entrusted the dog to you – she was well aware that her sister would lead you to fight her sweetheart. You must understand that she despises her because of him, for he's brought to grief every knight who passed this way, and the damsel who gave you the dog knew that sooner or later a knight would come who'd avenge all the others.'

Then Perceval asked if it was far to her castle, and he said: 'If you keep to this path here to the left, you'll reach it before nightfall.'

Perceval was overjoyed at this, and set off at once. But he first made the knight promise to declare himself a prisoner to the great King Arthur, to which he agreed, and he made his way to Arthur's court and submitted to him in the name of Perceval the Welshman, and the king gladly accepted him into his company and declared him free of imprisonment.

*

Meanwhile Perceval, after leaving the knight, rode swiftly on until he came to the castle of the damsel who had given him the hound. She was at the windows of the tower, and as soon as she saw him coming she came down to meet him and welcomed him with the greatest joy, saying: 'Sir knight, I was about to be angry with you! I wouldn't have been without my hound so long for anything, if I'd had my way.'

'Damsel,' Perceval replied, 'I couldn't help it: there are very good reasons for my delay.'

Then he told her the whole story from start to finish: of the old woman who had stolen the dog and how she had sent him to the tomb; how he had done battle with the knight and vanquished him, and how the knight had fled back into the tomb; how the other knight had taken the dog and how he had searched for it, not wanting to return without it; and how he had tracked the knight down in the wood and defeated him in combat. He told her everything exactly as it had happened, relating all the hardships he had endured since he left her. The damsel was delighted by the story, and pardoned him very graciously. She had him disarm, and then took him with her most welcomingly, saying:

'Since you've vanquished the one I hated so much, my sister's sweetheart, I wish to be at your command evermore: you shall be lord of this castle, and I'd have you stay here with me forever.'

But Perceval was downcast at this, and excused himself as kindly as he could, for he had no desire to stay.

'Damsel,' he said, 'I'm eager to do your will: I'll do whatever you reasonably ask. But at the court of the great King Arthur I vowed to lie no more than one night wherever I took lodging until I'd fulfilled my quest. I'd have you honour this.'

At this time it was the custom that a man would rather be beheaded than break his oath, and when the damsel heard his words she said: 'Truly, sir, anyone who made you break your promise would be no friend to you: I wouldn't dare to plead against what you've said. But I'd ask this much: that if God grants you success in your quest, you'll return to me swiftly.'

'Damsel,' he replied, 'there's no need to ask! There's nothing I desire so much as to spend time with you, if God grants that I achieve my goal.'

With that he asked her leave and called for his arms. Hearing this, she said: 'In God's name, sir, what do you mean? Won't you stay with me tonight?'

'It's impossible, lady,' he replied. 'I'd be breaking my oath, for I've already lain here before.'

The damsel was desperately upset, but saw there was nothing she could do; so she commended him to God – weeping as she did so, for she would much rather he had stayed than gone. But Perceval had no desire to sin, and Our Lord was not willing to let him. So he left her, and once he was on his way he rode at great speed, and slept that night in the forest.

*

And I tell you, after that he rode for seven years through the lands and forests in search of adventures, and every adventure and marvel and test of chivalry he encountered he brought to a successful outcome. And in those seven years he sent more than a hundred prisoners to the court of the great King Arthur. But for all the wonders he found and the things he saw, he could not find the house of his grandfather the rich Fisher King, and he became so distracted and lost his senses and memory to such a degree that in those seven years he gave no thought to God and never set foot in any holy church or minster. And on the day of the blessed cross when Our Lord suffered death for sinners, Perceval was riding along, fully armed, ready to defend himself and to do others damage if he met with a challenge; but what he met was a band of ladies and knights with heads bowed, wrapped in cloaks and hoods, praying to Christ for forgiveness for their sins. They stopped him and asked what could possibly be the matter, that on the day when Our Lord suffered on the cross he should be armed and ready to kill men and to seek adventures. When Perceval heard them speak of God he was brought back to his senses by the will of Christ, and he deeply repented of his long madness and swiftly disarmed. And the story says that, by the will of God, he found his way to the house of his uncle the hermit, where his sister had once taken him to make confession. And he made confession now, and accepted the penance he imposed, and stayed with him for two months.

But Chrétien de Troyes says nothing of this – nor do the other trouvères who have turned these stories into jolly rhymes. But we tell only what matters to the story: the things that Merlin dictated to his master Blaise who lived in Northumberland, and who was so old that he could barely support himself. Merlin saw and knew exactly what befell Perceval each day, and he had Blaise record these adventures for the worthy people who would be eager to hear them told. And we find in Blaise's writings, dictated with authority by Merlin, that Perceval stayed at his uncle's house for two months. Now, by the time he arrived there, his sister had died and passed from this world. He said: 'Sir, I'm going to go and see my sister, for I love her dearly.'

And when the hermit heard this he began to weep, and replied: 'Dear nephew, you'll never see her again, for she died a year and a half ago. I was most upset when I heard of her death, and went and had her brought back here, and buried her outside my house.'

When Perceval heard his sister had passed away he was filled with grief: he could not have stopped weeping for all the gold in the world. And he said to his uncle: 'In God's name, sir, take me to where my sister lies, who loved me so much.'

'Gladly,' said the worthy man, and he led him straight to her tomb and said: 'Dear nephew, this is where your sister lies buried.'

At this Perceval began to weep; and together they said prayers for her soul. After they had prayed the hermit said to him: 'Dear nephew, why don't you go to your family home – to the house of Alain li Gros, your father and my brother? You are its master now.'

'So help me God, sir,' he replied, 'I wouldn't go there for all King Arthur's kingdom! It would grieve me terribly to see my father's house bereft of loved ones, for I wouldn't find a soul there that I knew.'

'It wouldn't be like that, dear nephew, truly,' said the hermit; but Perceval said: 'Uncle, I'm going now by your leave. And I tell you, I'll never rest until I've found the house of my grandfather – your father.'

When the hermit heard this he said: 'Dear nephew, I shall pray to Our Lord, the Lord God Jesus Christ, that He may guide you there.'

*

With that Perceval took his leave and departed, and rode on through the forest until the eighth day of Pentecost. All that day he rode till none[14] without encountering any adventure; then he looked ahead and saw four squires riding along, each with a shield slung at his neck. They were leading horses and packhorses by the bridle, and pulling a cart laden with lances. As

14 See note 4 above, p. 120.

soon as he saw them Perceval spurred after them, and asked where they were taking all that equipment and in whose service they were.

'Good sir,' they replied, 'we serve Melian de Lis, and we're on our way to the tournament that's taking place at the White Castle, home of one of the loveliest damsels in the world. All who've seen her swear that if the beautiful features of all the world's ladies were combined in one they wouldn't match hers! And her beauty is equalled by her wealth. Many knights have asked for her hand, and counts and dukes and other lords, but she refuses to listen to any of them! But now the lady of the White Castle has announced a tournament to be held in the presence of this illustrious daughter of hers, with the promise that whoever wins the tourney will have the damsel – no matter how poor a young knight he may be, for she will make him a rich man, placing her and all she possesses at his command. I tell you, whoever God blesses with such fortune will be the wealthiest man in the world and the best provided in the land of Britain, except King Arthur. That's why Sir Melian de Lis is going there, for he's been in love with her for a good while and longs to win the tournament and have the damsel for his wife.'

Then Perceval asked them when they thought the tournament would be, and they replied: 'In three days from now, good sir.'

And he asked if there would be many knights there. One of the boys laughed and said: 'There's no need to ask that, sir knight! For the tournament was announced at the court of the great King Arthur, and I know for sure that all the knights of the Round Table will be coming, for they all returned at Pentecost from the quest of the Grail where they've had no success at all. King Arthur held the greatest feast at Pentecost that he's ever done, and that's when the tourney was announced; and I tell you, more than five thousand will be coming from his court. I know Sir Gawain's coming, and Lancelot of the Lake, and Kay the seneschal and Bedivere; and Mordred and Guirres and Garries, Sir Gawain's three brothers. Kay the seneschal boasted before all the barons that he would win her hand by deeds of arms and bring her back to Arthur's court! The knights found this hilarious and ludicrous, and even King Arthur – after a stern rebuke – kept mocking him. The king also said that if Perceval heard of the tournament he'd be there, and that he'd find no-one who could withstand him, for he's sent more than a hundred and fifty knights as prisoners to Arthur's court. The king's very upset that Perceval's not there with him now, and is sure he's dead. We've told you the truth about what you asked: now tell us if you'll come with us.'

Perceval replied that he wouldn't for the time being, and the boy said: 'You're right, so help me God, for it wouldn't help you much in achieving your goal.'

And with that the boys left Perceval and continued their journey. Perceval headed the other way, but thought he would make for the tournament. He rode on at a walk until evening, when he looked ahead along the path and saw a modest vassal's house, all enclosed by a wall. Perceval was very pleased to find this, and rode swiftly up and found the nobleman sitting on the bridge, and six boys with him, all watching passers by on their way to the tournament. As soon as the gentleman saw Perceval approaching he stepped forward to greet him, welcoming him heartily and gladly offering him lodging. Perceval was delighted and thanked him deeply and dismounted at once. The boys jumped up and helped him to disarm, and one took his horse to the stable and made him as comfortable as he could while the others took his arms to a chamber, leaving him quite undressed. The gentleman looked at him in admiration, for he was the most handsome knight in the world, and muttered to himself, out of Perceval's hearing: 'It would be a great shame if such a handsome knight lacked valour.'

Then two boys came and dressed him in a mantle, and he sat beside the gentleman and watched the stream of knights and equipment that was passing that way. He asked him if it was far to the White Castle, and he replied: 'You'll be there in the morning before prime.'[15]

Then Perceval asked: 'Have many knights passed by today on their way to the tourney?'

'Just before you arrived,' he replied, 'the knights of Arthur's court came by. I tell you, there were more than five hundred in the company, with the most magnificent equipment you ever saw.'

When Perceval heard this he was overjoyed. They sat there until nightfall, when the gentleman asked his servants if they could eat soon, and they said: 'Yes, in just a moment.'

So he went up to the hall, taking Perceval by the hand and treating him with the greatest honour. He gave orders for the tables to be set and it was done at once. And when all was ready his wife came from her chamber, accompanied by her two daughters, who were beautiful, intelligent and well-mannered girls. They gave Perceval a most noble welcome, and were seated at the table beside him. The lady and her daughters paid Perceval a deal of attention that night: they were sure they had never seen a knight so handsome. After they had dined the table was cleared away, and the gentleman asked Perceval if he had come that way because of the tournament. Perceval replied: 'I was only told about it yesterday by Melian de Lis's squires: they were on their way there with his equipment.'

'He's the one for whom the tournament's being held!' the gentleman said. 'The vespers[16] are due to take place tomorrow. If I may be so bold, I'd ask you to come with me.'

'Dear host,' Perceval replied, 'I'd be glad to repay you by doing so, but I'll not take up arms tomorrow at any price.'

'I shan't press you against your will,' he said.

---

[15] See note 12 above, p. 142.
[16] Preliminary engagements, effectively a practice session, usually held the day before a tournament proper.

Then the beds were prepared, and four boys took Perceval to lie in a splendid bed until the next morning, when the boys were soon up and about in the courtyard; and as soon as Perceval saw it was light he arose to find that the gentleman of the house was already up; and they went to hear mass in a most handsome chapel. And when mass had been sung they returned to the hall and ate with great pleasure, after which the gentleman went down to the yard and called for the horses to be made ready. He had Perceval's arms loaded on a packhorse; then they mounted at once and went to see the tournament.

It had begun with fearsome vigour. Before they even got there the tourneyers' banners had appeared on the field; there were so many handsome shields and magnificent horses to be seen, and splendid arms and rich silken banners: never in Arthur's time had a tournament been graced with so much fine armour and so many fine knights. And I tell you, Melian de Lis had ridden onto the field magnificently armed, with a gold shield superbly emblazoned with two lions, and around his arm was tied the sleeve of the damsel of the castle. With the utmost pride he rode, accompanied by fifty knights in splendid array. Then the heralds cried:

'On with your helms!'

– at which there was a great roar, and the hearts of cowards trembled. You never saw a tournament engaged with such fury: Melian de Lis went charging ahead of everyone, faster than an arrow from a bow, desperate to impress his love with his chivalry; and as soon as Sir Gawain saw him he charged to meet him, and they came at one another faster than a falcon or a swallow and exchanged such awesome blows with their lances that their shields split and shattered; but the lances were stopped by their mailcoats and the broken shafts flew skywards, and they rode past each other, heads held high, neither having lost his stirrups.

Then the companies assembled rapidly, and charged at each other to strike through shield and mailcoat; and when lances splintered, swords were drawn. There you would have seen the most fearsome tournament ever witnessed, with banners charging one at another in more than five hundred places. Melian de Lis charged time and again, winning horses and sending them back to the damsel in the castle, much to her delight. On the wall of the White Castle, I promise you, more than three hundred ladies and damsels stood watching, pointing out to each other the most accomplished knights, inspiring all those involved in the tournament to drive themselves to the limit. Sir Gawain and Lancelot and the knights of the Round Table were ploughing through the battle-lines, toppling every knight they met; and on the other side Melian de Lis and his company were performing wonders. The tournament continued until nightfall when it finally broke up. Sir Gawain and Yvain and Lancelot and Kay the seneschal had all done brilliantly, but so had Melian de Lis, and the ladies of the castle did not know who should have the prize: they said they had all performed so well that they could not choose a winner. The damsel said that Melian de Lis had done best, but her mother, the lady of the White Castle, did not agree, and most of them declared in favour of Gawain. A great argument broke out, until the damsel said: 'Tomorrow we'll see who's the finest and who should have the prize!'

They left it at that. And Melian de Lis entered the castle, as did Sir Gawain and Lancelot and Kay the seneschal and the knights of the Round Table; and I tell you, such magnificent lodging was never seen at any tournament.

Meanwhile, when the vespers tourneying broke up, Perceval returned with his host to his castle, which was not far away; and as soon as they dismounted boys came out to meet them, and took their horses away and stabled them splendidly. Perceval and his host took each other by the hand and climbed up to the hall, where the gentleman called for the table to be set, which was done at once, and they sat down to dine. Then he began to talk of the tournament, and asked Perceval who he thought had done best; and Perceval replied that the one with the gold shield with the two lions had performed like a very good knight, but the one with the white shield had done best of all.

'The one with the gold shield with the two lions,' said his host, 'was Melian de Lis, and the knight with the white shield was King Arthur's nephew Gawain.'

'I wouldn't exchange donning my arms and jousting tomorrow,' said Perceval then, 'for a mound of gold as big as this castle! And, by God, I'd like Gawain and Melian de Lis to fight on the same side, so that I could joust against them!'

When the gentleman and his daughters heard this they were overjoyed, and he said to Perceval: 'I'll take up arms, too, out of love for you, and accompany you tomorrow!'

Perceval was delighted and thanked him heartily. And so it was agreed; and soon the time came for them to take to their beds.

They slept till morning when Perceval and his host arose and went to hear mass in the chapel; and after mass they returned to the hall and breakfasted on bread and wine. Then the elder of the gentleman's daughters came and asked Perceval out of love for her to wear her sleeve at the tournament. He was pleased indeed, and said that out of love for her he hoped to do greater feats of arms that day than he had ever done before: her father was filled with joy. Then the boys mounted with all the equipment, and Perceval and his host did likewise, and off they rode to the White Castle.

By the time they reached the place where the tourneyers were lodged they were arming and some were already mounted. They looked at all the knights, and the ladies and damsels who had climbed up to the walls, and when Perceval saw they were all preparing he called for his arms and clad himself in splendid armour that he had borrowed from his host – he did not want to use his own because he wished to go unrecognised. And know this: Melian de Lis had lodged that night with Sir Gawain, and they had brashly determined to smash the outsiders.[17] The damsels were not pleased, for the day before he had been against Sir Gawain; but the lady's daughter was willing to forgive them, saying that the outsiders had gained three new banners since the previous day, so the castle company would struggle without Melian's help. The outsiders were dismayed at the news, but Saigremor said it was not going to stop him engaging; and when Perceval heard the news he was elated, and said to his host: 'They'll wish they'd stayed out of it altogether!'

Then the tourneyers came riding from the castle, and both sides deployed in magnificent array. As soon as they were in order the squires and heralds cried:

'On with your helms!'

And at that cry you would have seen both sides surge forward, and the knight with the swiftest horse was a happy man indeed. Melian de Lis went charging ahead of them all, and Perceval's heart leapt at the sight of him. He charged to meet him furiously, the damsel's sleeve on his arm; and when the damsels on the wall saw him they all said together: 'Look there – the most handsome knight you ever beheld!'

They came galloping with all the speed their mounts could summon, and shattered their lances on their shields, the splinters flying skyward; and Perceval, brimming with strength and courage, struck him so mightily on chest and helm that he sent him crashing to the ground, almost breaking his neck; his right arm indeed was broken in two, and he fainted with the pain fully fourteen times. Perceval had spurred to such a speed that as he galloped on past he met Kay the seneschal, and struck him such a blow that he did not know whether it was day or night, and sent him flying from his horse and left him stretched out on the ground. When the outsiders saw Perceval's wondrous feat of chivalry they went spurring after him; Sir Gawain and Lancelot charged to meet them, and the companies clashed so mightily that they made the earth tremble. Saigremor the Rash, who had joined the outsiders, fought splendidly, and performed such feats of arms that day that he earned the praise and admiration of all who saw him. Lancelot and Sir Gawain for their part fought awesomely, and made the battle-lines buckle before them. But Perceval surpassed all other knights, bringing horse and rider crashing to the ground whenever he met an opponent; and the ladies and damsels on the wall said that the woman who had given him her sleeve had chosen well, for whoever won that knight's love should count herself lucky – he toppled every knight he met. So said the damsels who were watching from the tower. Sir Gawain was most upset at seeing Perceval do such damage to his company, and he collected a lance from a squire and came charging at him; but when Perceval saw him he showed little fear, even

---

[17] In the early thirteenth century a tournament was a mass combat of knights divided into two or more teams. Here it is being fought between a company from the castle and 'those outside'.

though he knew Gawain to be a most worthy knight. They exchanged great blows on their shields – their lances shattered and flew into splinters – and they struck each other mightily as they passed; Sir Gawain had the worst of it, both he and his horse crashing to the ground, and his horse broke his neck and died.

The castle company were aghast at this and turned tail, and when Sir Gawain saw his side in flight he was distraught, and leapt to his feet and drew his sword, and a knight cried out: 'By God, sir knight, so you're holding out against us!'

And he flung himself at Gawain, intent on tearing the helmet from his head; Gawain was incensed and came to meet him, and raised his sword and dealt the knight such a terrible blow that he clove his head right down to the teeth and struck him to the ground. He grabbed the knight's horse and mounted and galloped after his men, bringing down four knights on the way. But his side had all rushed into the castle, the outsiders pursuing them right to the gates, taking a good deal of equipment and horses and prisoners.

As soon as the victory was complete, Perceval came to his host and presented him with three of the finest horses he had captured, asking that his daughter should have them in return for the sleeve he had worn. His host thanked him deeply, and then Perceval said: 'Let's go now, sir, for I'd like to lodge with you again tonight.'

As Perceval and the gentleman and his squires were making their way back, they saw a man approaching, old and bearded but decently dressed, and carrying a scythe on his shoulder: he appeared to be a reaper. He came to meet them, grabbed Perceval's horse by the reins and said: 'You silly fool! You shouldn't be tourneying!'

Perceval was astounded and said: 'What's it to do with you, old man?'

'A lot,' he replied. 'It matters to me and to others. It's your business, and mine, and other men's – and mine more than anyone's, I assure you.'

Perceval, thoroughly taken aback, asked him: 'Who are you?'

And the man replied: 'I'm the son of one you barely know – he knows you better than you know him. But I tell you, no man benefits from his knowing them – it's likely to bring nothing but grief!'

Perceval was bewildered by his words and said: 'Would you explain yourself if I dismounted?'

'There's something I'd tell you,' he replied, 'but not in front of others.'

Perceval was relieved at this, and said to his host: 'Carry on, good sir, and wait for me at your house. I'm going to talk to this worthy man and then I'll follow you.'

'Gladly, sir,' his host replied, and rode away, leaving Perceval with the old man. He stepped up to him and asked him who he was, and he replied: 'I'm a reaper, you can see.'

'Then who told you so much about me?' Perceval asked.

'I knew your name,' he answered, 'before you were born.'

Perceval was amazed and said: 'I implore you in God's name, tell me what this is about. What's your business? Tell me, for God's sake, I beg you.'

'I won't lie to you,' the old man said. 'My name is Merlin, and I've come from Northumberland to speak to you.'

Perceval was astonished and said: 'By God, Merlin, I've heard so much about you and what a great seer you are. So tell me, in God's name, how I can find the house of the rich Fisher King.'

'I will indeed,' Merlin replied. 'Know this: God has set obstacles in your path because of your broken vow. You swore you'd lie no more than one night at any lodging, but you've spent two nights at that gentleman's house and were intending to spend another now!'

'I'd completely forgotten!' said Perceval.

'Then it's easier to forgive you,' Merlin answered. 'I'll put you on a path to your grandfather's house that'll bring you there in less than a year.'

'In God's name, Merlin,' Perceval said, 'can't you get me there sooner?'

'It's simple and not simple,' Merlin replied. 'You could be there by tonight, but you'll make it in under a year. But don't be a fool when you get there: make sure you ask about the things you see.'

'I will indeed, sir,' said Perceval, 'if God grants that I reach that house.'

'I'm going now,' said Merlin. 'I'm not saying any more to you, but your faith should now be stronger. And when the time comes that you have Christ's vessel in your keeping, I'll bring my tutor who's recorded your deeds – and some of mine, though not all. But now I'm going.'

And he went: Perceval looked, and he was nowhere to be seen. He raised his hand and crossed himself, and then went to his horse and mounted, and set off along the path that Merlin had shown him. He rode on until, by Our Lord's will, he saw – on the very day that Merlin had said – his grandfather's house. He rode up to the gate and dismounted outside the hall.

Two servants came to meet him and welcomed him heartily, and helped him to disarm and stabled his horse with the utmost care; then they led him to the hall where his grandfather the king lay. And as soon as he saw Perceval he did his best to rise, overjoyed at his coming; and Perceval sat down beside him, and they spoke together of many things. Finally the king called for the table to be set; it was no sooner said than done, and they sat down to dine.

Just after the first course had been served, the lance with the bleeding head came out of a chamber, and after it came the Grail, and the damsel carrying the little silver platters. And Perceval, who could not wait to ask the question, said to the king: 'Sire, by the faith you owe me and all men, tell me the purpose of these things I see.'

And as soon as he had said this, he looked up and saw that the Fisher King was utterly changed, cured of his sickness, as fit as a fish! Perceval was filled with wonder. And the king jumped up and was about to kiss Perceval's feet, but he would not let him. Then all the boys of the house came running up and hailed Perceval with the utmost joy. At last he came to his senses and said: 'Sire, you should know that Alain li Gros – your son, sire – was my father.'

When the Fisher King heard this his elation redoubled, and he said: 'Dear grandson, I'm very glad you've come!' And with that he knelt down and gave thanks to Our Lord; then he took Perceval by the hand and led him before the vessel and said: 'Dear grandson, this is the lance with which Long-inus struck Christ on the cross. And this vessel, called the Grail, holds the blood that Joseph gathered as it flowed from His wounds to the earth. We call it the Grail because it delights[18] the hearts of all worthy men and all those who can stay in its presence – it will not tolerate the presence of the sinful. Now I shall pray to Our Lord to send me guidance in regard to you.'

With that Bron knelt before his vessel and said: 'Dear Lord God, as surely as this is your blessed blood, which you granted I should be given after the death of Joseph, and which I have guarded ever since, send me a true sign of what should become of it henceforth.'

And thereupon the voice of the Holy Spirit descended, and said to him:

'Bron, the prophecy that Our Lord made to Joseph will now be fulfilled. Our Lord bids you entrust to this man's keeping the sacred words that He taught Joseph when He gave him[19] the Grail in prison. And in three days from now you will leave this world and join the company of the apostles.'

With that the voice departed. And Bron did as it had instructed, and taught Perceval the sacred words that Joseph had taught him, which I cannot – and must not – tell you. And he taught him all about the faith of Our Lord, and how he had seen Him as a little child and in the temple where He had disputed with the elders; and how the great men of the land of Judaea had taken against Him, and how He had had a false disciple who had sold Him to the Jews; how he had seen Him crucified, and how his brother-in-law Joseph had asked for His body, which Pilate granted, and had taken Him down from the cross; and when he laid Him on the ground he had seen His blood flowing into the earth and, distressed by this, had gathered it in a vessel – 'the very one you see here, which cannot abide the presence of sinners'.

He told him all about the life his good ancestor had led; and Perceval delighted in his words, and at once was filled with the grace of the Holy Spirit. Then the aged Bron placed the vessel in Perceval's hands, and from it came a melody and a perfume so sweet that they thought they were with the angels in Paradise.

Bron, who was well advanced in years, spent the whole of the next three days with Perceval; and on the third day he came and lay before the vessel, his arms spread wide to form a cross, and offered thanks to Our Lord. And with that he passed away. And at his passing Perceval looked up and saw

---

[18] The play on words that appears in *Joseph of Arimathea* (above, p. 36) is made again here, juxtaposing *graal* and the verb *agreer* ('to delight').

[19] The manuscript accidentally reads 'you'.

David with his harp and a great host of angels with censers waiting to receive Bron's soul, and they carried him away to dwell in majesty with his heavenly Father whom he had served so long.

And there the illustrious Perceval remained; and all the enchantments that had beset the world were cast out and broken. And on that very day King Arthur was seated at the Round Table established by Merlin, and they all heard a grinding so terrible that they were filled with fear, and the stone that had split apart when Perceval had sat in the empty seat joined together once more. They were filled with awe, not knowing what this signified.

Then Merlin came to Blaise and told him of these things, and Blaise replied: 'Merlin, you told me that when this business was done you would put me in the company of the Grail.'

'Blaise,' said Merlin, 'you'll be there before tomorrow dawns.'

And with that Merlin took Blaise and led him to the house of the Fisher King – whose name was Perceval – and there he stayed in the company of the Grail.

When Merlin had brought this business to a close he came to Arthur's court at Carduel. Arthur was delighted to see him, and his men said he should ask Merlin the significance of the stone that had mended at the Round Table.

'I shall indeed,' said the king, 'if he's willing.'

'Arthur,' Merlin replied, 'you should know that your reign has seen the fulfilling of the greatest prophecy of all time. For the Fisher King is healed, and the enchantments of the land of Britain are cast out. And Perceval is lord of the Grail by Our Lord's decree. You can clearly see what a worthy man he is, when Our Lord entrusts His precious blood to his keeping; and that is why the stone that split beneath him is now repaired. And Gawain and Kay the seneschal should know that it was Perceval himself who won the tournament at the White Castle and laid them out on the ground. But now, I promise you, he has taken his leave of chivalry, and wishes to live henceforth in the grace of his Creator.'

When the king and his barons heard this they all wept as one, and prayed to Our Lord to bring Perceval to a good end. Then Merlin took his leave of the king and returned to Blaise and Perceval, and had Blaise set everything down in writing.

*

But the barons at Arthur's court were most downcast at the news that the enchantments and adventures were ended, and the young men and squires and knights of the Round Table said they would stay with King Arthur no longer, but would cross the sea to seek out knightly deeds. When Kay the seneschal heard this he was most distressed, and came to the king and said:

'Sire, all your barons are intending to leave you and go to foreign lands in search of adventure. But you're the most esteemed king of all time in the land of Britain, and have the finest company of knights ever known. Remember, there have been three kings of Britain who've also been king of France and emperor of Rome, and Merlin said you would be likewise, and you know very well that Merlin's the wisest man in the world and not inclined to lie. If your knights leave you and go seeking adventure abroad, you'll never assemble them all again. Don't be dilatory, my lord, or you'll lose the mighty reputation you've enjoyed so long! Cross the sea and conquer France and Normandy, and divide them amongst your barons who've given you long service. We'll do everything in our power to help you.'

Arthur was inspired by these words, and he came to his barons and sought their advice in the matter. Each gave his own reaction, all offering help most willingly. When Arthur heard he had the support of the finest men of his kingdom he leapt for joy, and had letters sealed and carried throughout the land by fifty messengers, declaring that no man able to give aid should fail to come, for he would repay each one with gifts enough to make them rich men. The messengers did their work, and assembled such a massive host that before the month was out they numbered more than a hundred thousand. The king was jubilant, and rode to see them with Sir Gawain and Kay the seneschal and King Lot of Orkney. He went to every tent, greeting each noble man with joy and winning their hearts and distributing splendid gifts. And they all cried:

'King Arthur, you're losing the whole world by your langour, for truly, if you shared our heart we'd conquer France and Normandy and Rome and all Lombardy for you – we'd have you bear the crown as far as Jerusalem, and you'd be lord of all the world!'

So said the Britons to their lord Arthur. The king was elated by their words, and swore upon his life that he would not stop until he had conquered France if nothing else. Then he summoned all the carpenters of the land and had them build the most magnificent fleet ever known, and when the ships and galleys were ready they came to port and provisioned them with bread and wine and meat and salt and arms and cloth. Then the knights embarked, taking with them the finest horses. In his absence the king entrusted his land to his wife the queen and to Mordred, who was Sir Gawain's brother and the son of King Lot of Orkney – and much disposed to evil. Then Arthur took his leave and came down to the port, and they sailed by the wind and the stars.

Across the sea they went, until the fleet reached Normandy. And as soon as they landed they rode out across the country seizing men, women and loot and laying waste the land. I tell you, no land was ever so woefully ravaged; and when the duke heard the news he pleaded for a truce until they had spoken together, and King Arthur agreed. And he came to Arthur's army and became his liegeman, saying he would hold the land as his vassal and pay him tribute; the king was delighted to accept his terms. And the duke had a most beautiful daughter, whom the king gave to Kay the seneschal along with lordship of all the duke's land.

Then Arthur set out and crossed the duchy and entered the land of the king of France. At this time France's king was named Floire. Alarmed at the news of Arthur's approach, he summoned his troops from every part of the land to meet at Paris. A vast number of knights assembled, and Floire declared that he would await Arthur there. Hearing this, Arthur rode to meet him, and came to within two leagues of the French host. When King Floire heard of his coming, he chose two messengers to go to Arthur's army and said: 'Good messengers, you're to go straight to the Britons and tell King Arthur there's no need to have knights killed for the sake of conquering the land. Tell him that if he's brave enough to contest the kingship of France in single combat, me against him, I'm ready to do battle; and either he'll have France or I'll have Britain.'

The messengers came at once to Arthur's army and asked for him, and they were shown to his pavilion. They rode up and dismounted, and went in and greeted him and delivered their lord's message word for word, keeping nothing back. And when he heard what they had to say, Arthur replied: 'Sirs, tell King Floire, whose subjects you are, that I'll do as he has bidden. Tell him I wouldn't fail to meet his challenge for all the land of Britain.'

'We want you to swear,' they replied, 'that he'll have nothing to fear from anyone but you.'

The king gave them his word, and all the greatest of the Britons swore that if King Arthur was killed they would return home and hold their lands as King Floire's vassals. The messengers for their part vowed that if King Floire was killed, they would surrender all the castles of France and pay homage to Arthur. It was agreed that the combat would take place in fifteen days. Then the messengers returned and delivered Arthur's reply to King Floire, while the Britons moved camp to within a stone's throw of the city walls. A truce was declared by both sides, so the Britons went into Paris to buy food.

The time passed and the day agreed by the king arrived. Both kings prepared for combat, donning the most magnificent royal armour; then they crossed to an island outside Paris and mounted their finest horses. The French and Britons, as agreed, stood in peace, unarmed spectators, praying for Our Lord's mercy as they watched their lords risking death to win honour. On the island the two kings drew apart, putting the range of two bowshots[20] between them, and then came charging at each other at such a speed and exchanged such mighty blows on their shields that their lances shattered and splinters flew, and they collided, chests and heads together, with such force that they brought each other crashing from their horses to the ground. Arthur was the first to leap to his feet, and he drew his fine steel sword Excalibur and advanced upon Floire. King Floire jumped up in turn and boldly drew his sword, and towards each other they came. I tell you,

---

20 See note 9 above, p. 133.

both the French and the Britons were praying for their lords while the two kings, with little love lost between them, attacked each other with their swords. King Floire was mightily brave and bold, and very sure of his strength. With sword clutched tight in his right hand he dealt a blow upon Arthur's shield, splitting it and hacking off a great piece; so mighty was the blow that as it flashed down it smashed three hundred rings from Arthur's mailcoat and cut into his thigh, taking with it a handful or more of flesh, and down it came still, severing a spur and three toes from his foot before it plunged a full yard into the earth. Arthur was stunned by the blow, and Floire gave a mighty barge with his shoulder that nearly brought him to the ground. When the Britons and Sir Gawain saw this they were aghast and in terror for their lord, for King Floire was a head and helmet taller than Arthur and now looked bolder and stronger, too. They feared the worst; and when King Arthur saw his people trembling and in fear for him, he was filled with shame and anguish. With his sword Excalibur in his right hand he advanced on the king who was waiting for him in the middle of the field and struck him on the shield with all his fury; he smashed it right down to the boss, cutting away what it hit, and the blow followed through on to his helmet, sending its metal band flying; and the hood of his mailcoat could not stop the blade slicing away a chunk of his head and a fistful of hair: if the sword had not turned in his hand, it would have killed him; even so the helmet flew from his head, for the laces were broken. King Floire was incensed and went to strike Arthur on the helm, but could inflict no damage. Now he was deeply dismayed, and with blood running over his face and into his eyes he lost all sight of Arthur. His heart failed him, and he collapsed face down in the middle of the field. King Arthur was jubilant, and strode up, took his sword, brought it down and cut off his head. When the French saw that their king was dead their hearts were filled with grief and they retreated into the city, while the Britons came to their lord Arthur, set him on a horse, and led him back to his pavilion amidst the greatest celebration and swiftly disarmed him.

The king now sent two messengers to the people in Paris to find out what they meant to do: these messengers were King Lot of Orkney and his son Gawain, a very fine speaker and regarded as one of the wisest men in the army; he was indeed a good knight and skilful and judicious in speech – certainly, there was no finer knight in the land of Britain now that Perceval had abandoned chivalry. So they rode to Paris, and when the men on the walls saw them coming they opened the gates. Gawain and his father King Lot entered and greeted the twelve peers of France who were there in the city, and saw the knights and messengers who had arranged the combat between Arthur and King Floire. Gawain now addressed them, saying:

'My lords, King Arthur bids you surrender the city as these messengers agreed. For it was decreed that Arthur and Floire would do battle on the terms I'm about to tell you – and I'll call as witnesses these very messengers who came to our king's tent to announce the combat. We vowed that if

Arthur was defeated we would come to King Floire and pay him homage and hold our land as his vassals: such was our oath; and your messengers swore that if your king Floire was defeated, you would come to King Arthur and place yourselves at his mercy – the conditions being that you would hold your castles as his vassals and France would be under his rule. Ask your messengers, whom I believe and trust to be worthy men, if this was the agreement.'

When the citizens heard Sir Gawain speak they were most impressed by his words, and said: 'We'll discuss this.'

And they retired to a splendid chamber, where the noblest men of France said: 'Sirs, we're powerless to resist this British king who's come against us, and haven't enough provisions to sustain us for long – and you can be sure he's not going to leave!'

And the messengers who had arranged the combat rose and said: 'Sirs, we wish to fulfil the promise we made to Arthur.'

And it was agreed that they should surrender the city and pay homage and hold France as King Arthur's vassals. Then they returned to King Lot and his son Gawain and said: 'Sirs, we clearly can't hold out against you, and even if we could we'd want to fulfil our promises. We will surrender France and pay homage to King Arthur, and ourselves and all we possess we place at his mercy. But in God's name, let him rule us justly: if he does otherwise, the sin will be on his head. Let him rule us as King Floire always did.'

'My lords,' Gawain replied, 'be assured that he will never treat you wrongly in any way.'

Then Gawain and his father King Lot returned to Arthur and reported everything the French had said. King Arthur was delighted by the news, and immediately ordered his army to strike camp and ride to Paris. When the people of Paris saw him approaching, churchmen and bishops and abbots came out to meet him with crosses and censers and holy relics; mint and flowers were strewn in his path; and throughout the city were set tables laden with bread and meat and game, and, for the most illustrious, fine wine and rich spices. The palace where King Arthur dismounted was draped with rich silks and festooned with decorations. Then they seated Arthur on the royal throne and brought him the crown, and crowned him king of France, swearing him faithful homage and loyalty. Arthur accepted them with a loving heart; and he spent fifty days in the land of France and bestowed many rich gifts upon his knights, and the knights of France and Normandy said they had never had such a good lord. Many of the barons of France loved Arthur more dearly than they had ever loved Floire, for he was fair of speech and knew how to gain men's affection – not with empty words but with generous favours.

After fifty days in Paris Arthur set out across France to see if any castles were being held against him; but at every one he persuaded them to bring him the keys as he won their hearts. The news had spread throughout the land that Arthur had slain the king of France, so every castle was surrendered to him. Then King Arthur gave his nephew Gawain the march of Brittany, and to Bedivere he gave all the Vermendois, a good and fertile land; every high lord in his company was given a city or a castle. Everything was duly arranged, with governors appointed in all the castles and marches.

With France conquered, Arthur said he would stay no longer. He took his leave of the barons of the land, who escorted him a long way before turning back. He rode to where his fleet was moored in Normandy – he had left five hundred knights to guard the vessels –and embarked with all his knights. Then the mariners set the sails, the wind filled them, and they sailed from port and across the sea to Dover, where they disembarked with all their horses and palfreys. They rejoiced to see their own land again.

When Gawain's brother Mordred heard that Arthur his uncle had returned, he mounted with the queen and fifty knights and rode to meet him, greeting him with joy. As the news spread throughout the land that King Arthur had returned and had conquered France there was jubilation among the common people, and the ladies and damsels whose sons and nephews had been with Arthur came to meet them: you never saw such joyous embraces as took place then! Then the king declared: 'My lords, I wish all those present to join me at court at Carduel in Wales at the feast of Saint John this summer.'

This was announced throughout the army, and the king summoned the highest men of his land who all vowed to be present on Saint John's Day. 'For I wish,' Arthur said, 'to make a common division of part of my wealth: even the poorest I shall make rich!'

With that they departed, Arthur retiring to spend a while at one of his castles; and all agreed he had succeeded in a wonderful adventure, culminating in the conquest of France.

Arthur waited while the season passed and Saint John's Day drew near. Then all the noble men of Britain assembled at his court, so many that they were beyond all counting, and a great many knights, both rich and poor. The day arrived and the king went to hear mass, sung by the archbishop who was a great support to him; and after mass he returned to his palace and had the water brought, announced by a fanfare, and the knights sat down for the feast. King Arthur was seated at the highest table, King Lot of Orkney with him. On the other side sat the kings of Denmark and Ireland: there were seven kings at the court, all at Arthur's command.

Just as Arthur had taken his seat and the first course had been brought before him, he and his barons and the other kings looked up and saw twelve men come through the door of the hall. They were white-haired and richly dressed and carrying twelve olive branches. As they entered they saw the array of lords and knights in the king's court and whispered to each other: 'Truly, sirs, this is a great king indeed.'

They walked past all the tables and strode aggressively up to Arthur.

There they stopped, and all remained silent except one, who spoke most haughtily, saying: 'May the God who is omnipotent and reigns over all the world protect first the emperor of Rome and then the Pope and the senators who safeguard and uphold the faith. And may that same God confound Arthur and all who follow him, for he has transgressed against God and Holy Church and the law of Rome by severing and annexing what is Rome's by right, and by slaying in combat the king who held his land as Rome's vassal and paid a yearly tribute. Our amazement is matched by our contempt that such base men as you, who should be despised by the whole world, and who are slaves through and through and always have been – your ancestors likewise! – should now mean to cast off slavery and live in freedom like other men.

'You know very well that you were all slaves to Julius Caesar and paid him tribute, and it has been received by other kings of Rome likewise: you have never been free of servitude, and we have nothing but contempt for your plans to be so. The emperor's disdain and scorn are such that he could not believe reports that you intended to free yourselves from your servitude. He bids and commands you by the twelve of us to send him the same tribute that your ancestors paid to Julius Caesar. If you do not, the emperor will march against you. I advise you to pay the tribute, for such is the Romans' anger that even the lowest in the land are saying to the emperor: "In God's name, sire, let us go and deal with those British curs who have destroyed France!" I tell you, if the emperor let them have their way they'd be upon you now! But he can't believe you're so mighty as to have conquered France. Be sure of this: if he marches against you, you'll not escape; wherever you flee he'll turf you out. He has sworn upon his crown that he will have your skin, and all the knights of your land will be boiled in cauldrons and burned on the fire – every last one will be treated the same: they'll be massacred.'

Arthur flushed scarlet and shook with shame that the messengers should speak so in the presence of all his barons at the tables in the hall; he rose swiftly to his feet and said: 'My lords, I don't know where you were born, but you speak good French and I understand you. Sit down and eat if you're hungry, I pray you.'

'We wouldn't eat at your court,' they replied, 'even if you threatened to cut off our hands: it's inconceivable!'

Arthur laughed at this and said: 'Sirs, I shall discuss your request with my counsellors, and I'll give you our answer shortly.'

Then he summoned his barons, the kings of Ireland and Orkney and Sir Gawain and his brother Mordred and Kay the seneschal and Bedivere and others till they numbered twelve, and they withdrew to a magnificent chamber, exquisitely painted. The painting depicted the story of the three goddesses and Paris, and how, after he had been given the apple, one promised him the most beautiful woman in the world, another the greatest riches in the world, and the third to make him the finest knight in the land. After each had made her offer – imagining that the others knew nothing of it – Paris thought to himself that he was already a fine knight and one of the most valiant in all his land, and needed no greater riches than he already enjoyed, so decided his best choice would be the pleasure of the beautiful woman! So he took the apple and gave it to the goddess who had promised him the woman: she was overjoyed to win it, for the apple gave her supremacy over the other goddesses. She duly united him with a woman more beautiful than any in the world; but her beauty was to cost Paris dear. Such was the story painted on the walls of the chamber where Arthur led the twelve to take counsel.

'Sirs,' he said at once, 'you are all my men and I am your lord. You all heard the emperor's messengers insulting and abusing me: it was an outrage, but I didn't show it. Now I pray you, give me your advice in all honour, and I promise I'll do exactly as you say.'

Then King Lot of Orkney, a most wise and worthy man, stood up and addressed the king, saying: 'Sire, you've asked for our advice and we'll counsel you well if you're willing to heed us. You've heard how the emperor of Rome's messengers have come to abuse you, and claim that Julius Caesar conquered Rome and France and your own kingdom of Britain. Well, that's true – but he took it by treachery, and treachery is not right. I'll tell you a little about how he won it. There was once a king who had a brother and two fair children, and when he died he left his land to those two, but the common people felt they were too young to safeguard the kingdom and entrusted it to their uncle, who became king and made one of his nephews a duke and the other a count. This king's name was Casibelan.[21] I don't know what his nephews had done wrong, but he summoned them to court and meant to have them killed; and when they realised their uncle hated them and had usurped their kingdom, they sent word to Julius Caesar that he could conquer England. Caesar had been twice before but had been unable to overcome Casibelan, but when he received the children's message he was overjoyed, and returned word that they were to supply hostages as a firm assurance, which they did, and he put to sea and sailed to this land. Meanwhile the two children had assembled great armies and now joined Julius Caesar, and they marched against Casibelan and defeated him in battle. And after the victory, Julius Caesar accepted the brothers' homage and made the elder the king and they paid him tribute. It's because of this that the Romans claim tribute from you. And I'll tell you something else.

'There were two other brothers in Britain, one named Brenes and the other Belin,[22] and such was their power that they crossed the sea and conquered France and advanced as far as Rome. When the Romans saw them

---

[21] Cassivellaunus, who led British resistance to Julius Caesar's invasions. His story appears in Geoffrey of Monmouth's *History of the Kings of Britain*.

[22] Brennius and Belinus, also in Geoffrey of Monmouth.

approaching they were terrified, and came out to meet them and vowed to submit to their command, giving them forty hostages. Once the hostages were given, Brenes and Belin said they'd return to Britain, which they did; but as soon as the Romans saw them go they said they'd been very wrong to let their hostages be led away, and decided to head the Britons off at a narrow pass in a deep defile. They assembled fifty thousand knights and positioned them in the pass. Meanwhile Brenes and Belin had divided their troops, each taking half, and each half numbered more than a hundred thousand men. Brenes came to the defile and was about to pass through, but the Romans leapt out and launched a savage attack. Brenes, in deep dismay, came to a squire and said: "Dear friend, go to my brother Belin and tell him we're betrayed! And tell him to march to the pass from behind the Romans and attack them in the rear!" The squire took the king's message to Belin, who was horrified; following a peasant's directions, he rode swiftly to the end of the defile to join the battle, in which Brenes had fought almost to exhaustion. Belin roared his battle cry and charged with fifty thousand men, crying: "Britain!", and Brenes cried: "France!" The Romans were aghast, and the Britons slew them: every last Roman was killed. Then Brenes and Belin returned to Rome and camped outside the city, set up gibbets, and hanged all the children given by the wealthy men of Rome as hostages. Then the city was surrendered, and Brenes was crowned emperor and the Romans paid him tribute. That's why it seems to me that you should have lordship over the Romans: you should be emperor of Rome! You both claim the same! I don't know what more to say, other than that you should meet and see who does best: whoever does will win what he claims!

'But one thing more, sire: remember how Merlin came to your court the very day you became king. He said there'd been two kings of Britain who'd been king of France and emperor of Rome. Sire, you are king of France, and I say you'll be king of Rome if you've the heart to conquer it! For Merlin has never lied but has always told the truth. So summon your knights and cross the sea and join battle with the Romans! I tell you, you'll be victorious, for you have the finest knights in all the world!'

And all twelve of the counsellors cried: 'Arthur, lord, ride in force and conquer Romenie and all the land of Lombardy, and we'll help you with all our might!'

Arthur was elated by his barons' words and said: 'It seems to me, sirs, that King Lot has spoken splendidly! From what he's told me, even if the Romans hadn't come here, I ought to go there and claim what my ancestor won!'

With that, Arthur returned to the hall and said to the Roman messengers: 'Sirs, know this: I am amazed the emperor has the nerve to demand the outrageous tribute that you claim. I assure you, I mean to free myself of servitude to him. You can tell him that before eight months are out my army will be within a javelin's throw of Rome, unless he comes to meet me. And I'm willing to fight him man to man or army to army.'

'We assure you,' the messengers replied, 'that the emperor will meet you with two hundred thousand men or more.'

And with that they haughtily strode from the hall without asking leave. They made their way to the sea and sailed across and rode day after day until they reached Rome and found the emperor. They told him how they had fared, and how the Britons were a proud and strong people and had gathered the finest knights in the world at a Round Table they had established.

'We gave Arthur your message and he said he'd take counsel. He took twelve of his barons to his chamber and they discussed it at great length. Their decision amounts to this: Arthur sends you word that within eight months his army will be within a javelin's throw of Rome unless you go to meet him.'

The emperor was enraged. He sent out sealed letters and scrolls and assembled the greatest army ever seen, summoning soldiers and archers and great bands of knights, and squires on foot and horseback carrying lances and javelins. And know this: he appealed to the king of Spain – a Saracen – and this Saracen brought the most immense army of all time. No king ever had a mightier force, and they all placed themselves at the emperor's command. I tell you, when the whole army was on the march it was reckoned to number three hundred thousand, all armed and equipped for war. When his forces were all assembled the emperor appealed to them, explaining how Arthur had risen against him and in single combat had killed King Floire who held his land as a vassal of Rome. 'And now he's claiming tribute from us! I pray you, give me your advice in these matters.'

Hearing this, the barons were filled with contempt and all cried as one: 'Rightful emperor, ride in force and cross the mountains and the sea and conquer Britain and avenge King Floire whom Arthur, king of Britain, has slain! We'll aid you with all our might!'

While the emperor was engaged in this debate, three messengers arrived and greeted him most nobly in their own tongue on behalf of the Sultan, and said: 'Lord emperor, the Sultan sends you word that he is coming to join you to destroy the Britons, because his brother the king of Spain is with you already. I promise you, his army numbers fifty thousand Saracens, and in three days they will be camped in the fields outside Rome.'

The emperor was elated; and when the third day came he mounted with all the senators of Rome and joyfully rode to meet the Sultan half a league outside the city. When the emperor saw him he spurred towards him and flung his arms around his neck. Neither his Christian faith nor his baptism stopped him kissing him full on the lips, and all the Roman senators bowed deeply to him: they knew well enough how he defied God, but their fear of the Britons was great! They camped outside Rome for fifteen days to rest their men, and during those fifteen days the emperor transgressed mightily against God and Holy Church, for he took the Sultan's daughter as his wife – a beautiful woman indeed, but an infidel. The common people of Rome were most distressed, and kept saying the emperor had lost much of his faith.

Then, when the fifteen days had passed, the army set out and marched across the lands; but Blaise says nothing about their daily marches and what befell them, for Merlin did not care to mention it. But I can tell you this much: they came to the land of Provence where they heard that Arthur's seneschal Kay was on the frontier of Brittany, guarding that land, and when the emperor heard this he rode that way. But Arthur's spies informed him of this and he was already at the port of Dover, preparing the fleet for his immense army. When the fleet was ready Arthur came to his nephew Mordred, Sir Gawain's brother, and entrusted his land and his castles and his wife to his keeping. But he would have done better to have boiled them both in cauldrons, for his nephew Mordred committed the greatest treason ever known; for he loved Arthur's wife, and persuaded the knights and stewards and keepers of the castles to receive him as their lord, and then married the queen, garrisoned every castle in the land and had himself crowned king. But Arthur, suspecting nothing of this, had his knights embark with all their arms and harness, and the mariners steered them to a port named Calais. Word of their landing was sent to the barons of France, who were overjoyed at the news; and the king, by the common consent of his army, sent two messengers to Paris, where the people joyously declared they would receive him as their lord. Hearing this, Arthur rode to Paris and assembled all his forces there.

The Romans and Saracens heard that Arthur was at Paris, and advanced to within three leagues of the city. Then Arthur sent Gawain and Bedivere to the enemy camp to find out if the emperor wished to do battle. Gawain and Bedivere, mounted on two splendid horses and magnificently armed, came to the emperor's tent. Gawain proudly delivered his message, insulting and slighting the emperor as he did so, until one of the legates had had enough and said: 'Britons are always boastful, foul-tongued braggarts! You wretched knight! If you say any more I'll drag you from your horse!'

At that Bedivere thrust a lance clean through him, and Gawain skewered one of the emperor's nephews before drawing his sword and dealing a knight such a blow on the head that he split him from his scalp to his waist. Then he spurred forward, beheading six as he went; he and Bedivere meant to ride off, but it was impossible: more than twenty thousand came galloping after them. Some overtook them by a bowshot's length,[23] and Bedivere and Gawain found themselves confronted by more than two thousand; they gathered around Gawain and Bedivere with drawn swords, lances, javelins, darts and sticks and stones, and dealt so many blows that death was inevitable. They killed both their horses. Then fury surged within Sir Gawain, and he drew his sword and clutched his shield and struck a Roman – the governor of a great

[23] See note 9 above, p. 133.

estate – such a blow that he split him down to his chest; and he seized his horse and mounted and rode to the aid of Bedivere who was defending himself ferociously. But before he could reach him he was unhorsed again and his mount killed beneath him; and when he realised he had lost the horse he had won, Gawain leapt up and stoutly defended himself on foot, hopeless though it was. Then suddenly a force of twenty thousand Britons who had been stationed in the wood came charging out to attack the Romans; they cut through them in a fury and killed them all – hardly a single man escaped. Messengers rode back to report to Arthur; as soon as he heard the news, he commanded his men to arm, and gave orders for two hundred horns and two hundred trumpets to be sounded, which was done – in a blast so mighty that it seemed as if all the earth were quaking and crumbling: God's thunder would have gone unheard. In perfect order they rode to battle, Saigremor entrusted with the royal banner. They met the twenty thousand who had rescued Sir Gawain and joined forces with them under Gawain's command.

Meanwhile those who had fled returned to the emperor's tent with the news that his brother Bretel was dead. He was filled with anguish, and swore he would make Arthur and the Britons pay dearly. He had the horn sounded at the royal pavilion to call them to arms, and when the Romans heard the horn's ringing blast they armed, and the infidels likewise. They formed their battalions and squadrons and rode out to find Arthur – and Arthur rode to meet them; soon they were close enough to see each other plainly. When the armies came within sight of one another, even the bravest felt fear. Then the Christians made confession to each other and forgave one another their mutual wrongs, and took communion with blades of grass; then they mounted once again.

I promise you, truly, such massive armies were never seen; and when they had advanced so close that there was nothing for it but to fight, Sir Gawain, leading the first squadron, spurred forward and struck a Saracen through shield and mailcoat alike, thrusting the lance-head clean through his chest and sending him crashing dead to the ground. Then both sides charged. Gawain had twenty thousand men confronting fifty thousand Saracens: they clearly could not last long. Even so they killed eleven thousand of the infidels, while seven hundred and sixty of Gawain's men were lost. All the same, they would not have survived had not Kay the seneschal come to Sir Gawain's aid with twenty thousand knights. They charged into the infidels from Spain and left huge piles of dead all over the field: the infidels could not resist, and took to flight; but they met the Sultan advancing with fifty thousand Saracens, who now attacked Sir Gawain and Kay the seneschal.

They fought from the third hour[24] till noon, when the field was so littered with dead knights and men-at-arms that it was impossible to ride and joust;

---

[24] See note 6 above, p. 122.

but they killed each other with their naked swords. And I tell you, Gawain fought so mightily that day that he himself killed one thousand two hundred and thirty knights and men-at-arms. It was true that his strength grew after midday, and when noon had passed every knight he attacked he cut down, man and horse together. He had become so wild that no-one would go near him, and by his efforts the Britons put the Sultan to flight.

But now the emperor engaged Sir Gawain – who had already endured so much – and Kay the seneschal, and his forces numbered a hundred and fifty thousand. So immense was the dustcloud that Kay took to flight and the Britons with him. But Gawain defended their rear; and then Arthur arrived with sixty thousand worthy and courageous knights, all superbly armed and equipped. They joined battle with the Romans, and it was the fiercest battle that any man could endure. In the fighting that followed, more than fourteen thousand knights from both sides died. And I tell you, King Arthur proved himself to be a great warrior indeed. Then the emperor came through the ranks, magnificently armed, crying: 'King Arthur, I'm ready to put our honour to the test – and I'll prove that you're my slave!'

Arthur heard this and galloped to meet him, and with sword clutched in his right hand he struck the emperor full on the head: with God's help he dealt such a blow that he split him to the waist and sent him toppling, dead. The cry went up that the emperor was slain; and then Gawain charged forward and struck the Sultan across the waist with his sword, slicing him in half; and King Lot struck the king of Spain through the chest with a javelin, sending him crashing dead to the ground. When the Romans and Saracens saw their lords fall they were aghast. More than a hundred thousand gathered around their bodies, intending to carry them back to their tents; but the Britons and the Norse and the Irish and the Scots descended with lances, darts and daggers and declared that they would take the bodies of the three traitors. But the Romans were determined to have them; and such blows rained down on them then that you could have filled two hundred waggons with the dead. I tell you truly, there had never been such a massacre since the days of Hercules who set up his pillars in Ethiopia.[25] Then Gawain returned, and he could not restrain himself, but continued to kill like a raging wolf devouring a lamb. Bedivere, too, wielded his sword until the fields were awash with blood. The Romans fled and abandoned the field.

But twenty thousand men-at-arms had reformed, with knights amongst them too, and the Romans joined them and returned to the field, where the bodies of so many knights lay colourless and pale. Then the Britons summoned all their strength and charged to meet them, and Guillac the king of Denmark clutched his sword in his right hand and struck the foremost

---

[25] A strange reference to the Greek hero. *Ethyope* is perhaps a half-memory of Erythia, where Hercules has a bloody encounter with the triple-bodied ogre Geryon shortly after setting up his mighty Pillars.

Roman such a blow that he cut him right down to the saddle of his horse.
Seeing their leader killed filled the Romans with alarm, and Arthur came
storming at them with thirty thousand Britons who struck them down and
slew them. The Romans and Saracens took to flight, and the Britons pursued
them for a long while, killing and capturing them at will. The chase lasted a
day and a night, and among the captives were fifteen Roman senators.

When the victory was complete, Arthur took counsel with his barons and
said he wished to be crowned in Rome, and his men all agreed he should
advance in force and be crowned there indeed. He sent for the captured senators, and when they came before him they fell at his feet and begged for
mercy, that he might spare their lives, promising to surrender Rome to him
and serve him forever. Arthur granted this, and accepted them as liegemen
and declared them free from captivity. Then the king commanded his men to
be ready to go to Rome in three days.

But the day before Arthur was due to march he was in the palace at Paris,
with his nephew Gawain and Kay the seneschal and Guillac the king of
Denmark and King Lot of Orkney, when four messengers dismounted at the
mounting-block and climbed up to the hall and greeted him in the name of
God; he recognised them instantly and asked them: 'Why have you come
here, sirs? In God's name, tell me how my wife is, and my nephew Mordred.
There's nothing wrong?'

And the messengers replied: 'Lord king, it's about them that we've
brought you news. We have to tell you that your nephew Mordred has acted
treacherously towards you: he's married your wife, and within a month of
your leaving the country he'd taken the crown. He's won over the people,
and every one of your castles is filled with crossbowmen and knights and
men-at-arms, for every knight in the land who opposed his will he's had put
to death! And know this: he's called upon the Saxons of Hengist's line –
Hengist, who fought so long against your father! – and throughout the land
of Britain he's banned the singing of mass or matins. Truly, if you don't come
to the country's aid you'll lose it – you'd do better to conquer your own land
than someone else's!'

When Arthur heard this his heart was filled with shame and rage. He
debated with his barons what he should do, and their advice was to return
and seek to recover his land – and if he could capture Mordred, to have him
burnt. Even Mordred's brother Gawain and his father King Lot of Orkney
said so – King Lot felt the deepest shame. Arthur thought this good advice,
and the next day he set out with all his knights and rode to Normandy and
put to sea.

But Mordred knew of this from spies he had in the king's camp, and
assembled Saxons and knights and men-at-arms and advanced to the shore to
confront Arthur. As Arthur prepared to land, Mordred was there to oppose
him. It was going to be a perilous landing. Sir Gawain sailed in with twenty
thousand men – and I tell you, he was burning with shame at Mordred's

treachery – but his brother confronted him with fifty thousand Saxons hurling spears and stones and darts and javelins; the Britons rained missiles in return. And I tell you now, ill befell Gawain: his helmet was not laced on, and a Saxon wielding an oar dealt him a blow to the head that struck him dead.

The anguish at Gawain's death! Ah God, what grief to lose the great righter of wrongs! He was a good knight, handsome and loyal and wise, elegant in speech and fair in judgement. God, what sorrow that he should die! There was such grieving on the ship that it could be heard two leagues away. And Saigremor was killed there, and Bedivere, and Kay the seneschal. The lives of so many worthy men ended there. I tell you, not one of the twenty thousand knights escaped: every last man was killed or drowned. Even their ship was lost, broken into four quarters and sinking into the sea.

When Arthur heard the twenty thousand had perished he was filled with grief. And when he knew the truth, that Gawain was dead, his rage and anguish were such that his heart failed him, and he collapsed on the deck and fainted more than fifteen times. The Britons revived him; but I tell you, no man ever heard such lamentation as that of King Lot for Gawain, his son.

King Arthur gave orders for the fleet to land, and they took the port by force and disembarked; but many were killed before they did so. It was then that another great misfortune befell Arthur, for as King Lot was leaving the ship a man-at-arms loosed a crossbow bolt at him and hit him in the chest. Once more there was bitter grieving over his body. Then the Saxons reformed and launched another attack upon Arthur; but as soon as the Britons were mounted they charged at the Saxons and slaughtered many, so mighty was their rage. Like the ravening wolf devouring the lamb, so the Britons devoured the Saxons; they slew so many that mounds of dead lay all over the fields. God granted victory to the Britons: they routed the Saxons, and Mordred took to flight. He fled to the castles he had garrisoned, thinking to take refuge; but when the knights and townsmen heard that Arthur was returning and had defeated him, they would not let him into their fortresses; and Mordred, in distress and fear that the castles were barred to him, fled to Winchester and summoned the Saxons from all over the land, saying he would wait to meet Arthur in battle.

Arthur was distraught at what had happened. First he went down to the shore and sent for the bodies of Gawain and Kay the seneschal and Bedivere and Saigremor and King Lot of Orkney, and had them buried; then he set out with the remainder of his men and tracked Mordred from castle to castle, until word came that he was at Winchester with a great army. So Arthur rode that way, summoning the barons and townsmen and citizens from all over his land; and they all came with their grievances, telling him how Mordred had ruined and abused them. Arthur was so distressed by what they said that he could not reply. Instead he ordered his knights to mount at once, and rode to Winchester.

When Mordred heard he had come he rode out to meet him, saying he would never go hiding away in castles for he had a mightier army than the king. Both sides were ready for combat, and came charging at each other in a fury. There you would have seen the fiercest battle in the world, with knights and men-at-arms strewn dead on the ground, enough to fill thirty waggons. So many Saxons were killed that very few remained, and Mordred fled away at speed with the remnants of his men. To Ireland he fled, and crossed the country until he came to an island ruled by a heathen Saxon king – a descendant of Hengist – who made him most welcome and valued him highly as a fine knight.

Hearing that Mordred had gone to Ireland, Arthur set off in swift pursuit, and rode on until he reached the land where he had taken refuge. When the Saxon king heard of his coming he summoned his army and marched against him. Battle was joined. I tell you, the Britons hated the Saxons deeply, as the Saxons did the Britons, and all the more died because of it.

The battle raged for a long while, and many fine knights were killed. The book does not tell of all who died, but I can tell you this much: Mordred was killed there, and so was the Saxon king who had harboured him. And King Arthur was mortally wounded, struck through the chest with a lance. They gathered about Arthur, grieving bitterly, but he said to them: 'Stop this grieving, for I shall not die. I shall be carried to Avalon, where my wounds will be tended by my sister Morgan.'

And so Arthur was borne to Avalon, telling his people to wait for him, for he would return.

The Britons made their way back to Carduel, and waited more than forty years before they named a new king, for they were daily expecting Arthur to reappear. And I tell you, some people have seen him since out hunting in the forests, and have heard his hounds with him; so that others have long lived in the hope that he would return.

When all this business was complete, Merlin came to Blaise and told him everything that had happened; and when Blaise had set it all down in writing he took him to the house of Perceval who had the Grail in his keeping, and who lived such a saintly life that he was often visited by the Holy Spirit. And he told him all that had befallen Arthur: how he had been carried off to Avalon, and how Gawain had been killed, and how the knights of the Round Table had ended their days. When Perceval heard this he wept with sorrow, and prayed to Our Lord to have pity on their souls, for he had loved them dearly.

Then Merlin came to Perceval and to his master Blaise and took his leave of them. He said that Our Lord did not want him to appear to people again, but he would not die until the end of the world.

'But then I shall live in eternal joy. Meanwhile I shall make my dwelling-place outside your house, where I shall live and prophesy as Our Lord shall instruct me. And all who see my dwelling-place will call it Merlin's *esplu-moir*.'[26]

With that Merlin departed; and he made his *esplumoir* and entered in, and was never seen again in this world.

Neither of Merlin nor of the Grail does the story say more, except that Merlin prayed to Our Lord to grant mercy to all who would willingly hear his book and have it copied for the remembrance of his deeds. To which you will all say: Amen.

Here ends the romance of Merlin and the Grail.

---

[26] This untranslatable – and probably invented – word has wonderful resonances. Its root is 'the shedding of feathers', implying moulting, transformation, renewal.

ARTHURIAN STUDIES